Arson

A Detective S...

Michae... ...go

GW01465851

Copyright © 2024 by Michael R. Hastings

All rights reserved. No part of this book may be used or reproduced in any form whatsoever without written permission except in the case of brief quotations in critical articles or reviews.

First Edition: June 2024

Table of Contents

Chapter 1
The New Arson Attack

The scene at Beacon Theater was a chaotic mix of flashing lights, billowing smoke, and the acrid smell of burnt wood and fabric. Detective Sarah Thompson stood amidst the wreckage, her keen eyes scanning the area for any clues that might have survived the inferno. Her partner, Ethan Drake, arrived on the scene, pulling his jacket tighter against the early morning chill.

"Sarah, what do we have so far?" Ethan asked, stepping carefully over the charred remains of what used to be the theater's entrance.

"Not much," Sarah replied, her voice tinged with frustration. "The fire chief confirmed it's arson. Same M.O. as the last three fires. Accelerant used, ignition point near the main electrical panel. Cameras were disabled before the fire started."

Ethan frowned, glancing around. "Whoever did this knew exactly what they were doing. Any witnesses?"

"Just a few," Sarah said, consulting her notepad. "A couple of night owls and a homeless man who was sleeping nearby. They're being interviewed now. But so far, no one saw anything useful."

"Great," Ethan muttered, crouching down to examine a scorched piece of debris. "We're dealing with a ghost."

Sarah sighed, rubbing her temples. "We need to find something, Ethan. This is the fourth fire in two months, and we're no closer to catching this guy."

"Let's talk to the fire chief again," Ethan suggested. "Maybe he found something new."

They made their way over to where Fire Chief Sam Turner was coordinating the cleanup. Turner looked up as they approached, his face grim and lined with soot.

"Chief Turner," Sarah greeted him. "Any new developments?"

Turner shook his head. "Nothing concrete. My team is still sifting through the debris, but it's the same pattern. Whoever's doing this is good. No prints, no DNA, nothing left behind but ashes."

Sarah nodded, feeling the weight of the case pressing down on her. "What about the accelerant? Can you tell what they used?"

"Same as before," Turner confirmed. "An industrial-grade accelerant, likely stolen from a construction site. We're running tests, but it's a long shot."

Ethan crossed his arms, his jaw tightening. "This guy is meticulous. There has to be something we're missing."

"We'll keep looking," Turner promised. "But you two need to find a lead. Fast. The media is already all over this, and people are scared."

"We're on it," Sarah assured him. "Thanks, Chief."

As they walked away, Ethan turned to Sarah. "What's our next move?"

"We need to revisit the old case files," Sarah said. "There has to be a pattern we're not seeing. And I want to re-interview the witnesses. Maybe someone remembered something they didn't think was important at first."

Ethan nodded. "Sounds like a plan. I'll start pulling the files. You want to handle the interviews?"

"Yeah," Sarah agreed. "Let's meet back at the precinct in an hour."

They parted ways, each lost in their own thoughts. Sarah approached the first witness, a middle-aged man who had been out for a late-night jog. He looked shaken, clutching a cup of coffee provided by one of the officers.

"Mr. Davis?" Sarah said gently, showing her badge. "I'm Detective Thompson. I understand you saw something last night?"

Davis nodded, his hands trembling slightly. "Yes, I was jogging past the theater when I smelled smoke. I didn't see anyone, but I heard a car speeding away. It sounded like it came from the alley behind the building."

"Did you get a look at the car?" Sarah asked, hopeful.

He shook his head. "No, it was too dark. But it was an older model, maybe a sedan. And it had a loud engine. That's all I remember."

"Thank you, Mr. Davis," Sarah said, making a note. "Anything helps."

As she moved to the next witness, a young woman named Lisa who had been walking her dog, Sarah's phone buzzed with a message from Ethan: "Found something in the old files. Meet me at the precinct."

Sarah finished her interview quickly and headed back, her mind racing. Maybe they were finally catching a break.

At the precinct, Ethan was waiting in the conference room, a stack of files spread out on the table. "Look at this," he said as Sarah entered. "All four fires were started in buildings owned by the same real estate company: Whitman Properties."

Sarah's eyes widened. "You think this is more than just a pyromaniac?"

"I think it's a pattern," Ethan replied. "And patterns lead to suspects. Let's dig into Whitman Properties and see what we find."

Sarah nodded, feeling a renewed sense of determination. They were on the trail now, and she wouldn't rest until they caught whoever was responsible for the devastation at Beacon Theater and the other fires.

The precinct buzzed with the usual morning activity as Sarah and Ethan sat down in the conference room, files and reports spread out before them. The coffee machine in the corner gurgled softly, providing a constant supply of caffeine to fuel their investigation.

"We need to start with the witness interviews," Sarah said, flipping through her notes. "Mr. Davis mentioned hearing a car speeding away from the scene. That's our first tangible lead."

Ethan nodded, pulling up a map of the area around Beacon Theater. "Let's map out the potential escape routes. If the arsonist used a car, they would've taken one of these streets."

Sarah leaned over the map, tracing the routes with her finger. "Here, here, and here. We should check traffic cameras in these areas. Maybe we'll get lucky."

"I'll call traffic control," Ethan said, reaching for his phone. "See if they have any footage from last night."

While Ethan made the call, Sarah opened her laptop and started searching for information on Whitman Properties. The connection between the fires and the real estate company was too strong to ignore.

As she typed, her mind wandered to the previous arson cases. Each fire had been meticulously planned, with no obvious connection between the locations other than the ownership. It was a sophisticated operation, and she had a nagging feeling that there was more to it.

Ethan finished his call and turned back to Sarah. "Traffic control is pulling the footage now. We should have something to review in a couple of hours."

"Good," Sarah said, glancing up from her laptop. "In the meantime, I found something interesting about Whitman Properties. They've been involved in several legal disputes over the past year. Mostly with small businesses and independent property owners."

Ethan raised an eyebrow. "Legal disputes? What kind?"

"Foreclosures, hostile takeovers, things like that," Sarah explained. "It seems like they're trying to expand aggressively, and not everyone is happy about it."

"Sounds like a motive," Ethan said, leaning back in his chair. "If someone wanted to sabotage their plans, arson would be a pretty effective way to do it."

Sarah nodded. "Agreed. We should look into anyone who's had recent conflicts with Whitman Properties. Start with the businesses affected by the previous fires."

"On it," Ethan said, jotting down notes. "I'll compile a list of all the businesses and property owners connected to Whitman Properties. We'll interview them and see if anyone stands out."

As they worked, the door to the conference room opened and Captain Donovan walked in. "How's it going, detectives?"

"We're making progress," Sarah replied. "We've identified a potential connection between the fires and a real estate company, Whitman Properties. We're looking into possible suspects now."

Donovan nodded, his expression serious. "Good. Keep at it. The mayor is breathing down my neck about this case. We need to show some results."

"We're on it, Captain," Ethan assured him. "We should have more leads by the end of the day."

"See that you do," Donovan said, turning to leave. "And keep me updated."

Once Donovan was gone, Sarah and Ethan resumed their work. The hours flew by as they sifted through documents, conducted phone interviews, and cross-referenced information. By late afternoon, they had compiled a list of potential suspects, all with recent disputes with Whitman Properties.

"Alright," Sarah said, rubbing her eyes. "Let's start with the most recent case. A coffee shop owner named Jane Roberts. She filed a lawsuit against Whitman Properties two months ago, claiming they were trying to force her out of her lease."

Ethan pulled up her file. "Jane Roberts. Small business owner, highly active in the local community. No criminal record. She might have a grudge, but is she capable of arson?"

"There's only one way to find out," Sarah said, standing up. "Let's pay her a visit."

They arrived at Jane Roberts' coffee shop, a quaint little place nestled between two larger buildings. The sign above the door read "Roberts' Brews," and the smell of freshly brewed coffee wafted out as they entered.

Jane was behind the counter, serving a customer. She looked up as Sarah and Ethan approached, her expression wary. "Can I help you?"

Sarah showed her badge. "Detective Thompson, Harborview Police. This is my partner, Detective Drake. We'd like to ask you a few questions about a recent arson case."

Jane's eyes widened, and she set down the coffee pot. "Arson? I don't know anything about that."

"We understand," Ethan said gently. "But we're looking into possible motives. You recently had a legal dispute with Whitman Properties, correct?"

Jane's expression darkened. "Yes, they're trying to force me out of my lease. It's been a nightmare. But I didn't start any fires, if that's what you're implying."

"We're not implying anything," Sarah assured her. "We're just gathering information. Can you tell us more about your dispute with Whitman Properties?"

Jane sighed, leaning against the counter. "They've been buying up properties in the area and jacking up the rent. They want to turn this neighborhood into some upscale shopping district. I've been fighting them, but it's been tough."

"Have you noticed any unusual activity around your shop or your home?" Ethan asked.

Jane shook her head. "No, nothing like that. Just the usual harassment from their lawyers. But I've never seen anyone suspicious hanging around."

"Thank you for your time, Ms. Roberts," Sarah said. "If you think of anything else, please give us a call."

As they left the coffee shop, Ethan turned to Sarah. "What do you think?"

"I think she's telling the truth," Sarah replied. "But we should keep her on our radar. Let's move on to the next name on the list."

They spent the rest of the day interviewing other business owners and property managers, gathering pieces of a puzzle that was slowly starting to take shape. By the time they returned to the precinct, they had a clearer picture of the motives and potential suspects involved.

As they sat down to review their findings, Sarah felt a renewed sense of determination. They were getting closer, and she wouldn't rest until they caught the arsonist.

Back at the precinct, the conference room was filled with a tangible sense of urgency. Sarah and Ethan spread out their collected evidence on the large table, trying to make sense of the information they had gathered throughout the day.

"Okay, let's review what we have so far," Sarah said, pinning a map of the city to the wall. She marked the locations of the four arson attacks, each one linked to a property owned by Whitman Properties.

Ethan added photos and notes from their interviews with business owners. "All these people had disputes with Whitman Properties, but none of them seem capable of something like this. It feels like we're missing a key piece."

Sarah nodded, tapping her pen against the table. "Let's look at the pattern of the fires again. They all happened late at night, when the buildings were empty. No casualties, but significant property damage."

"Who benefits the most from these fires?" Ethan asked, leaning back in his chair.

"Whitman Properties," Sarah replied without hesitation. "If the buildings are damaged or destroyed, they can buy them out at a lower price, rebuild, and profit from the new developments."

Ethan frowned, considering this. "So, we're looking at someone within Whitman Properties who has the motive and the resources to pull this off. Someone high enough to benefit from the scheme, but careful enough to avoid detection."

Sarah stood and paced the room, her mind racing. "We need to dig deeper into Whitman Properties. Find out who's really pulling the strings. Let's start with the executive team."

Ethan pulled up the company's website on his laptop. "Here's the executive board: CEO Richard Whitman, CFO Julia Bennett, and COO Paul Andrews. They all have the motive, but we need to find out if they have the means."

Sarah nodded. "Start with financials. See if any of them have unusual transactions or connections to known arsonists. I'll look into their backgrounds and see if there are any red flags."

As they worked, the room filled with the sound of clicking keys and rustling papers. Hours passed as they dug through public records, financial statements, and news articles.

"Got something," Ethan said suddenly, breaking the silence. "Paul Andrews has a history of shady business deals. A couple of years ago, he was involved in a scandal where he was accused of bribing city officials to secure building permits."

Sarah looked up, intrigued. "That's a start. Anything else?"

Ethan scrolled through the documents. "Andrews also has several offshore accounts. Large sums of money moving in and out, not easily traceable. It's suspicious, to say the least."

Sarah leaned over his shoulder, examining the records. "If Andrews is behind this, he's covering his tracks well. But why take the risk of arson?"

"Desperation, maybe," Ethan suggested. "If Whitman Properties is struggling financially, he might see this as a way to turn things around quickly."

Sarah nodded. "Let's bring him in for questioning. We need to apply some pressure, see if he cracks."

They called Captain Donovan into the room, briefing him on their findings. Donovan listened intently, his expression serious.

"Good work, detectives," Donovan said. "Bring Andrews in. But be careful. If he's involved in this, he's dangerous."

Sarah and Ethan left the precinct, heading to the upscale office building where Whitman Properties was headquartered. The sun was setting, casting long shadows across the city as they arrived at the sleek, glass-fronted building.

They approached the reception desk, showing their badges. "Detectives Thompson and Drake, Harborview Police. We need to speak with Paul Andrews."

The receptionist, a young woman with a nervous smile, nodded and made a call. "Mr. Andrews, there are two detectives here to see you... Yes, sir, right away."

A few minutes later, Paul Andrews appeared, his expression calm and composed. He was a tall man in his early fifties, with sharp features and a confident demeanor.

"Detectives, what can I do for you?" Andrews asked, his tone polite but guarded.

"We have a few questions about the recent fires at properties owned by Whitman Properties," Sarah said, watching his reaction closely.

Andrews' smile faltered slightly. "Of course. Anything I can do to help."

Sarah and Ethan exchanged a glance. "We'd prefer to discuss this in private," Ethan said. "Your office, perhaps?"

Andrews nodded, leading them to his office on the top floor. The room was spacious and luxuriously furnished, with a panoramic view of the city.

"Please, have a seat," Andrews said, gesturing to the chairs in front of his desk. "What's this about?"

Sarah got straight to the point. "Mr. Andrews, we've noticed a pattern. All the properties targeted by arson were owned by Whitman Properties. And you have a history of controversial business practices. Care to explain?"

Andrews' expression hardened. "I assure you, detectives, I have no involvement in any criminal activities. My business dealings are all above board."

Ethan leaned forward, his gaze steady. "What about the offshore accounts? Large sums of money moving in and out, right around the time of the fires. That doesn't look above board to us."

Andrews' eyes narrowed. "I don't know what you're insinuating, but I have nothing to hide. Those accounts are for legitimate business purposes."

Sarah held his gaze. "Then you won't mind if we take a closer look at your financials and communications."

Andrews stood, his demeanor turning cold. "I think this interview is over. If you want to look at my records, get a warrant."

Sarah and Ethan stood as well. "We'll be in touch," Sarah said, leading the way out.

As they exited the building, Ethan glanced at Sarah. "He's hiding something."

Sarah nodded. "We need that warrant. Let's get back to the precinct and start the paperwork."

With a clearer picture forming and a prime suspect in their sights, Sarah and Ethan felt a renewed sense of determination. They were getting closer to uncovering the truth behind the arson attacks, and they wouldn't stop until they had all the answers.

Back at the precinct, the atmosphere was thick with tension and anticipation. Sarah and Ethan had returned from their confrontational meeting with Paul Andrews, and they were now waiting for the warrant that would allow them to dig deeper into his financials and communications.

Captain Donovan entered the conference room, holding a folder. "Good news. We've got the warrant," he said, handing it over to Sarah. "Start with his financial records. If he's involved, there will be something there."

"Thanks, Captain," Sarah replied, taking the folder. She turned to Ethan. "Let's get started."

Ethan nodded, already pulling up Andrews' financial records on his laptop. As the data loaded, Sarah spread out the documents they had gathered earlier. "We need to look for any irregularities. Large transactions, unusual patterns, anything that stands out."

For the next few hours, the two detectives sifted through the data, their focus unwavering. As the clock ticked past midnight, Ethan's eyes lit up. "Sarah, look at this."

Sarah leaned over, her eyes narrowing as she examined the screen. "What did you find?"

"Several large transfers to an account registered under the name 'Samuel Harper.' These transfers were made shortly before each fire," Ethan explained. "The name didn't come up in our initial search, but it's definitely suspicious."

Sarah nodded. "Let's run a check on Samuel Harper. See if we can find any connections to Paul Andrews or Whitman Properties."

Ethan quickly typed the name into their database. After a few moments, a file appeared on the screen. "Got him. Samuel Harper, 45, a known arsonist for hire. He's been linked to several suspicious fires over the past decade but has always managed to avoid conviction."

Sarah's eyes widened. "That's our guy. Andrews must have hired him to set the fires. We need to bring Harper in for questioning."

Just as they were about to leave, Sarah's phone buzzed with an incoming call. It was Officer Lisa Chen from the traffic control division. "Detective Thompson, we've reviewed the traffic footage from the night of the Beacon Theater fire. We found something."

Sarah put the call on speaker. "What did you find, Lisa?"

"We spotted a car speeding away from the theater shortly after the fire started. It matches the description Mr. Davis gave—an older model sedan with a loud engine. We traced the license plate, and it's registered to Samuel Harper," Lisa reported.

Ethan exchanged a triumphant glance with Sarah. "That's the evidence we need. Good work, Lisa. Can you send us the footage?"

"Already on its way," Lisa confirmed. "Anything else you need?"

"No, that's it for now. Thanks, Lisa," Sarah said, ending the call. She turned to Ethan, her eyes blazing with determination. "We have our lead. Let's move."

They gathered their team and briefed them on the situation. Within minutes, they were on their way to Harper's last known address, a rundown apartment complex on the outskirts of the city.

As they arrived, the team moved quickly and quietly, surrounding the building. Sarah and Ethan led the way to Harper's apartment on the third floor. Sarah knocked on the door, her hand resting on her holstered weapon. "Samuel Harper, this is the Harborview Police. Open up."

There was a tense silence, followed by the sound of hurried movement inside. "He's trying to run," Ethan muttered, drawing his gun.

Sarah signaled to the officers to cover the back entrance. "Harper, we know you're in there. Open the door, or we're coming in."

When there was no response, Sarah nodded to Ethan. He kicked the door open, and they rushed inside, weapons drawn. Harper was halfway out the window, trying to escape down the fire escape.

"Stop right there!" Sarah shouted. "Hands where I can see them!"

Harper froze, his eyes darting around desperately. Realizing he was trapped, he slowly raised his hands and turned to face them. "Alright, alright, don't shoot."

Ethan cuffed him and led him back inside. "Samuel Harper, you're under arrest for arson and conspiracy. You have the right to remain silent. Anything you say can and will be used against you in a court of law."

Harper scowled but said nothing as he was led away. Sarah felt a surge of triumph. They had their suspect, and now they had the leverage they needed to bring down Paul Andrews and uncover the full extent of the conspiracy.

Back at the precinct, Harper was taken to an interrogation room. Sarah and Ethan sat across from him, ready to get the answers they needed.

"Harper, we know you've been setting fires for Paul Andrews," Sarah began. "We have the evidence—financial records, witness statements, and traffic footage. It's all over for you."

Harper glared at them, his defiance wavering. "What do you want?"

"The truth," Ethan said, leaning forward. "Tell us everything, and maybe we can work out a deal."

Harper hesitated, then sighed. "Fine. I'll talk. But you better keep your end of the bargain."

Sarah nodded. "Start talking."

As Harper began to recount his dealings with Andrews, Sarah and Ethan listened intently, knowing they were finally getting closer to unraveling the conspiracy behind the arson attacks.

Chapter 2
Shadows in the Dark

The morning after Samuel Harper's arrest, the precinct was a hive of activity. Sarah and Ethan, having barely slept, were already in the conference room, poring over the latest developments. Captain Donovan had called for a meeting to discuss the next steps and to address the growing concerns about security.

As the officers gathered, Donovan took his place at the head of the table. "Alright, everyone, listen up. Last night, Detectives Thompson and Drake made significant progress in the arson case. Samuel Harper, a known arsonist, is in custody, and he's started talking. But we're not out of the woods yet."

Sarah glanced at Ethan, who nodded. She took a deep breath and began, "Harper confirmed he was hired by Paul Andrews from Whitman Properties to set the fires. Andrews' motive appears to be financial gain by driving down property values and acquiring them cheaply."

The room buzzed with murmurs. Donovan raised a hand for silence. "We need to tighten security measures around all key locations linked to Whitman Properties. We also need to ensure the safety of all potential witnesses and anyone connected to the case."

Ethan stood up, addressing the team. "We've already identified several high-risk locations. These include buildings owned by Whitman Properties, the homes of the business owners who were targeted, and our own precinct. We can't afford to let our guard down."

Officer Lisa Chen raised her hand. "What about our personnel? Should we increase security for our officers as well?"

Donovan nodded. "Absolutely. Effective immediately, all officers involved in the case will be provided with additional protection. No one goes anywhere alone. We're up against a well-organized operation, and we can't take any chances."

Sarah turned to Lisa. "We also need to monitor communication channels more closely. Harper mentioned that Andrews used burner phones and encrypted messages to communicate. If we can intercept those, we might get ahead of any further plans."

Lisa took notes. "I'll get on it. We'll set up surveillance and tap into any suspicious communications."

Donovan looked around the room, his gaze serious. "This case has taken a dangerous turn. We're dealing with a network that's willing to go to extreme lengths to protect their interests. Stay vigilant and report anything unusual immediately."

Ethan spoke up again. "We should also consider coordinating with other departments. The more eyes we have on this, the better. I'll reach out to neighboring precincts and see if they've had any similar incidents."

Sarah added, "And let's not forget about the press. They're going to be all over this once word gets out. We need to control the narrative and ensure that the public remains informed but not panicked."

Donovan nodded in agreement. "I'll handle the media. We need to present a unified front and reassure the public that we're on top of this."

Officer Jake Martinez, who had been listening intently, leaned forward. "Do we have any intel on Andrews' next move? If he knows Harper has been caught, he might try to run or destroy evidence."

Sarah sighed. "That's a possibility. Harper's information has given us a lot, but we're still piecing everything together. We need to move fast to stay ahead of Andrews. We're executing a search warrant on his properties today."

Donovan looked at his team, his expression resolute. "Alright, everyone. You know what to do. Stay sharp and stay safe. Dismissed."

As the officers filed out, Sarah and Ethan lingered, discussing their next steps. "We need to be ready for anything," Ethan said, his voice low. "Andrews is a cornered animal now. He could lash out in unpredictable ways."

Sarah nodded. "Agreed. Let's make sure all our bases are covered. I'll coordinate with the surveillance team and ensure Harper's information is verified. You handle the search warrant for Andrews' properties."

Ethan patted her shoulder. "We've got this, Sarah. We're close to bringing him down."

Sarah gave a determined smile. "Yes, we are. Let's finish this."

As they walked out of the conference room, the sense of urgency and determination in the air was palpable. The case was reaching a critical point, and every step they took brought them closer to unraveling the dark conspiracy that had cast shadows over their city. With heightened security measures in place and a clear plan of action, Sarah and Ethan were ready to face whatever challenges lay ahead.

The interrogation room at the precinct was stark and sterile, with harsh fluorescent lights that cast sharp shadows on the walls. Sarah and Ethan sat across from Victor Sanchez, a man in his early thirties with a wiry build and nervous eyes. He had been picked up earlier that morning based on information from Samuel Harper. Sanchez was a known associate of Paul Andrews, and they hoped he could provide more insight into the conspiracy.

Sarah leaned forward, her voice calm but firm. "Victor, we know you've been working with Paul Andrews. We need you to tell us everything you know about his operations."

Sanchez shifted uncomfortably in his seat. "I don't know what you're talking about. I'm just a real estate agent."

Ethan interjected, his tone harsher. "Don't play dumb with us, Sanchez. We have evidence linking you to several of the properties that were burned down. We know you were involved."

Sanchez's eyes darted around the room, looking for an escape that wasn't there. "I... I just do what I'm told. Andrews is the one in charge. I didn't want any part of it."

Sarah's gaze softened slightly, sensing an opportunity. "If you cooperate with us, it will go a lot easier for you. Help us bring down Andrews, and we can talk about a deal."

Sanchez hesitated, then nodded slowly. "Alright. What do you want to know?"

Ethan leaned back, giving Sarah the floor. She placed a digital recorder on the table. "Start from the beginning. How did you get involved with Andrews, and what role did you play in his operations?"

Sanchez took a deep breath, his hands trembling slightly. "It started about a year ago. Andrews approached me with a business proposition. He wanted to buy up properties in certain areas, but the owners wouldn't sell. He said he needed someone to convince them, to apply a little pressure."

Sarah raised an eyebrow. "Pressure? What kind of pressure?"

"Harassment, mostly," Sanchez admitted. "Legal threats, bogus fines, things like that. But then it escalated. He started talking about more extreme measures. That's when the fires began."

Ethan leaned forward. "And your role in all this?"

"I was the middleman," Sanchez confessed. "I found the targets, set up the deals, made sure the money flowed. Andrews handled the big picture, but I made it happen on the ground."

Sarah nodded, making notes. "Did you know about Harper? The arsonist?"

"Yeah," Sanchez said, his voice barely above a whisper. "I knew. Andrews brought him in for the dirty work. He wanted plausible deniability, you know? If things went south, Harper would take the fall."

Ethan's jaw tightened. "And the other properties? Are there more targets?"

Sanchez swallowed hard. "There were a few more on the list. But after Harper got caught, Andrews went to ground. He's paranoid now, cutting ties with everyone. He's probably trying to cover his tracks."

Sarah exchanged a glance with Ethan. "We need names, locations, anything you can give us to find Andrews and stop him."

Sanchez nodded, scribbling down addresses and contact names. "This is everything I know. Just... just promise you'll keep me safe."

"We will," Sarah assured him, taking the paper. "You did the right thing, Victor."

As they left the interrogation room, Sarah felt a mixture of relief and determination. They were getting closer to bringing down Andrews, but the danger was far from over.

Ethan looked at her, his eyes serious. "We need to move fast. If Andrews is cutting ties, he might be planning to disappear."

"Agreed," Sarah replied. "Let's get a team together and follow up on these leads. Andrews won't get away."

Back in the conference room, they briefed Captain Donovan on Sanchez's confession. Donovan listened intently, his expression grim.

"Good work," Donovan said. "We'll put a team on these addresses immediately. Andrews won't know what hit him."

Sarah and Ethan nodded, feeling the weight of the case pressing down on them. They were close, but there was still work to be done.

As they prepared for the next phase of their investigation, Sarah couldn't shake the feeling that they were about to uncover something even bigger. The shadows were closing in, but they were ready to face whatever lay ahead.

The team moved quickly, setting up surveillance on the new targets and preparing for the possibility of more arrests. Sarah and Ethan worked tirelessly, knowing that every second counted. The web of conspiracy was unraveling, and they were determined to see it through to the end.

The following days were a whirlwind of activity as Sarah and Ethan chased down every lead provided by Victor Sanchez. They worked long hours, driven by the need to bring Paul Andrews to justice and dismantle his network. Each new clue brought them closer, but the path was fraught with false trails and dead ends.

The precinct's war room was cluttered with maps, photographs, and notes. Sarah stood by the whiteboard, marking new locations as Ethan briefed the team.

"Alright," Ethan began, pointing to a map. "Based on Sanchez's information, these are the properties Andrews was targeting next. We need to hit these locations and see if we can find any more connections."

Officer Lisa Chen, who had been helping with the investigation, raised her hand. "What about the surveillance on Andrews' known associates? Any movement?"

Sarah shook her head. "So far, nothing. It's like they've all gone to ground. But we can't afford to miss anything. We need to keep the pressure on."

Ethan glanced at his notes. "Let's start with the warehouse on 5th Street. It's been flagged as a potential meeting place. We'll split into teams and cover all exits."

The team nodded, gathering their gear. As they prepared to leave, Captain Donovan entered the room. "Detectives, I just got word that Andrews might be planning something big. We need to find him before he disappears for good."

"We're on it, Captain," Sarah replied, her voice filled with determination. "We'll find him."

The drive to the warehouse was tense, each member of the team focused on the task ahead. As they arrived, they spread out, covering all possible exits.

"Remember, we're looking for anything that can link back to Andrews," Sarah reminded them. "Documents, computers, anything."

They entered the warehouse, moving quietly and methodically. The place was empty, but signs of recent activity were evident—footprints in the dust, discarded coffee cups, and a few scattered papers.

Ethan picked up one of the papers, his brow furrowing. "This looks like a shipping manifest. Could be useful."

Sarah nodded, taking a photo of the document. "Bag it. We'll analyze it back at the precinct."

As they continued to search, Officer Martinez called out, "Detectives, over here!"

They rushed over to find Martinez standing by a locked door. "It's the only door we haven't checked."

Ethan nodded. "Let's see what's behind door number one."

They forced the door open to reveal a small office, cluttered with files and a computer. Sarah immediately moved to the computer, booting it up while Ethan searched the desk.

"Bingo," Ethan said, holding up a ledger. "This could be what we're looking for."

Sarah scanned the computer's contents. "Looks like emails and transaction records. Andrews was definitely here."

Just then, Ethan's phone buzzed with an incoming call. "It's Lisa," he said, answering it. "What's up?"

Lisa's voice was urgent. "We've got a problem. One of Andrews' associates, a guy named Tom Granger, just showed up at a safe house we've been watching. He's packing up files and looks ready to run."

"Stay on him," Ethan instructed. "We're wrapping up here and heading your way."

He turned to Sarah. "We need to move. Granger could lead us straight to Andrews."

They gathered the evidence and headed to the safe house. As they arrived, they saw Lisa and her team watching from a distance.

"Granger's inside," Lisa reported. "He's been moving fast, like he knows we're closing in."

Sarah nodded, formulating a plan. "Ethan and I will go in through the front. Lisa, you and Martinez cover the back. No one gets out."

They moved quickly, breaching the front door and sweeping through the house. Granger, caught off guard, tried to make a run for it but was quickly subdued by Martinez at the back door.

"Tom Granger, you're under arrest," Ethan said, cuffing him. "We have some questions for you."

Granger glared at them but said nothing. As they searched the house, they found more documents and a laptop.

"Let's get this back to the precinct," Sarah said. "Maybe Granger's files will give us the final piece we need."

Back at the precinct, they began sifting through the new evidence. Sarah felt a mix of frustration and determination. Each lead seemed to bring them closer, yet Andrews remained elusive.

"Look at this," Ethan said, pointing to an email on Granger's laptop. "It's from Andrews, dated yesterday. He's arranging a meeting at a location we haven't checked yet—the old factory on Pine Street."

Sarah's eyes lit up. "This could be it. Let's gear up and move out."

As they prepared for the raid, the sense of urgency intensified. They were closing in on Andrews, and they knew this might be their best chance to catch him.

The team moved out, ready for whatever awaited them at the factory. The shadows were closing in, but Sarah and Ethan were determined to bring the case to light and put an end to Andrews' arsonist network once and for all.

The precinct was buzzing with anticipation as Sarah and Ethan returned with the evidence from the safe house. They headed straight to the forensics lab, where the team was already at work decoding the ledger and analyzing the files they had retrieved.

Dr. Linda Keller, the head of forensics, greeted them as they entered. "We've made some progress," she said, gesturing to a whiteboard covered in notes and diagrams. "The ledger you found is a goldmine. It's detailed with financial transactions linking directly to several known associates of Paul Andrews."

Sarah's eyes widened. "Can you show us?"

Dr. Keller nodded, pulling up a digital version of the ledger on her computer. "Here, look at this entry. Large sums of money transferred to an account registered to a 'John Ryder.' He's a known enforcer in Andrews' network."

Ethan leaned in, examining the screen. "And what about these other names?"

"Several of them are on our watch list," Dr. Keller confirmed. "But the most interesting one is this—an account linked to a shell company called 'Phoenix Holdings.' We did some digging, and it's directly connected to Andrews. He's been using it to launder money and fund the arson attacks."

Sarah felt a surge of excitement. "This is the breakthrough we needed. With this information, we can track down Andrews and dismantle his entire operation."

Ethan nodded. "We need to move fast. If Andrews gets wind that we're onto Phoenix Holdings, he could disappear for good."

Dr. Keller handed them a stack of printouts. "I've highlighted all the significant transactions and connections. This should help you narrow down your targets."

"Thank you, Linda," Sarah said, taking the documents. "You've just helped us make a huge leap forward."

Back in the war room, Sarah and Ethan spread out the new information on the table, bringing the team up to speed. "We've got a solid lead on Andrews and his network," Sarah began. "Phoenix Holdings is our key target. We need to hit them hard and fast."

Ethan pointed to a map. "We've identified several properties linked to Phoenix Holdings. We'll split into teams and raid these locations simultaneously. Our goal is to apprehend Andrews and his associates, and secure any further evidence."

Officer Lisa Chen raised her hand. "What about the shell company's main office? Do we have an address?"

Sarah nodded. "Yes, it's an office building downtown. We'll need to approach carefully. Andrews is likely to have it heavily guarded."

Captain Donovan entered the room, listening to the plan. "This is a critical operation, folks. We need to be coordinated and precise. Andrews has slipped through our fingers before, but this time, we have the upper hand."

Ethan looked around the room, meeting the eyes of each team member. "Stay sharp. This is our best chance to bring him down. Let's make it count."

As the team prepared to move out, the sense of urgency and determination was palpable. They donned their gear and double-checked their equipment, ready for the simultaneous raids that would hopefully end Andrews' reign of terror.

The convoy of police vehicles moved through the city streets, splitting off to their designated targets. Sarah and Ethan led the team assigned to the main office of Phoenix Holdings, their adrenaline pumping as they approached the building.

They parked a block away, moving in on foot. The office building loomed ahead, its glass facade reflecting the afternoon sun. Sarah signaled for the team to take positions around the entrances, ensuring no one could escape.

"Remember," she whispered into her radio, "we're looking for Andrews and any critical evidence. Move in on my mark."

Ethan nodded, his eyes focused on the building. "Ready when you are."

Sarah took a deep breath. "Go."

The team moved in quickly and efficiently, breaching the doors and sweeping through the building. Inside, they found several of Andrews' associates, who were swiftly apprehended.

"Clear!" one of the officers called out as they secured the main office.

Sarah and Ethan entered the office, finding stacks of documents and computer equipment. "This is it," Sarah said, her voice filled with determination. "Let's gather everything. Andrews won't escape this time."

As they secured the evidence, Ethan's phone buzzed with an incoming call. He answered it, his expression growing serious. "We've got Andrews. He was trying to flee from one of the other properties. He's in custody."

Sarah felt a wave of relief wash over her. "We did it," she said softly. "We finally got him."

Back at the precinct, the mood was one of triumph. Andrews' arrest marked a significant victory, but there was still work to be done. As they began processing the evidence, Sarah and Ethan knew they had taken a major step toward dismantling the entire network.

Captain Donovan addressed the team, his voice filled with pride. "Excellent work, everyone. This was a critical operation, and you handled it with precision and professionalism. We've dealt a significant blow to organized crime in our city."

Sarah and Ethan exchanged a satisfied glance. They had faced countless obstacles and false trails, but their persistence had paid off. The shadows were starting to lift, and they were ready to bring the case to a definitive close.

Chapter 3
The First Clue

The raid at the docks had been intense, but successful. Marco's operations were disrupted, and they had managed to seize crucial evidence. Back at the precinct, Sarah and Ethan began sorting through the items recovered from the raid. They hoped to find something that would finally link Marco directly to the arson attacks.

Sarah spread the confiscated documents across the table. "There's got to be something here. Financial records, blueprints, anything that ties Marco to the fires."

Ethan picked up a folder marked "Confidential" and started flipping through it. "Look at this. It's a ledger. Dates, amounts, and locations. These look like payments, but they're coded."

Sarah leaned over, her eyes scanning the pages. "We need to get this to Garcia. If anyone can crack these codes, it's him."

As they walked over to Garcia's office, Sarah couldn't shake the feeling that they were on the brink of a breakthrough. The evidence they had collected so far was substantial, but they needed concrete proof.

"Garcia," Sarah called as they entered his office. "We need your expertise. We've got a ledger here with coded entries. Can you take a look?"

Garcia adjusted his glasses and took the folder. "Coded, huh? Let's see what we've got." He began examining the pages, his eyes narrowing in concentration.

Ethan crossed his arms, watching Garcia work. "If we can decode this, we might be able to track the money back to Marco and link it to the arson materials."

Garcia nodded, scribbling notes. "This is intricate, but not impossible. I'll need some time, but I should be able to crack it."

Sarah's phone buzzed with a new message. She glanced at it and frowned. "Another taunt from our arsonist. 'Think you're smart? You're just chasing shadows.'"

Ethan shook his head. "He's getting desperate. We're closing in on him, and he knows it."

Garcia looked up from his work. "I'll get on this right away. You'll have the results as soon as possible."

"Thanks, Garcia," Sarah said. "Let us know if you find anything."

As they left Garcia's office, Sarah felt a mix of hope and frustration. They were so close, but the final pieces were still out of reach.

Back at their desks, Ethan started organizing the other evidence they had collected. "We need to go through these items methodically. There might be something we overlooked."

Sarah nodded, pulling out a stack of photographs. "Agreed. Let's start with these. We need to find any detail that connects Marco to the arson scenes."

As they reviewed the photos, one caught Sarah's attention. It was a close-up of a charred piece of paper found at the warehouse, partially burned but still legible. "Ethan, look at this. It's a delivery receipt for industrial chemicals. The kind used in arson."

Ethan examined the photo closely. "If we can trace where these chemicals were delivered and who signed for them, we might have our direct link to Marco."

Sarah grabbed her phone and dialed the number on the receipt. "Hello, this is Detective Sarah Thompson with the Harborview Police. I need information on a delivery made to the docks recently. It's crucial to an ongoing investigation."

The voice on the other end responded, and Sarah took detailed notes. "Thank you, I appreciate your cooperation."

As she hung up, she turned to Ethan, her eyes shining with determination. "The delivery was made to a warehouse registered under a shell company. The same company we linked to Marco's financial records. We've got him."

Ethan grinned, the first real sign of optimism in days. "That's the connection we needed. Let's get a warrant and bring him in."

Sarah and Ethan moved quickly, the pieces finally falling into place. They had the evidence, the leads, and now, they had the determination to see it through. They were ready to take Marco down once and for all.

Sarah and Ethan returned to Garcia's office, their anticipation palpable. Garcia looked up from his desk, a triumphant gleam in his eye. "You're in luck. I managed to decode the ledger."

Sarah leaned in, eager to hear the details. "What did you find?"

Garcia spread the decoded pages across his desk. "These entries correspond to payments made to various suppliers for arson materials. We've got dates, amounts, and recipients. It's all here."

Ethan scanned the pages quickly. "This is gold. We can use this to track down the suppliers and link them back to Marco."

Garcia nodded. "Exactly. And there's more. Some of the payments were made to a known associate of Marco's, a guy named Luis Ortega. He's been on our radar for a while."

Sarah's mind raced. "If we can bring in Ortega, he might flip on Marco. This could be our chance to get a direct testimony linking Marco to the arson attacks."

Ethan turned to Garcia. "Can you get us the addresses for these suppliers? We need to move fast."

Garcia handed them a list. "Already done. Be careful out there. These guys won't go down without a fight."

Sarah and Ethan gathered their team and briefed them on the plan. "We're hitting these locations simultaneously," Sarah explained. "We need to catch them off guard and secure as much evidence as possible."

Ethan nodded in agreement. "Our priority is to bring in Ortega. He's our key to linking everything back to Marco."

They moved out swiftly, the urgency of their mission driving them forward. The first location was a small warehouse on the outskirts of the city. As they approached, Sarah signaled for the team to take their positions.

"Ready?" Ethan whispered.

Sarah nodded. "Let's do this."

They breached the door, moving in with precision. Inside, they found stacks of chemical containers and equipment. The workers, caught off guard, raised their hands in surrender.

"Police! Everyone down on the ground!" Sarah shouted, securing the area.

Ethan began questioning the workers while Sarah checked the office. She found a ledger matching the one they had decoded, confirming their suspicions. "Ethan, we've got a match. This place is definitely connected to Marco."

Ethan cuffed one of the workers and brought him over. "Who runs this operation?"

The man hesitated, then mumbled, "Luis Ortega. He's in charge."

Sarah's eyes lit up. "Where is he?"

"Usually at the main warehouse downtown," the man replied, fear evident in his voice. "Please, I don't want any trouble."

Ethan secured the scene, making sure all evidence was collected. "Sarah, we need to move. Ortega's the key."

They left the warehouse, adrenaline pumping. The team regrouped and headed to the main warehouse. As they arrived, Sarah noticed a familiar figure slipping inside.

"That's Ortega," she whispered to Ethan. "Let's move."

They approached the building cautiously. Inside, they found Ortega overseeing a shipment. Sarah stepped forward, her gun drawn. "Luis Ortega! Harborview Police! You're under arrest!"

Ortega froze, then turned to run. Ethan tackled him, pinning him to the ground. "It's over, Ortega. You're coming with us."

Ortega struggled, but Sarah cuffed him securely. "We know about the payments, the arson materials. You're done."

Ortega glared at them. "You think you can stop Marco? He's untouchable."

"Maybe," Sarah replied, her voice firm. "But we're going to try. And you're going to help us."

Back at the precinct, they began questioning Ortega. Ethan played the good cop, trying to coax information from him. "Luis, you're looking at serious charges. Help us, and we can work something out."

Ortega remained silent, his defiance apparent. Sarah leaned in, her tone cold. "You can protect Marco all you want, but when he finds out you're in custody, he'll cut you loose. Think about your options."

Ortega's resolve started to crack. "Alright. I'll talk. But I want protection. Marco's got eyes everywhere."

Ethan nodded. "You'll get protection. Now, tell us everything."

Ortega took a deep breath, then began spilling details about Marco's operations, his associates, and his plans. With each word, the net tightened around Marco Alvarez.

As the interrogation continued, Sarah and Ethan felt the momentum shifting in their favor. They were getting closer to bringing Marco to justice, and nothing would stop them now.

Sarah and Ethan sat in the interrogation room with Luis Ortega, the tension in the air palpable. Ortega's initial resistance had waned, and now he looked more resigned than defiant.

"Alright, Luis," Sarah began, her voice steady. "We've got you on record. You're involved in Marco Alvarez's operations. If you want any chance of a deal, you need to give us everything."

Ortega shifted in his chair, eyes darting between Sarah and Ethan. "I told you already. Marco's planning something big. The fires were just a distraction."

Ethan leaned forward, his gaze intense. "A distraction for what?"

"Money laundering," Ortega replied, his voice low. "Marco's using the chaos to cover his tracks. He's moving large sums of money through legitimate businesses, making it look clean."

Sarah glanced at Ethan, then back to Ortega. "We need specifics. Names, locations, dates."

Ortega sighed. "Fine. He's got a guy named Victor handling the finances. The money gets funneled through several shell companies. One of them is called Green Horizon Enterprises. They're fronting as an environmental consulting firm."

Ethan jotted down the information. "Where is Victor now?"

"He operates out of a small office downtown," Ortega said. "But he moves around a lot. Marco's paranoid about getting caught."

Sarah's mind raced. "What about the chemicals used in the fires? Where are they coming from?"

Ortega hesitated, then relented. "There's a supplier named Javier. He's got a warehouse near the industrial district. Supplies everything Marco needs."

"Good," Sarah said, her voice firm. "This is useful. But we need more. What's Marco's next move?"

Ortega's eyes flickered with fear. "He's planning another fire. This time, it's the central bank. He wants to destroy evidence linking him to the money laundering."

Ethan's expression hardened. "When is this supposed to happen?"

"Two days from now," Ortega admitted. "He's got everything in place."

Sarah stood up, determination burning in her eyes. "Alright, Luis. You've done the right thing. We'll make sure you're protected. But if you're lying or holding back, there won't be any deals."

Ortega nodded, looking relieved. "I'm telling you everything. I don't want to go down for this."

Sarah and Ethan left the interrogation room, immediately heading to Chief Donovan's office. The urgency of the situation pressed heavily on them.

"Chief, we've got intel on Marco's next target," Sarah said as they entered. "He's planning to hit the central bank in two days."

Donovan's eyes widened. "That's serious. We need to mobilize all units and coordinate with bank security. This could be catastrophic."

Ethan handed over his notes. "We also have leads on his financial handler, Victor, and the chemical supplier, Javier. We need to move on these immediately."

Donovan nodded, already making calls. "Get teams ready. We're hitting all these locations simultaneously. We can't afford any slip-ups."

Sarah and Ethan left the office, their minds racing with the plan. "I'll take the team to Javier's warehouse," Sarah said. "You handle Victor."

Ethan agreed. "We need to be quick and efficient. Marco's not going to wait around for us to catch him."

They gathered their teams, briefing them on the new intel. The atmosphere was tense but focused. Every officer knew the stakes.

As they prepared to move out, Sarah took a deep breath. "Remember, Marco's dangerous. Stay sharp and watch each other's backs. We bring him down tonight."

With that, they split into their respective units, ready to take on the task ahead. The clock was ticking, and failure was not an option.

The precinct was abuzz with activity as the teams prepared for the simultaneous raids. Sarah gathered her team in the briefing room, the tension palpable.

"Alright, everyone," Sarah began, her voice clear and authoritative. "We have intel that Marco Alvarez's supplier, Javier, is operating out of a warehouse near the industrial district. Our objective is to secure the location, apprehend Javier, and seize any chemicals or evidence linking him to the arson attacks."

One of the officers, Lisa, raised her hand. "Detective, do we have any intel on the security at the warehouse?"

"Good question," Sarah replied. "From what we know, the warehouse isn't heavily guarded, but we can't take any chances. Assume that Javier has a few men on the lookout. We go in fast and secure the area."

Ethan, leading a separate team, gave his final instructions as well. "My team will head downtown to Victor's office. Our goal is to apprehend him and seize any financial records that can link Marco to the money laundering. We need to be thorough and quick."

Sarah's phone buzzed with a message from Chief Donovan: "All teams ready. Commence operation on your command."

Sarah looked at her team, their faces set with determination. "Remember, this is a coordinated effort. Timing is crucial. We move in five. Stay safe out there."

As the teams moved out, Sarah and Ethan exchanged a nod of solidarity. "Good luck," Sarah said. "Let's bring this guy down."

Ethan gave a tight smile. "You too. We've got this."

The drive to the industrial district was tense. Sarah reviewed the plan in her head, ensuring every detail was covered. "Lisa, you take the rear entrance with two officers. We'll secure the front. No one gets in or out without our say."

"Got it," Lisa responded, her grip on her weapon firm.

They arrived at the warehouse, the dim lighting casting eerie shadows across the area. Sarah signaled for the team to take their positions. "Go," she whispered into her radio.

They moved swiftly, the element of surprise on their side. Sarah and two officers breached the front entrance, weapons drawn. Inside, they found a group of men around a table, similar to the scene at the docks.

"Police! Don't move!" Sarah shouted, the men freezing in their spots.

One of the men, presumably Javier, bolted for the back door. Lisa's team intercepted him, tackling him to the ground. "Got him!" Lisa called out.

Sarah secured the other men, cuffing them quickly. "Where are the chemicals?" she demanded.

Javier glared at her but remained silent. Sarah searched the room, finding a hidden compartment filled with industrial-grade chemicals. "We've got the evidence," she said, her voice steady.

Meanwhile, Ethan's team faced their own challenges. They breached Victor's office, finding him in the middle of shredding documents. "Victor!" Ethan barked. "Step away from the shredder and put your hands where I can see them!"

Victor hesitated but complied, raising his hands. "You're making a big mistake," he said, his voice shaking.

"We'll see about that," Ethan replied, cuffing him. "Search the place," he ordered his team.

They found financial records, ledgers, and digital files linking Marco to the money laundering scheme. Ethan felt a surge of triumph. "We've got him."

Back at the precinct, Sarah and Ethan reconvened, their evidence laid out before them. Chief Donovan joined them, his expression one of cautious optimism.

"Good work, both of you," Donovan said. "We've disrupted Marco's operations significantly. Now, let's prepare to take him down once and for all."

Sarah looked at the evidence, feeling a sense of accomplishment but knowing the hardest part was yet to come. "We're ready, Chief. Marco's not slipping through our fingers this time."

The teams began coordinating the final phase of their plan. Every detail was meticulously reviewed, every possible outcome considered. They knew Marco would be a formidable opponent, but they were prepared.

As they moved into position for the final raid, Sarah felt a sense of unity among her team. They were all driven by the same goal: to bring Marco Alvarez to justice and put an end to his reign of terror.

With a final nod to her team, Sarah gave the command. "Move in. Let's finish this."

The night was far from over, but for the first time, Sarah felt they were on the verge of victory. The pieces were falling into place, and soon, Marco Alvarez would face the consequences of his actions.

Chapter 4
Personal Stakes

The precinct was buzzing with activity, the culmination of their efforts against Marco Alvarez creating an electric atmosphere. Sarah Thompson, however, felt a mixture of exhilaration and dread. She had been waiting for this moment for years, ever since the unsolved case of Jamie Reed had left an indelible mark on her career and psyche.

Sarah sat at her desk, staring at the old case file of Jamie Reed. It was worn from countless readings, the edges frayed. She traced her fingers over Jamie's photo, a young man full of life and potential. His tragic death had haunted her, driving her to pursue justice with relentless determination.

Ethan walked over, sensing her turmoil. "Sarah, we're ready to move on Marco. You okay?"

Sarah nodded, though her eyes remained fixed on Jamie's photo. "I've waited a long time for this, Ethan. Jamie's death... it changed everything for me. I need to see this through."

Ethan placed a reassuring hand on her shoulder. "We will. Jamie deserves justice, and so do all the other victims. We're going to bring Marco down."

Taking a deep breath, Sarah closed the file and stood up. "Let's do this."

The team assembled in the briefing room, a large map of the city pinned to the wall with various locations marked. Chief Donovan stood at the front, outlining the final phase of their operation.

"Listen up, everyone," Donovan began, his voice commanding attention. "We've gathered enough evidence to make a move on Marco Alvarez. Our intel indicates he's currently at a safe house on the outskirts of the city. This is our chance to take him down once and for all."

Sarah and Ethan stood at the front with Donovan, ready to lead the charge. "Marco is dangerous," Sarah emphasized. "He won't go down without a fight. Stay sharp and watch each other's backs. This is it."

The team nodded, a mixture of determination and resolve on their faces. They moved out, the tension mounting as they approached their vehicles. Sarah and Ethan rode together, the weight of the moment pressing heavily on them.

"Do you think Marco knows we're coming?" Ethan asked, breaking the silence.

Sarah shook her head. "We've been careful, but he's always one step ahead. We need to be ready for anything."

The drive to Marco's safe house was tense, the city lights blurring past as they sped through the streets. Sarah's mind raced with memories of Jamie and the countless hours she had poured into this investigation. This was personal, and she wouldn't rest until Marco was brought to justice.

As they neared the location, the team coordinated their positions, surrounding the safe house to cut off any escape routes. Sarah and Ethan led the main assault team, their movements precise and silent.

"Remember, we need Marco alive," Sarah reminded her team. "He has to answer for his crimes."

They approached the house, the darkness providing cover. Sarah signaled for the team to breach the front door, their entry swift and efficient. Inside, the house was dimly lit, the silence almost deafening.

"Clear the rooms," Ethan ordered, his voice a low whisper.

The team moved methodically, checking each room and securing any occupants. As they reached the back of the house, they found Marco in a small office, his back to the door, working on a laptop.

"Marco Alvarez," Sarah announced, her gun trained on him. "You're under arrest."

Marco turned slowly, a chilling smile on his face. "Detective Thompson, I've been expecting you."

"Hands where we can see them," Ethan commanded, stepping forward.

Marco complied, his demeanor eerily calm. "You think you've won? This is far from over."

Sarah's eyes burned with anger. "We'll see about that. Cuff him."

As Ethan secured Marco, Sarah scanned the room, her eyes landing on a series of documents spread across the desk. Financial records, blueprints, and a list of names—evidence of Marco's extensive operations.

"We've got everything we need," Sarah said, feeling a sense of triumph. "Let's get him out of here."

The team moved quickly, escorting Marco out of the house and into a waiting vehicle. As they drove back to the precinct, Sarah couldn't help but feel a weight lifting off her shoulders. They had finally captured Marco Alvarez, and justice for Jamie Reed and the other victims was within reach.

Back at the precinct, they processed Marco, securing him in an interrogation room. Sarah stood outside, watching through the one-way glass. This was the moment she had been waiting for, the culmination of years of relentless pursuit.

Ethan joined her, a look of satisfaction on his face. "We did it, Sarah. We finally got him."

Sarah nodded, a mixture of relief and determination in her eyes. "Now it's time to make sure he pays for everything he's done."

As they prepared to question Marco, Sarah felt a renewed sense of purpose. The shadows of the past had led them here, but now, with Marco in custody, they had the chance to bring everything into the light. Justice was within reach, and Sarah was ready to see it through to the end.

The interrogation room was dimly lit, casting long shadows across Marco Alvarez's face as he sat at the metal table, his hands cuffed in front of him. His expression was unreadable, a mix of defiance and smugness. Sarah Thompson stood outside the room, watching through the one-way glass, her emotions a turbulent mix of anger and determination.

Ethan Drake entered the observation room, his face serious. "Are you ready for this, Sarah?"

She nodded, her eyes never leaving Marco. "I've been ready for this moment for years. He's going to answer for everything."

Ethan placed a reassuring hand on her shoulder. "Let's go in together. We've got this."

They entered the interrogation room, the door closing with a heavy thud behind them. Sarah took a seat across from Marco, while Ethan stood to the side, his presence a silent but formidable support.

"Marco Alvarez," Sarah began, her voice steady but cold. "You're facing charges of arson, murder, money laundering, and conspiracy. We have enough evidence to put you away for life."

Marco leaned back in his chair, a faint smile playing on his lips. "You think you've got it all figured out, don't you, Detective? But this is just the beginning."

Sarah's eyes narrowed. "What do you mean by that?"

Marco's smile widened. "You've disrupted some of my operations, sure. But you have no idea how deep this goes. There are others out there, and they're not going to stop just because I'm behind bars."

"We'll take down every single one of them," Ethan interjected, his voice firm. "Starting with you."

Marco chuckled, a low, chilling sound. "You're welcome to try. But you're in over your heads."

Sarah leaned forward, her gaze piercing. "We've already taken down your suppliers and seized your assets. It's over, Marco. The sooner you accept that, the better."

For a moment, Marco's mask of arrogance slipped, revealing a flicker of uncertainty. But it was gone as quickly as it appeared. "You think you've won because you've captured me. But my reach extends far beyond this city."

Sarah felt a surge of anger but kept her composure. "You killed Jamie Reed. You burned him alive to cover your tracks. You've caused countless other deaths and destruction. You're a monster, Marco, and you're going to pay for your crimes."

Marco's eyes flashed with something unreadable. "Jamie was a loose end. He knew too much, and he was a liability. Just like anyone else who gets too close."

Ethan stepped closer, his voice cold. "You're not untouchable, Marco. You're just a criminal who finally got caught."

Marco's gaze shifted to Ethan, his smile returning. "Maybe. But you'll never get the whole truth. There are things in motion you can't even begin to understand."

Sarah stood up, her resolve hardening. "We'll see about that. For now, you're going to sit here and think about all the lives you've destroyed."

She and Ethan left the room, the door closing with a finality that felt satisfying. Outside, they took a moment to collect themselves, the weight of the confrontation heavy on their shoulders.

"Do you think he's bluffing?" Ethan asked, concern evident in his voice.

"I don't know," Sarah admitted. "But we can't take any chances. We need to dig deeper into his operations and find out who else is involved."

Ethan nodded. "Agreed. Let's start with the leads we've got from his files and see where they take us."

They returned to the evidence room, where the confiscated documents were spread out on a large table. Sarah picked up a blueprint marked with several locations around the city.

"These are the places we need to check out," she said, tracing the marks with her finger. "If Marco has associates still operating, they'll be here."

Ethan joined her, studying the blueprint. "We'll need to coordinate with other units and move quickly. We can't let them regroup or retaliate."

Sarah felt a renewed sense of determination. "We've come this far, Ethan. We can't let up now. We'll bring down every last one of them."

They spent the next few hours planning their next moves, their focus unwavering. The precinct buzzed with activity as officers prepared for the upcoming raids. Sarah felt a sense of camaraderie and purpose among her colleagues, a shared resolve to see justice served.

As the night wore on, Sarah found herself alone in the evidence room, the quiet allowing her a moment of reflection. She thought of Jamie Reed and the promise she had made to his family. They were close to fulfilling that promise, but there was still work to be done.

Ethan re-entered the room, breaking the silence. "Everything's in place. We move at dawn."

Sarah nodded, grateful for his steadfast support. "We're going to finish this, Ethan. For Jamie, and for all the victims."

Together, they stood ready to face whatever challenges lay ahead, united in their mission to bring justice to those who had suffered at Marco Alvarez's hands. The final showdown was imminent, and they were prepared to see it through to the end.

The precinct buzzed with activity as officers prepared for the next phase of the operation. Sarah and Ethan, however, were focused on the task at hand—getting Marco Alvarez to reveal more about his network. They reentered the interrogation room, determined to break his silence.

Marco sat at the table, still exuding an air of defiance. Sarah took a seat across from him, while Ethan stood beside her, a silent yet formidable presence.

"Marco, we've got enough evidence to put you away for life," Sarah began, her tone firm. "But we need more. Who are your associates? Who's still out there?"

Marco smirked. "You really think I'm going to give up my people? You're more naïve than I thought, Detective."

Ethan leaned forward, his eyes narrowing. "You're looking at serious time, Marco. Cooperate, and maybe we can work something out. Keep stonewalling, and you're only making it worse for yourself."

Marco shrugged, feigning nonchalance. "I've got nothing to say."

Sarah took a deep breath, her mind racing for another angle. "You said earlier that this is just the beginning. What did you mean by that?"

Marco's eyes flickered with a hint of amusement. "You think taking me down stops everything? There are others who will take my place. You've only scratched the surface."

Ethan crossed his arms, his voice steady but intense. "Then help us dig deeper. Give us names, locations, anything. This is your chance to make a deal."

Marco leaned back, considering his options. "Why should I trust you? You'll just throw me in a cell and forget about me."

Sarah met his gaze, her expression resolute. "You help us, and we'll make sure you're protected. We're offering you a way out, Marco. Don't waste it."

For a moment, Marco seemed to waver, but then he shook his head. "I'm not saying a word."

Ethan exchanged a frustrated glance with Sarah. "You're making a mistake, Marco. This is your last chance."

Marco's defiance returned. "I guess I'll just have to take my chances."

Realizing they were getting nowhere, Sarah stood up, signaling to Ethan. "We'll see how long your loyalty lasts, Marco. Think about what you stand to lose."

As they left the room, Sarah felt a surge of frustration. "He's not going to break easily."

Ethan nodded. "We need to find another way to pressure him. Maybe we can leverage someone else in his network."

Sarah agreed. "Let's go over the evidence again. There has to be something we missed."

They returned to the evidence room, poring over the documents and files. Hours passed, their determination unwavering. Finally, Sarah found a lead—a series of payments made to a secondary supplier not previously identified.

"Ethan, look at this," she said, pointing to the documents. "These payments were made to a company called Silver Star Imports. We need to check this out."

Ethan nodded, already making calls. "I'll get a team together. We can't afford to waste any time."

They gathered their team and briefed them on the new lead. "This could be the break we need," Sarah explained. "We're hitting Silver Star Imports. Stay sharp and be ready for anything."

The team moved out, the anticipation building. Sarah and Ethan led the charge, their focus unrelenting. The stakes were higher than ever, but they were ready to see it through.

The drive to Silver Star Imports was tense, the team brimming with anticipation. Sarah and Ethan reviewed the plan, their minds focused on the task at hand. They arrived at the nondescript warehouse, its exterior giving no hint of the illicit activities within.

"Alright, everyone," Sarah said, addressing the team. "We go in quick and secure the area. No mistakes."

The team nodded, their faces set with determination. They moved to their positions, ready to breach the entrance on Sarah's signal. "Go," she whispered into her radio.

The door burst open, and the team flooded in, their movements swift and precise. Inside, they found a group of men gathered around pallets of chemicals and supplies. The men froze, caught off guard by the sudden intrusion.

"Police! Hands up!" Ethan shouted, his voice echoing through the warehouse.

The men complied, raising their hands in surrender. Sarah moved quickly, securing the area and directing the team to search the premises. "Check every corner. We need to find anything that links this place to Marco."

As the team conducted their search, Ethan approached one of the detained men. "Who's in charge here?"

The man hesitated, then pointed to a burly figure at the back of the warehouse. "Him. He runs the place."

Sarah and Ethan approached the man, who glared at them defiantly. "You're making a big mistake," he spat. "You have no idea who you're dealing with."

"We know exactly who we're dealing with," Sarah replied coldly. "And we're shutting you down."

Ethan cuffed the man, securing him with the others. "We've got this place locked down, Sarah. Let's see what we can find."

The team uncovered a hidden office in the back, filled with ledgers, invoices, and shipping records. Sarah sifted through the documents, her eyes widening as she realized the scale of the operation.

"Ethan, look at this," she called, holding up a series of documents. "These records show shipments to multiple locations across the city. This isn't just about arson. It's a full-scale criminal enterprise."

Ethan joined her, examining the papers. "We've been focusing on the fires, but this is so much bigger. Money laundering, drug trafficking, illegal arms—Marco's network is extensive."

Sarah felt a chill run down her spine. "We've been looking at this all wrong. Marco's just a piece of a much larger puzzle."

Ethan nodded, his expression grim. "We need to bring this to Donovan. He needs to know what we're dealing with."

Back at the precinct, Sarah and Ethan presented their findings to Chief Donovan. The gravity of the situation was clear as Donovan reviewed the evidence.

"This is huge," Donovan said, his voice tense. "We've been targeting Marco, but his network is far more extensive than we realized. We need to expand our investigation and bring in federal agencies."

Sarah nodded. "Agreed. We're going to need all the help we can get to take down this operation."

Ethan looked at Sarah, determination in his eyes. "We've come this far. We can't stop now."

Donovan stood, his resolve firm. "I'll make the calls. In the meantime, you two keep digging. Find every connection, every link. We're going to dismantle this network piece by piece."

As they left Donovan's office, Sarah felt a renewed sense of purpose. The battle against Marco Alvarez had revealed a much larger war, but she was ready to fight it. She and Ethan returned to the evidence room, their determination unwavering.

"We need to track down every lead, follow every thread," Sarah said, her voice steady. "We're not just bringing down Marco. We're taking down the whole operation."

Ethan nodded, already diving into the files. "We'll find them, Sarah. We'll bring them all to justice."

As the night wore on, they worked tirelessly, driven by the knowledge that they were making a difference. The shadows of Marco's network loomed large, but they were ready to bring everything into the light. Justice would be served, and they would see it through to the end.

Chapter 5
The Threat

The atmosphere in the precinct was thick with tension as Sarah Thompson and Ethan Drake prepared for the next phase of their mission. The realization that Marco Alvarez's criminal network was far more extensive than they had initially believed had cast a new light on their investigation. The stakes were higher, and the dangers more pronounced.

In the briefing room, Chief Donovan stood before the assembled officers, his face grave. "We have new information indicating that Marco's network extends beyond arson and into money laundering, drug trafficking, and illegal arms. This is a full-scale criminal enterprise, and we need to be prepared for increased threats."

Sarah and Ethan exchanged a glance, the weight of the situation settling on their shoulders. They knew the risks were escalating, but so was their resolve to see justice served.

Donovan continued, "We'll be coordinating with federal agencies, but for now, we need to tighten security and ensure the safety of everyone involved in this investigation. That includes witnesses, officers, and our own families."

Sarah nodded, stepping forward. "Chief, I recommend we establish a secure communication line with the federal agencies. We need to stay coordinated and make sure no information slips through the cracks."

"Agreed," Donovan replied. "Ethan, you'll handle the logistics for the secure line. Sarah, I need you to brief the witness protection team. We can't afford any slip-ups."

As the meeting adjourned, Sarah and Ethan moved swiftly to their tasks. The urgency of their mission had never been clearer. They met in the hallway, their expressions mirroring the seriousness of the situation.

"Ethan, once you've set up the secure line, meet me in the witness protection unit. We need to make sure everyone's on the same page," Sarah said, her voice steady but intense.

"You got it," Ethan replied, heading towards the tech room.

Sarah made her way to the witness protection unit, her mind racing with the new developments. She entered the unit, where Officer Jenny Morris was coordinating the protection details.

"Jenny, we need to update the protection protocols," Sarah began, her tone urgent. "Marco's network is bigger than we thought. We need to ensure that every witness is secure and that our officers are prepared for any escalation."

Jenny nodded, already making notes. "I'll increase the patrols and double-check the security measures at the safe houses. We can't leave anything to chance."

Sarah appreciated Jenny's efficiency. "Good. Make sure every officer knows the risks. We need to be vigilant."

As she left the unit, Sarah's phone buzzed with a message from Ethan: "Secure line set up. Meet in conference room."

She made her way to the conference room, where Ethan was waiting with a laptop set up for the secure communication. "We're connected to the federal task force," Ethan said, gesturing to the screen.

On the screen, Agent Marcus Lawson from the FBI appeared, his expression serious. "Detective Thompson, Officer Drake, thank you for coordinating with us. We've reviewed your intel and agree that the threat level is significant. We're mobilizing resources to assist with the investigation."

"Thank you, Agent Lawson," Sarah replied. "We need to ensure that all our efforts are synchronized. We can't afford any missteps."

Lawson nodded. "Agreed. We'll have agents on the ground by tomorrow morning. In the meantime, keep us updated on any new developments."

As the call ended, Sarah felt a sense of relief knowing they had federal support, but the pressure remained. She and Ethan returned to their desks, preparing for the long night ahead.

"Ethan, let's go over the plan one more time," Sarah said, spreading out the maps and documents on the table. "We need to hit every location linked to Marco's network simultaneously. We can't give them time to regroup."

Ethan nodded, his focus unwavering. "We've got teams ready to move on your command. The key is coordination. If we can disrupt their operations all at once, we have a better chance of bringing them down."

Sarah agreed. "And we need to be ready for retaliation. Marco's not going to go down without a fight. Make sure everyone's on high alert."

The hours ticked by as they fine-tuned their strategy, ensuring every detail was covered. The weight of their responsibility was immense, but so was their determination. They knew the risks, but they also knew the stakes. This was their chance to dismantle a criminal empire and bring justice to those who had suffered.

As dawn approached, the precinct buzzed with activity. Officers geared up, final briefings were given, and the teams prepared to move out. Sarah and Ethan stood ready, their resolve unshaken.

"Remember," Sarah said, addressing the assembled officers. "We're in this together. Watch each other's backs and stay focused. We're taking down Marco and his entire network today."

Ethan added, "We've come a long way, and this is our moment. Let's make it count."

With a final nod, the teams moved out, the anticipation palpable. The battle against Marco Alvarez was far from over, but they were ready for whatever lay ahead.

The morning sun cast a harsh light over the city as Sarah and Ethan drove towards the headquarters of Green Horizon Enterprises. This supposedly legitimate business was a key link in Marco Alvarez's money laundering operation. Their goal: to gather concrete evidence that would solidify their case and expose the full extent of Marco's criminal network.

As they approached the sleek, modern building, Ethan glanced at Sarah. "You ready for this?"

Sarah nodded, her expression determined. "We need to get in there and find something that ties this place directly to Marco. Let's stay sharp."

They parked and entered the building, flashing their badges at the receptionist. "Detective Thompson, Harborview Police," Sarah announced. "We need to speak with your manager."

The receptionist's eyes widened slightly but she quickly composed herself. "Of course, one moment please." She picked up the phone and spoke in hushed tones. "Mr. Hayes, the police are here to see you."

A few moments later, a tall man with a stern expression approached them. "I'm Robert Hayes, the manager. How can I help you?"

Sarah and Ethan exchanged a glance before Sarah spoke. "Mr. Hayes, we're here as part of an ongoing investigation. We need to look at your financial records."

Hayes frowned. "Is there a problem, Detectives?"

"We have reason to believe this company is being used for illegal activities," Ethan said bluntly. "We need to see your records."

Hayes hesitated, clearly conflicted. "This is highly irregular. Do you have a warrant?"

Sarah handed him the warrant, her voice firm. "We do. Now, please show us to your records."

Hayes sighed and led them to a large office filled with filing cabinets and computers. "Everything is here. Our financial officer, Linda, will assist you."

Linda, a middle-aged woman with sharp eyes, looked up as they entered. "What's going on, Robert?"

"They're here to see our financial records, Linda," Hayes explained. "Cooperate fully."

Linda nodded, clearly uneasy but compliant. "What exactly are you looking for, Detectives?"

"Any transactions that seem out of the ordinary," Sarah replied. "Large sums, unusual recipients, anything that stands out."

Ethan started going through the digital records while Sarah combed through the physical files. The room was silent except for the rustle of papers and the occasional click of the mouse.

After an hour of searching, Ethan's eyes lit up. "Sarah, take a look at this." He pointed to a series of transactions on the screen. "These payments don't match the company's regular business activities. They're all funneled through multiple shell companies."

Sarah examined the screen closely. "These are significant amounts. This is exactly what we need."

She turned to Linda. "Can you explain these transactions?"

Linda looked visibly nervous. "I don't handle these specific accounts, but they've been authorized by upper management."

"Who exactly authorized these?" Ethan asked, his tone insistent.

Linda hesitated, then pulled out a file. "Mr. Hayes and a few others at the top level."

Sarah exchanged a glance with Ethan. "We need copies of all these records. This is critical evidence."

As they gathered the documents, Sarah turned to Hayes, who had been watching the entire process. "Mr. Hayes, you're going to need to come with us for further questioning."

Hayes looked resigned. "I didn't know what was happening. I was just following orders."

"We'll sort that out back at the precinct," Ethan said, his voice firm. "For now, you're coming with us."

They escorted Hayes out of the building and back to the precinct. Once there, Sarah and Ethan began the interrogation.

"Mr. Hayes," Sarah started, "We need you to tell us everything you know about these transactions and who's behind them."

Hayes sighed, rubbing his temples. "Look, I honestly didn't know the full extent of what was going on. I was given instructions to authorize certain transactions. They came from someone higher up, someone I never met directly. The orders were always very clear, and there were threats if I didn't comply."

"Who gave you these orders?" Ethan pressed.

Hayes shook his head. "I don't know his real name. We always referred to him as 'The Handler.' He's the one coordinating everything, but he's a ghost. No one knows who he really is."

Sarah felt a chill. "And you have no idea how to contact him?"

"No," Hayes replied. "He contacts us. It's always through encrypted messages or phone calls from untraceable numbers."

Ethan leaned forward, his gaze intense. "We need to find this Handler. He's the key to dismantling Marco's entire operation."

Hayes nodded, his face pale. "I'll give you access to all my communications. Maybe you can find something I missed."

As they left the interrogation room, Sarah turned to Ethan. "We're getting closer. We need to find this Handler. He's the missing link."

Ethan nodded, determination in his eyes. "Let's dig through Hayes's communications and see what we can uncover. We're not stopping until we bring this whole operation down."

With renewed resolve, they began the painstaking task of sifting through Hayes's communications, determined to find the elusive Handler and bring an end to Marco Alvarez's criminal empire.

Back at the precinct, Sarah and Ethan were hunched over their desks, pouring over Hayes's communications. The office was quiet, the usual buzz of activity muted by the weight of their investigation. The dim light from the desk lamps cast long shadows, adding to the intensity of their work.

Sarah's phone buzzed with a notification. She glanced at it and then turned to Ethan. "I've got something. An encrypted message from 'The Handler.'"

Ethan looked up, his eyes narrowing. "What does it say?"

Sarah read aloud, "'Ensure the transfer is complete. The bank needs to be ready by Thursday.'"

"The bank?" Ethan echoed. "Which bank?"

Sarah quickly scanned through more of the messages. "Here it is. Central Savings Bank. They're planning something there."

Ethan's expression hardened. "We need to move fast. If Marco's planning to hit a bank, it could be catastrophic."

Sarah stood up, her resolve unwavering. "Let's brief the team. We need to secure that bank and stop whatever Marco has planned."

They gathered the team in the briefing room, the tension palpable. Sarah addressed the assembled officers, her voice steady. "We've uncovered a plan to target Central Savings Bank. We don't have all the details yet, but we know it's happening soon. We need to secure the bank and prevent any attacks."

One of the officers, Lisa, raised her hand. "Do we know what kind of attack it could be?"

Ethan responded, "It could be anything from a heist to another arson. We need to be prepared for any scenario."

Sarah added, "We'll coordinate with bank security and have officers stationed at all entry points. We can't afford to let anything slip through the cracks."

The team nodded, their faces set with determination. They moved out quickly, heading towards Central Savings Bank. The streets were bustling with the usual midday activity, but the officers were focused on their mission.

Upon arrival, they met with the bank's head of security, Mr. Turner, a tall man with a stern expression. "Detectives, what's going on?"

Sarah explained the situation. "We have credible intel that your bank is a target. We need to secure the premises and ensure everyone's safety."

Turner frowned. "This is serious. What do you need from us?"

Ethan stepped in. "We need access to your security feeds and a list of all personnel. We'll station officers at every entrance and patrol the interior."

Turner nodded, already making calls to his team. "Consider it done."

Sarah and Ethan coordinated the security measures, ensuring every corner of the bank was covered. They set up a command post in Turner's office, monitoring the security feeds for any suspicious activity.

Hours passed, the tension mounting with each passing minute. The bank's regular operations continued, but there was an underlying sense of unease among the staff and customers. Sarah kept a close eye on the feeds, her mind racing with possibilities.

Suddenly, Ethan pointed to one of the screens. "Sarah, look at this. That man by the vault—it's one of Marco's known associates."

Sarah's eyes narrowed. "We need to move. Now."

They rushed out of the office, signaling to the other officers. "You, with us," Sarah commanded, pointing to two nearby officers.

As they approached the vault, the man spotted them and bolted. "Stop! Police!" Ethan shouted, chasing after him.

The man ducked into a side corridor, but Sarah and Ethan were right behind him. They cornered him at a dead end, their guns drawn. "It's over. Hands where we can see them," Sarah ordered.

The man hesitated but then raised his hands, his face a mask of defiance. "You have no idea what you're dealing with."

Ethan cuffed him, his grip firm. "We'll see about that. Let's get him out of here."

Back at the precinct, they began interrogating the man, whose name was revealed to be Carlos. Sarah and Ethan sat across from him, determined to get answers.

"Who are you working for?" Sarah demanded.

Carlos smirked. "You already know the answer to that."

"Marco Alvarez," Ethan stated. "What's the plan for the bank?"

Carlos remained silent, his smirk infuriatingly persistent.

Sarah leaned in, her voice cold. "You can either talk now and maybe help yourself, or you can stay quiet and go down with Marco. Your choice."

Carlos sighed, his defiance waning. "Alright. Marco's planning to hit the bank tomorrow. Big score, lots of cash. He's desperate and needs to fund his operations."

Ethan pressed further. "How many people are involved? What's the exact plan?"

Carlos shook his head. "I don't know all the details. I was just supposed to scope the place out and report back."

Sarah stood up, her resolve firm. "We've got enough. We need to stop this now."

As they prepared for the next phase, Sarah felt a mix of anxiety and determination. The threat was imminent, but they were ready to face it head-on.

The air was thick with anticipation as Sarah and Ethan finalized their strategy. They gathered the team in the briefing room one last time before the operation. The room buzzed with the murmurs of officers checking equipment and reviewing their roles.

"Alright, everyone," Sarah began, her voice steady. "We have intel that Marco's planning to hit the bank tomorrow. We need to be in position early and stop this before it starts."

Ethan continued, "Our goal is to apprehend Marco and his associates without putting civilians at risk. We'll have plainclothes officers inside the bank and uniformed officers at all entrances."

Sarah nodded. "We need to stay coordinated. Communication is key. Any sign of trouble, report immediately. Let's move out."

The officers filed out, ready to execute the plan. Sarah and Ethan led the way, their minds focused on the task ahead. They arrived at Central Savings Bank before dawn, the city still cloaked in darkness.

Inside the bank, plainclothes officers mingled with the early morning staff, their eyes sharp and watchful. Outside, uniformed officers took up their positions, blending into the surroundings to avoid drawing attention.

Sarah and Ethan monitored the situation from the command post in Turner's office, their eyes fixed on the security feeds. The tension was palpable, each moment stretching into an eternity.

As the morning progressed, the bank began to fill with employees and customers. Sarah's heart pounded in her chest, every face on the screen a potential threat.

"Stay sharp," she reminded the team over the radio. "We need to be ready for anything."

Hours passed with no sign of Marco or his associates. The anticipation was nerve-wracking, but the team remained vigilant. Suddenly, Ethan spotted something on one of the feeds.

"Sarah, look at the main entrance. That's Marco," Ethan said, his voice urgent.

Sarah's eyes snapped to the screen, where Marco Alvarez was entering the bank, flanked by two men. "This is it. Everyone, be ready," she commanded over the radio.

Marco and his men moved purposefully, heading towards the vault. The plainclothes officers inside discreetly followed, maintaining a safe distance.

"Let's go," Sarah said to Ethan, grabbing her weapon. They moved swiftly through the bank, converging on the vault.

Marco and his men had just started their operation when Sarah and Ethan burst in, their guns drawn. "Freeze! Harborview Police!" Sarah shouted.

Marco spun around, his face a mask of fury. "You think you can stop me?"

Ethan's eyes were steely. "It's over, Marco. Hands up, now."

Marco hesitated, then reached for his weapon. Before he could draw, Sarah fired a warning shot into the air. "Don't even think about it."

The tension was electric as Marco slowly raised his hands, his expression seething with rage. His associates followed suit, realizing the futility of resistance.

"Secure them," Sarah ordered. The officers moved in, cuffing Marco and his men.

As they were led away, Marco turned to Sarah, his eyes burning with defiance. "This isn't over, Detective. You'll never take down my entire network."

Sarah met his gaze, unflinching. "We'll see about that. We've already started, and we're not stopping."

Back at the precinct, the atmosphere was charged with a mix of relief and triumph. Marco Alvarez was finally in custody, and his immediate threat neutralized. But Sarah knew their work was far from over.

Chief Donovan approached them, a rare smile on his face. "Good work, both of you. This is a major victory."

Sarah nodded, feeling a weight lift off her shoulders. "Thank you, Chief. But we still have a lot to do."

Ethan agreed. "Marco's network is vast. We need to keep digging, find every connection, and dismantle it completely."

Donovan's smile faded slightly. "I know. But for now, take a moment to appreciate what you've accomplished. You've made a significant impact."

As the precinct buzzed with activity, Sarah and Ethan took a moment to reflect on their journey. They had faced immense challenges and uncovered a web of crime far greater than they had imagined. But they had also proven their resilience and dedication to justice.

Sarah looked at Ethan, a sense of camaraderie and respect in her eyes. "We've come a long way, haven't we?"

Ethan smiled. "We have. And we're not done yet. There's still a lot of work to do."

Sarah nodded, feeling a renewed sense of purpose. "Let's get back to it. We've got a network to dismantle and justice to serve."

With Marco behind bars and their resolve stronger than ever, Sarah and Ethan were ready to continue their fight against crime, knowing that they were making a difference, one step at a time.

Chapter 6
The Pursuit

The sun was setting over Harborview as the precinct buzzed with activity. Despite the recent victory in apprehending Marco Alvarez, the work was far from over. Sarah Thompson and Ethan Drake were at the center of the storm, sifting through mountains of evidence and new leads, trying to dismantle the remnants of Marco's vast criminal network.

Sarah sat at her desk, her eyes glued to a computer screen filled with spreadsheets and coded messages. She rubbed her temples, feeling the weight of exhaustion, but she knew they couldn't afford to slow down.

Ethan walked over with two cups of coffee, setting one down in front of her. "Thought you could use a pick-me-up."

"Thanks," Sarah said, taking a sip. The bitterness was a welcome jolt. "We've got a lot to go through. These financial records from Green Horizon Enterprises are a labyrinth."

Ethan nodded, taking a seat next to her. "I've been cross-referencing the names we found in Marco's documents with known associates. It's a mixed bag—some leads look promising, others are dead ends."

Sarah sighed. "We need to be thorough. We can't let anyone slip through the cracks. Marco's network is like a hydra—cut off one head, and two more take its place."

Ethan tapped a few keys on his laptop. "I found a potential lead. A guy named Ramon Silva. He's been receiving large payments from one of Marco's shell companies. On paper, he runs a logistics firm, but there's something off about his transactions."

Sarah looked at the information on Ethan's screen. "This could be something. Let's dig deeper into Silva. Any known addresses or recent activities?"

Ethan pulled up another file. "He's got a warehouse on the outskirts of the city. I checked the records—it's been flagged for suspicious activity a few times, but nothing ever stuck."

Sarah's eyes narrowed. "Sounds like the perfect place to hide illicit operations. Let's get a team together and check it out."

They quickly assembled a team and briefed them on the plan. "We're heading to Silva's warehouse," Sarah explained. "Stay alert. If he's part of Marco's network, he could be dangerous."

The drive to the warehouse was tense, the anticipation building with each passing mile. As they approached the industrial area, the setting sun cast long shadows, giving the place an eerie atmosphere.

They parked a block away and approached the warehouse on foot, moving quietly. The building was old and dilapidated, with broken windows and faded paint. It looked abandoned, but Sarah's instincts told her otherwise.

"Ethan, take the back entrance with a couple of officers. The rest of you, follow me through the front," Sarah directed, her voice low but firm.

Ethan nodded, leading his group around the building. Sarah and her team approached the front door, which was slightly ajar. She signaled for silence and pushed the door open, her flashlight cutting through the darkness.

Inside, the warehouse was a maze of crates and machinery. Sarah moved cautiously, her senses heightened. They navigated through the labyrinthine space, checking every corner.

"Clear," one officer whispered after inspecting a side room.

"Clear," another echoed from the opposite direction.

Sarah reached a large office at the back of the warehouse. She motioned for the team to stay back and carefully opened the door. The office was cluttered with papers, maps, and a computer that was still on.

"Ethan, we found something," Sarah said into her radio. "Get in here."

Ethan and his team arrived moments later. "What do you have?"

Sarah pointed to the desk. "Looks like Silva's been busy. Let's see what he's been up to."

They began searching the office, sifting through documents and files. Sarah found a ledger with coded entries similar to the ones they had seen before. "This is it. These codes match the ones from Marco's records."

Ethan nodded, examining a map pinned to the wall. "And look at this. It's a map of the city with several locations marked. These must be safe houses or other operation sites."

Sarah felt a surge of determination. "We need to decode this ledger and figure out what these locations are. This could be the breakthrough we need."

As they gathered the evidence, a noise from outside the office caught their attention. Sarah drew her gun, signaling for the others to be ready. They moved towards the source of the noise, finding a man trying to escape through a side door.

"Stop! Police!" Sarah shouted, her weapon trained on him.

The man froze, his hands raised. "Don't shoot! I'm just the janitor!"

Ethan quickly restrained him, patting him down. "What are you doing here?"

"I clean this place at night," the man stammered. "I didn't know anything about what's going on here, I swear."

Sarah's eyes narrowed. "We'll see about that. Take him back to the precinct for questioning. He might know more than he's letting on."

As they secured the warehouse and prepared to return to the precinct, Sarah felt a mix of frustration and hope. They had uncovered more pieces of the puzzle, but there was still a long way to go. Marco's network was vast and elusive, but they were closing in.

Back at the precinct, they began the painstaking process of decoding the ledger and analyzing the map. Sarah knew they were getting closer, but the stakes were higher than ever. Every step brought them nearer to the heart of Marco's operations, and they couldn't afford any missteps.

The precinct was alive with activity as Sarah and Ethan began piecing together the information from Ramon Silva's warehouse. The evidence they had gathered pointed to several key players in Marco Alvarez's network, and they knew they had to act quickly to apprehend them.

Sarah sat at her desk, surrounded by maps, ledgers, and photographs. She tapped a pen against the table, deep in thought. "Ethan, look at this," she said, pointing to a series of names in the decoded ledger. "These individuals received substantial payments from Silva's accounts. They must be significant players in Marco's network."

Ethan leaned over, studying the names. "Yeah, and check this out." He held up a photograph of a man with a distinctive scar on his cheek. "This is Raul Garcia. He's a known enforcer for Marco. His name is all over these documents."

Sarah nodded, her mind racing. "We need to bring him in. If we can flip him, he might give us the information we need to dismantle the rest of the network."

Just then, Chief Donovan entered the room, his expression serious. "What have you got?"

"We've identified several key players," Sarah explained. "Raul Garcia is one of them. We believe he's heavily involved in Marco's operations."

Donovan nodded. "Good work. What's the plan?"

Sarah outlined their strategy. "We'll coordinate with the SWAT team for a simultaneous raid on Garcia's known locations. We need to catch him off guard."

Ethan added, "We've also got a list of other associates. We'll need to hit them all at once to prevent them from warning each other."

Donovan considered this. "Alright. Let's get it done. We can't let them slip through our fingers."

The team quickly mobilized, gearing up for the operation. As they gathered in the briefing room, Sarah and Ethan detailed the plan.

"Raul Garcia has been spotted at a warehouse on the south side," Sarah began. "SWAT will take point on the raid. We'll move in right after to secure any evidence and apprehend Garcia."

Ethan continued, "We've identified four other locations linked to Marco's associates. Each team will be responsible for one location. Move quickly and be ready for anything."

The officers nodded, their expressions determined. They knew the risks, but they also understood the importance of their mission.

As they prepared to move out, Sarah felt a mix of anticipation and resolve. "This is it," she said to Ethan. "We're finally closing in on them."

Ethan nodded. "Let's bring them down."

The convoy of police vehicles moved through the city streets, lights flashing but sirens off to maintain the element of surprise. Sarah and Ethan led the team to the warehouse, their hearts pounding with adrenaline.

They arrived at the location, a dilapidated building surrounded by a chain-link fence. SWAT took their positions, ready to breach the entrance.

"Go, go, go!" the SWAT commander ordered, and the team moved in, the door crashing open.

Inside, the warehouse was a flurry of activity. Raul Garcia and his men were caught off guard, scrambling to react. The SWAT team moved with precision, quickly subduing the suspects.

"Police! Get down!" Sarah shouted, her weapon trained on Garcia.

Garcia hesitated, then dropped his weapon and raised his hands. "Alright, alright! Don't shoot!"

Ethan moved in, cuffing Garcia while Sarah secured the area. "We've got you now," he said. "You're going away for a long time."

Garcia sneered but said nothing as he was led away. Sarah turned to the SWAT commander. "Good work. Let's search the place. There might be more evidence here."

As they combed through the warehouse, Sarah found a hidden room filled with documents and computer equipment. "Ethan, over here," she called.

Ethan joined her, his eyes widening at the sight. "This could be the jackpot."

They began collecting the evidence, carefully bagging and tagging each item. Sarah found a laptop that was still on, displaying a series of emails. "Look at this," she said. "These emails detail shipments and transactions. This is exactly what we need."

Ethan nodded, a sense of triumph in his eyes. "We're getting closer."

Back at the precinct, they began analyzing the new evidence. The documents and emails provided a detailed look at Marco's operations, revealing the full extent of his network.

Chief Donovan entered the room, his expression a mix of pride and urgency. "Good work today. This evidence is crucial. We need to act fast and take down the rest of Marco's network."

Sarah nodded. "We've got the names and locations. We're ready to move."

Donovan placed a hand on her shoulder. "You've done an incredible job. Let's finish this."

As they prepared for the final phase of their operation, Sarah felt a renewed sense of purpose. They were on the brink of dismantling Marco's entire network, and nothing would stop them now. The pursuit had been long and grueling, but the end was in sight.

The precinct was abuzz with energy and anticipation. The new evidence had given them a clear path to follow, but Sarah knew they needed more resources to take down the remaining key players in Marco's network. She and Ethan had a crucial meeting with representatives from the FBI and DEA to coordinate their efforts.

In the conference room, the air was thick with tension as Agent Marcus Lawson from the FBI and Agent Maria Hernandez from the DEA took their seats. Chief Donovan stood at the head of the table, flanked by Sarah and Ethan.

"Thank you for coming on such short notice," Donovan began. "We have significant evidence linking Marco Alvarez's network to various criminal activities, and we need your assistance to take them down."

Agent Lawson nodded, his expression serious. "We've reviewed the evidence you sent over. This is a large-scale operation, and we're ready to provide support. What's your plan?"

Sarah spread out a detailed map of the city on the table, marking several locations. "These are the known hideouts and operation points for Marco's associates. We plan to hit them simultaneously to prevent any communication or escape."

Agent Hernandez leaned forward, examining the map. "How many targets are we looking at?"

"Five key locations," Ethan answered. "We'll need coordinated teams at each site to ensure we capture everyone involved."

Lawson exchanged a glance with Hernandez. "We can allocate agents to each location. Our goal is to secure the sites and gather as much evidence as possible. We also need to be prepared for armed resistance."

Hernandez added, "DEA will focus on the drug trafficking aspects. We've been tracking some of these players for a while. This is our chance to bring them down."

Sarah nodded, appreciating their readiness. "We'll divide the teams. Local officers will work alongside your agents. We need to move quickly and efficiently. Time is of the essence."

Donovan addressed the room, his voice commanding. "This operation needs to be airtight. No leaks, no mistakes. We coordinate everything through a secure channel. Sarah and Ethan will lead the charge on the ground. Let's synchronize our watches and prepare to move out."

As the meeting adjourned, Sarah and Ethan stayed behind to finalize the details. "We need to make sure everyone's on the same page," Sarah said. "One slip-up and these guys will scatter."

Ethan agreed. "I'll brief our team and ensure they're ready. We've come too far to let this fall apart now."

Later that evening, the teams gathered at the precinct, the atmosphere charged with determination. Sarah and Ethan briefed their officers one last time, ensuring every detail was covered.

"Remember," Sarah said, her voice clear and strong, "we move in fast and secure the targets. Watch each other's backs and stay sharp. We're taking down an entire network tonight."

Ethan added, "We'll be coordinating with federal agents. Follow the plan, and we'll bring them all in."

The officers nodded, their resolve evident. As they moved out, Sarah felt a mix of anticipation and resolve. They were ready to finish what they had started.

The operation was in full swing. Sarah and Ethan, along with their team, arrived at the first location—a high-end apartment complex known to house one of Marco's top lieutenants. They moved swiftly through the building, their weapons drawn and eyes alert.

Sarah signaled for her team to take positions around the target's door. She knocked firmly, announcing their presence. "Police! Open up!"

There was a tense silence before the door burst open, and a man tried to bolt past them. Ethan tackled him to the ground, cuffing him quickly. "We've got one," he said, pulling the man to his feet.

Sarah scanned the apartment, finding evidence of drug transactions and large sums of cash. "Bag it all," she instructed her team. "We need every piece of evidence."

As they secured the scene, Sarah's radio crackled to life. "Team Bravo, we've secured our target," came the voice of Agent Lawson. "Moving to the next location."

"Copy that," Sarah responded. She turned to Ethan. "Let's move. We've got more ground to cover."

The next location was a rundown warehouse on the outskirts of the city. As they approached, they saw figures moving inside. "Stay alert," Sarah warned. "This could get messy."

They breached the entrance, the dim light inside revealing stacks of illegal goods and a group of men scrambling to escape. "Freeze!" Ethan shouted, but the men opened fire, forcing the team to take cover.

A tense firefight ensued, the air filled with the sound of gunfire. Sarah and Ethan moved strategically, returning fire and advancing towards their targets. One by one, the men were subdued, either surrendering or being taken down.

"Clear!" Sarah shouted once the last man was secured. She approached a table laden with documents and electronic devices. "This is a goldmine. We need to get this back to the precinct for analysis."

As they wrapped up the operation, Sarah's phone buzzed with an incoming call from Donovan. "What's the status?" he asked.

"We've secured two locations and apprehended multiple suspects," Sarah reported. "We've also recovered significant evidence. How are the other teams doing?"

"All targets are secured," Donovan replied, relief evident in his voice. "We've got a lot of evidence to sort through, but it looks like we've dealt a significant blow to Marco's network."

Sarah felt a surge of triumph but knew the work was far from over. "We'll bring everything back and start processing it immediately. This is a huge step forward."

Back at the precinct, the teams worked tirelessly through the night, cataloging evidence and interrogating suspects. Sarah and Ethan led the efforts, their determination unwavering.

As dawn broke, they gathered in the briefing room, exhausted but satisfied. Donovan addressed the assembled officers and agents. "Outstanding work, everyone. We've dismantled a major part of this operation, but there's still more to do. Let's keep the pressure on and finish what we started."

Sarah looked at Ethan, a sense of camaraderie and shared purpose in her eyes. "We're making progress. This is what we've been working for."

Ethan nodded, a tired but triumphant smile on his face. "We'll get them all, Sarah. We're not stopping until we do."

With the dawn of a new day, they were ready to continue their relentless pursuit of justice, knowing that their efforts were bringing them closer to dismantling Marco Alvarez's entire criminal empire.

Chapter 7
Unraveling the Web

The precinct was bathed in the harsh glow of fluorescent lights, casting stark shadows on the walls. Detective Sarah Thompson sat at her cluttered desk, her eyes scanning the new intel laid out before her. The web of connections was growing clearer, but the sense of urgency was mounting. The recent attacks had left the city on edge, and the pressure to find and stop the remaining members of the network was intense.

Ethan Drake walked in, his expression grave. He dropped a thick file onto Sarah's desk. "We've got a lead on one of Raines' top operatives. Name's Michael Dorn. He's been seen around the old shipyard on the west side."

Sarah looked up, her eyes narrowing. "Dorn's known for his expertise in logistics. If he's involved, he's probably coordinating the movement of materials for the next attack."

Ethan nodded. "Exactly. We need to move fast. If we can get to Dorn, we might be able to prevent the next hit."

Garcia approached, his face lined with concern. "I've got some bad news. The surveillance on the communications hub was compromised. Someone got to our cameras. We're blind over there."

Sarah's frustration was evident. "We need eyes on that site immediately. Get a team to replace the cameras and set up additional patrols. We can't afford any more slip-ups."

Garcia nodded. "Already on it. They'll be operational within the hour."

Sarah turned back to Ethan. "Alright, let's head to the shipyard. We'll take Dorn down and see what he knows."

The drive to the shipyard was tense, the air thick with anticipation. Sarah and Ethan reviewed their plan, knowing that any mistake could be costly. The shipyard was a sprawling complex of rusted cranes and abandoned warehouses, a perfect hideout for someone like Dorn.

As they arrived, Sarah signaled for the team to spread out. "Remember, Dorn is dangerous. Approach with caution. We need him alive."

Ethan nodded, his weapon at the ready. "Let's move."

They navigated the narrow passageways between the warehouses, the sound of distant waves crashing against the docks adding to the eerie atmosphere. Sarah spotted movement near one of the buildings and signaled for the team to halt.

"Ethan, take Bravo team and circle around. I'll lead Alpha team through the front," she whispered into her radio.

Ethan acknowledged with a nod and led his team into position. Sarah took a deep breath, then moved forward, her senses heightened. They approached the entrance, and Sarah motioned for an officer to breach the door.

"Police! Hands up!" she shouted as they stormed in.

The interior was dimly lit, filled with crates and old machinery. Dorn was in the center, surrounded by a few armed men. He looked up, a sneer on his face. "Detective Thompson. I've been expecting you."

Sarah's eyes locked onto him. "Drop your weapons. Now."

Dorn's men hesitated, then dropped their guns. Dorn raised his hands slowly, his sneer never fading. "You think you've won? This is just the beginning."

Ethan entered from the rear, his weapon trained on Dorn. "We'll see about that. Cuff him."

As they secured Dorn, Sarah stepped closer, her voice cold. "You're going to tell us everything. Who's left, where they're hiding, and what the next target is."

Dorn's eyes flickered with defiance. "You think I'm afraid of you? I'd rather rot in prison than betray my comrades."

Ethan's voice was calm but firm. "You might change your mind once you see the inside of a cell. Or we can make a deal. It's up to you."

Dorn laughed, a harsh sound that echoed through the warehouse. "Deals? You're desperate. But fine, I'll talk. Not because of you, but because I want to see you squirm. There's a safe house in the industrial district. That's where they're planning the next attack."

Sarah's eyes narrowed. "What's the target?"

Dorn shrugged. "All I know is it's big. Bigger than anything we've done before."

Ethan stepped closer. "And who's in charge now? Who's coordinating the attacks?"

Dorn hesitated, then smirked. "You'll find out soon enough."

As they led Dorn out of the warehouse, Sarah's mind raced. They had a lead, but the details were still vague. The industrial district was vast, and finding the safe house would be like searching for a needle in a haystack.

Back at the precinct, Sarah and Ethan debriefed the team, outlining the next steps. "We need to locate that safe house immediately. Garcia, coordinate with local law enforcement and start canvassing the area."

Garcia nodded. "I'm on it. We'll have units covering every corner of the district."

Ethan added, "We also need to tighten security around all potential targets. We can't leave anything to chance."

Sarah looked at her team, determination in her eyes. "We're getting closer. Let's stay focused and see this through. We can't let them win."

As the team dispersed to carry out their tasks, Sarah felt a renewed sense of purpose. They had Dorn in custody and a lead on the next attack. The pieces of the puzzle were falling into place, but the clock was ticking, and the stakes were higher than ever. They had to act swiftly and decisively to protect the city and bring the remaining members of the network to justice.

The interrogation room was dimly lit, casting long shadows across the walls. Michael Dorn sat in the metal chair, his hands cuffed to the table, a smug expression on his face. Sarah and Ethan stood on either side of the table, their eyes locked on him, determination etched into their features.

Sarah began, her voice steady but intense. "Dorn, we know you're involved in the attacks. We've got enough to put you away for a long time. But if you cooperate, maybe we can work something out."

Dorn smirked, leaning back in his chair. "You think I'm scared of a prison cell? I've faced worse."

Ethan leaned forward, his voice low and menacing. "This isn't just about you, Dorn. There are lives at stake. If you know something, now's the time to speak up."

Dorn's eyes flickered with a hint of amusement. "You're wasting your time. I'm not saying anything more without a deal."

Sarah's patience was wearing thin. "We're not here to play games. You told us about the safe house in the industrial district. What else do you know?"

Dorn shrugged, his demeanor infuriatingly calm. "I know that no matter what you do, you're too late. The plan is already in motion."

Ethan slammed his hand on the table, making Dorn flinch. "Enough with the cryptic answers. What's the next target?"

Dorn's smile faded slightly. "Fine. You want details? The next target is the Grand Plaza Hotel. They're hitting it during the charity gala tomorrow night. Hundreds of people, including some high-profile figures. It's going to be a massacre."

Sarah's eyes widened, her heart pounding. "Who's coordinating the attack? Give us a name."

Dorn hesitated, his defiance wavering. "It's... it's someone called The Architect. That's all I know. I've never met him."

Ethan exchanged a look with Sarah, then turned back to Dorn. "Where can we find The Architect?"

Dorn shook his head. "I don't know. He's a ghost. We get our orders through encrypted messages. No face, no voice, just text."

Sarah's frustration was palpable, but she pressed on. "How do you communicate with him?"

Dorn sighed. "There's a drop site near the docks. We leave messages in a dead drop and wait for instructions."

Ethan's voice was cold. "You're going to show us this drop site."

Dorn looked at him, his expression resigned. "Alright. But you better keep your end of the deal."

Sarah nodded. "If this information checks out, we'll talk about a deal. Let's move."

As they prepared to leave, Garcia entered the room, his face grim. "We've got a problem. There's chatter on the dark web about an imminent attack. They're saying it's going to be the biggest one yet."

Sarah felt a chill run down her spine. "The Grand Plaza. We need to secure it now."

Ethan turned to Garcia. "Get every available unit to the hotel. We need to evacuate the guests and secure the perimeter."

Garcia nodded and hurried out, his phone already in hand, barking orders.

Sarah grabbed her jacket, her mind racing. "Ethan, take Dorn to the drop site. See if we can get anything on The Architect. I'll head to the hotel and coordinate with the team there."

Ethan nodded. "Be careful, Sarah. This could be a trap."

Sarah's eyes met his, a fierce determination in them. "I know. But we don't have a choice."

The drive to the Grand Plaza Hotel was tense, the city lights blurring past as Sarah sped through the streets. She arrived to find the area already swarming with police and emergency services. Officers were guiding guests out of the building, their faces a mix of confusion and fear.

Sarah approached the incident commander, a stern-faced man named Captain Miller. "What's the status?"

Miller looked grim. "We've evacuated most of the guests, but there are still some stragglers. We're sweeping the building for any suspicious packages or devices."

Sarah nodded. "Good. We need to find out if there's anyone inside who shouldn't be. Check all staff and security personnel."

As the minutes ticked by, the tension grew. Sarah coordinated with the bomb squad, ensuring every corner of the hotel was searched. Her phone buzzed, and she answered it quickly.

"Ethan, what's the update?"

Ethan's voice was steady but urgent. "We found the drop site. There was a message waiting. It's a code, but we think it's instructions for the attack. I've sent it to the cyber team for decryption."

Sarah felt a surge of hope. "Good work. Keep me posted."

Just then, an officer approached, his face pale. "Detective Thompson, we found something. A device in the ballroom. It's armed."

Sarah's heart pounded. "Get the bomb squad in there now. Evacuate the rest of the building."

As the team moved into action, Sarah felt a mix of fear and determination. They were close, but the danger was far from over. She watched as the bomb squad carefully approached the device, their movements precise and cautious.

Minutes felt like hours as they worked to disarm the bomb. Finally, the squad leader gave a thumbs up. "We're clear."

Sarah let out a breath she didn't realize she was holding. "Thank God. Let's sweep the rest of the building, just to be sure."

As the officers continued their search, Sarah's phone buzzed again. It was Ethan. "We decrypted the message. It was a diversion. The real target is the city's main water supply. They're planning to poison it."

Sarah's blood ran cold. "I'll head there now. Get every available unit to the water treatment plant."

The race was on. The city's safety hung in the balance, and time was running out. Sarah and her team were determined to stop the attack and bring the remaining members of the network to justice. Every second counted, and failure was not an option.

The precinct was a storm of activity as the team prepared for the imminent threat. Sarah and Ethan were at the center of the chaos, coordinating efforts and relaying orders. The gravity of the situation was palpable; the city's main water supply was under threat, and the stakes had never been higher.

Garcia rushed over, a map in hand. "We've pinpointed the most vulnerable access points to the water treatment plant. There are three main entryways. We need to secure each one."

Sarah nodded, her mind racing. "Ethan, take Bravo team and cover the south entrance. Garcia, you're with me on the west. We'll have Alpha team on the north. We need to be synchronized. Any misstep, and we could lose everything."

Ethan's jaw tightened. "Got it. We'll be in position in ten."

Sarah turned to Garcia. "Let's move."

As they sped towards the water treatment plant, Sarah's phone buzzed with an incoming call. She answered quickly. "Thompson."

It was Captain Reynolds. "Sarah, we've got intel that suggests the attack could happen within the next hour. You need to be ready for anything."

Sarah's grip on the steering wheel tightened. "Understood, Captain. We'll stop them."

Arriving at the plant, the teams dispersed to their designated positions. The air was thick with tension as they moved into place. Sarah glanced at her watch, feeling the seconds tick by with agonizing slowness.

Ethan's voice crackled over the radio. "Bravo team in position."

Sarah responded, "Copy that. Alpha team, status?"

"Alpha team ready," came the reply.

Sarah took a deep breath. "All units, stay sharp. We're expecting heavy resistance. Engage only if necessary. Our priority is to secure the plant."

Minutes passed in silence, each one stretching longer than the last. Suddenly, movement in the shadows caught Sarah's eye. A group of figures approached the west entrance, moving stealthily.

Sarah whispered into her radio, "Contact west side. Hold positions."

Garcia, crouched beside her, nodded. "Looks like four of them. Armed."

The figures reached the entrance, beginning to tamper with the lock. Sarah signaled to Garcia, and they moved in quietly, weapons drawn. "Police! Drop your weapons!"

The intruders froze, then sprang into action. Shots rang out, and Sarah dove for cover, returning fire. Garcia took down two of them, while Sarah neutralized the remaining pair. Breathing heavily, they secured the area.

Ethan's voice came over the radio, urgent. "We've got contact south side! Multiple hostiles!"

Sarah responded quickly. "Hold your ground, we're on our way."

She and Garcia sprinted to the south entrance, finding Ethan and his team engaged in a fierce firefight. Sarah joined the fray, her focus sharp. One by one, they took down the attackers, pushing them back.

Ethan glanced at her, a grim smile on his face. "Nice of you to join the party."

Sarah returned the smile briefly. "Wouldn't miss it. Status?"

Ethan reloaded his weapon. "We've got them contained for now, but I don't know how long we can hold."

Just then, a loud explosion rocked the facility. Sarah's heart sank. "The north entrance! They're breaching!"

They raced towards the explosion, finding Alpha team pinned down by heavy fire. Sarah's mind raced, searching for a solution. She spotted a vantage point above the attackers and signaled to Ethan.

"Cover me. I'm going up."

Ethan nodded, providing suppressive fire as Sarah climbed to the higher ground. From her new position, she had a clear shot at the intruders. She took a deep breath, aimed, and fired. One by one, the attackers fell, the tide turning in their favor.

With the immediate threat neutralized, Sarah climbed down, joining Ethan and Alpha team. "Is everyone okay?"

One of the officers nodded. "A few injuries, but we're holding."

Sarah looked around, the destruction evident. "We need to secure the explosives they planted. Move, now."

They spread out, locating and disarming the devices. Each second felt like an eternity, the pressure immense. Finally, the last bomb was defused, and Sarah allowed herself a moment of relief.

Ethan approached, his expression serious. "We've secured the plant, but there's no sign of The Architect. This was a distraction."

Sarah's frustration was evident. "He's always one step ahead. We need to regroup, find out what we're missing."

Just then, Garcia's voice crackled over the radio. "Sarah, we've intercepted a communication. It's from The Architect. He's taunting us."

Sarah's eyes narrowed. "Play it."

Garcia patched the message through. The Architect's voice was smooth, almost mocking. "Congratulations, Detectives. You've won this round, but the game is far from over. You can't stop what's coming."

Sarah's grip tightened on her radio. "We'll see about that. We're coming for you."

The message ended, leaving a chilling silence in its wake. Sarah turned to her team, determination burning in her eyes. "We need to find him, and we need to do it now. Let's get back to the precinct and figure out our next move."

As they gathered their equipment and prepared to leave, Sarah couldn't shake the feeling that time was running out. The Architect was out there, planning his next move, and the clock was ticking. But with her team by her side, she knew they had the strength and resolve to face whatever came next. Together, they would stop The Architect and bring peace back to their city.

The precinct was alive with activity as Sarah, Ethan, and their team returned from the water treatment plant. The air was thick with tension, the threat of The Architect's next move hanging over them like a dark cloud. Sarah's mind was racing, each step she took echoing with urgency. They had to find The Architect before he struck again.

Ethan walked beside her, his face etched with determination. "We need to review everything we have on The Architect. There's got to be something we're missing."

Sarah nodded, her eyes scanning the room. "Garcia, get everyone into the briefing room. We need to go over the intel again."

Garcia quickly gathered the team, and within minutes, the room was filled with the buzz of conversation. Sarah stood at the front, facing her team. "Alright, listen up. We've been playing catch-up with The Architect, and it's time we got ahead of him. Let's review what we know."

Ethan pulled up the map of the city, marked with the locations of the recent attacks. "We know he's been targeting critical infrastructure— power, water, communications. Each attack has been a diversion, buying him time for something bigger."

Sarah pointed to the map. "He's methodical, always one step ahead. We need to think like him. What's his endgame?"

Garcia chimed in. "Total chaos. If he can cripple the city's infrastructure, he can cause widespread panic and instability."

Sarah nodded. "Exactly. But why? What's his motive?"

A young officer, Jamie, raised her hand. "Maybe it's personal. Revenge or a vendetta against the city."

Ethan considered this. "Could be. But we need more than theories. We need hard evidence."

Just then, Garcia's phone buzzed. He answered quickly, his expression shifting to one of surprise. "Sarah, you need to hear this. It's from the cybercrimes unit."

He put the call on speaker. "Detective Garcia, we've decrypted more of the data from Travers' laptop. There's a reference to a location—an abandoned factory on the outskirts of town. It's mentioned multiple times, always in connection with The Architect."

Sarah's eyes lit up with determination. "That's our lead. We need to move now."

Ethan turned to the team. "Gear up. We're heading out in five."

The drive to the abandoned factory was tense, the city lights giving way to the darkened outskirts. Sarah's mind was a whirlwind of thoughts, each possibility more dire than the last. They had to find The Architect and stop him before he could execute his plan.

As they approached the factory, Ethan signaled for the team to halt. "We go in quiet. We don't know what we're walking into."

Sarah nodded, her senses on high alert. "Stay sharp. Let's move."

They approached the factory, its looming structure a stark silhouette against the night sky. Sarah and Ethan led the team through the broken gates, their footsteps echoing in the eerie silence. They spread out, scanning for any signs of movement.

Sarah's radio crackled. "Bravo team in position. No visual on targets."

She whispered back, "Copy that. Stay alert."

As they moved deeper into the factory, Sarah spotted a faint light coming from a room at the end of the corridor. She signaled to Ethan, and they approached cautiously, weapons drawn.

Inside the room, they found a makeshift command center—computers, maps, and stacks of documents. And standing in the center, calmly typing on a laptop, was The Architect.

Sarah's heart pounded as she raised her weapon. "Freeze! Hands where I can see them!"

The Architect turned slowly, a cold smile on his face. "Detective Thompson. I must say, I'm impressed. You've been quite persistent."

Ethan moved to flank him. "It's over. Step away from the computer."

The Architect's smile widened. "You think you've won? This is just the beginning."

Sarah's eyes narrowed. "Shut it down. Now."

He raised his hands, stepping away from the laptop. "You're too late. The final phase is already in motion."

Sarah glanced at the screen, seeing a countdown timer ticking away. "What is this? What's the target?"

The Architect's eyes gleamed with malicious glee. "The heart of the city. The financial district. In less than an hour, it'll all come crashing down."

Ethan stepped forward, cuffing him. "You're coming with us. We'll see how smug you are in a cell."

The Architect's laughter echoed through the room. "You can't stop it. It's inevitable."

Sarah turned to the team. "We need to find that bomb. Now."

Garcia's voice came through the radio. "We're searching the area, but it's huge. We need more time."

Sarah's mind raced. "We don't have time. We need to split up, cover more ground."

Ethan nodded. "You heard her. Move out."

They fanned out through the factory, searching every room, every corner. Sarah's heart pounded as the timer ticked down. They had minutes left—minutes to save the city from catastrophe.

Suddenly, Garcia's voice crackled through the radio. "I've found it! Northwest corner, under the main floor. It's rigged to blow."

Sarah and Ethan raced to the location, finding Garcia kneeling by a large device, wires running in every direction. The timer showed less than five minutes.

Garcia looked up, sweat dripping down his face. "I can disarm it, but I need a steady hand. Cover me."

Sarah and Ethan stood guard, weapons ready, as Garcia worked. Each second felt like an eternity, the tension unbearable.

Finally, with seconds to spare, Garcia cut the last wire. The timer stopped, and Sarah let out a breath she hadn't realized she was holding. "Good work, Garcia."

Ethan placed a hand on her shoulder, his expression one of relief and admiration. "We did it."

Sarah nodded, her eyes meeting his. "Yeah. But it's not over. We still need to take down the rest of the network."

They secured the factory, gathering all the evidence they could find. As they led The Architect away, Sarah felt a mix of triumph and resolve. They had averted disaster, but the fight was far from over. Together, they would dismantle the network piece by piece, bringing justice to those who sought to bring chaos to their city.

Chapter 8
Closing In

The interrogation room was filled with a heavy silence, punctuated only by the faint hum of the air conditioning. Sarah and Ethan sat across from Diane Hayes, the finance manager who had been implicated by both Linda Matthews and Michael Turner. Diane's hands were clasped tightly in her lap, her knuckles white, betraying the fear she tried to hide behind a mask of defiance.

Sarah started the conversation, her tone calm but firm. "Ms. Hayes, we have substantial evidence linking you to a network of illegal financial activities. We need your cooperation to bring this operation down."

Diane's eyes flicked nervously between Sarah and Ethan. "I don't know what you're talking about. I'm just a finance manager. I handle accounts and budgets."

Ethan leaned forward, his eyes boring into hers. "We have records of your transactions, Diane. Large sums of money funneled through shell companies, bribes to city officials. You're in deep, and denying it won't help you."

Diane's facade cracked slightly, her lips pressing into a thin line. "I was just doing my job. I didn't have a choice."

Sarah nodded, her expression sympathetic but unyielding. "We understand that you might have been coerced, but we need you to give us names. Who else is involved?"

Diane hesitated, her fear palpable. "If I talk, they'll come after me. After my family."

Ethan's voice softened, though it remained firm. "We can protect you, Diane. Witness protection, relocation—whatever it takes to keep you safe. But you need to give us something to work with."

Diane looked down, her voice barely above a whisper. "There's a man named Richard Lawson. He's the one who recruited me. Said it was an opportunity I couldn't pass up."

Sarah took notes, her pen moving swiftly across the paper. "What can you tell us about Lawson?"

"He's a lawyer," Diane replied, her voice gaining strength as she spoke. "Handles all the legal aspects, makes sure everything looks legitimate on the surface. He's very careful."

Ethan interjected, "And who does he report to?"

Diane's eyes widened slightly. "I've heard him mention someone called The Broker, but I've never met him. Lawson is the only one I had direct contact with."

Sarah nodded, processing the information. "What about the money? Where does it come from?"

"Various sources," Diane said, her voice steadier now. "Corporate donations, government grants, all funneled through legitimate channels. Once the money's clean, it's used for whatever they need—bribes, payoffs, you name it."

Ethan exchanged a glance with Sarah. "This is good, Diane. Very good. But we need more. Can you give us any locations? Where does Lawson operate from?"

Diane thought for a moment, then nodded. "He has an office downtown. And there's a safe house in the suburbs. They use it to store documents and money when things get too hot."

Sarah stood up, her eyes meeting Diane's. "You've done the right thing, Diane. We'll make sure you're protected."

As they left the room, Ethan turned to Sarah, a determined glint in his eyes. "We're getting closer. Lawson could be the key to bringing down The Broker."

Sarah nodded, feeling a surge of determination. "Let's get a team together. We're raiding his office and the safe house tonight."

The precinct was buzzing with activity as the team prepared for the raids. Warrants were issued, tactical gear was distributed, and the atmosphere was charged with anticipation. This was the breakthrough they had been working toward, and no one wanted to let it slip through their fingers.

A few hours later, they arrived at Richard Lawson's office building. The night was dark, the city lights casting eerie shadows on the streets. Sarah and Ethan led the team, moving swiftly and silently through the building. They reached Lawson's office and breached the door, finding Lawson at his desk, his expression one of shock and anger.

"Richard Lawson," Sarah announced, her voice echoing through the room. "You're under arrest for conspiracy, money laundering, and bribery."

Lawson stood up, his hands raised in mock surrender. "You have no idea what you're getting into, Detective. You can arrest me, but you'll never touch The Broker."

Ethan cuffed him, his grip firm. "We'll see about that. Now, you're coming with us."

As they escorted Lawson out of the building, Sarah felt a sense of triumph but also a growing sense of urgency. The operation was far from over, and The Broker was still out there, a shadowy figure orchestrating everything from behind the scenes.

Back at the precinct, Lawson was placed in an interrogation room. Sarah and Ethan prepared to question him, knowing that this could be their best chance to unravel the entire operation.

Ethan looked at Sarah, his expression resolute. "This is it. We're going to take them all down."

Sarah nodded, feeling the weight of their mission but also the thrill of the hunt. "One step at a time, Ethan. Let's get to work."

They entered the interrogation room, ready to confront Lawson and extract every piece of information they could. The walls were closing in on The Broker, and Sarah knew they were closer than ever to bringing him to justice.

The raid on Richard Lawson's office had been a success, but the night was far from over. Sarah and Ethan, accompanied by a team of officers, now headed toward the suburban safe house that Diane Matthews had mentioned. The drive was tense, the weight of their mission pressing heavily on everyone.

The safe house was located in a quiet, upscale neighborhood, its exterior giving no hint of the illicit activities it concealed. As they approached, Sarah's mind raced with the possibilities of what they might find inside—documents, money, perhaps even more key players in The Broker's operation.

They parked a few houses away, moving silently through the shadows. The team took their positions, surrounding the property. Sarah and Ethan moved to the front door, weapons drawn.

Ethan nodded to Sarah, signaling that they were ready. She took a deep breath, then knocked loudly. "Police! Open up!"

There was a moment of silence, then the sound of hurried footsteps inside. Sarah nodded to Ethan, and he kicked the door open, the team pouring in behind them. Inside, the safe house was a flurry of activity as several men tried to escape or hide evidence.

"Get down! Hands where we can see them!" Sarah shouted, her voice cutting through the chaos.

The men hesitated, then slowly raised their hands, realizing they had no way out. The team moved quickly, securing the suspects and beginning to search the house.

Sarah and Ethan moved through the rooms, finding stacks of documents, computer equipment, and large sums of cash. The scale of the operation was staggering.

"Over here!" one of the officers called from a back room.

Sarah and Ethan hurried to the room, finding a hidden compartment in the wall. Inside were more documents, including ledgers and correspondence, detailing the network's activities and financial transactions.

"This is it," Sarah said, her voice filled with a mix of triumph and disbelief. "We've got them."

Ethan nodded, his expression serious. "We need to get this back to the precinct and start going through it. This is the evidence we need to bring The Broker down."

As the team finished securing the house and the suspects, Sarah and Ethan gathered the most crucial evidence and headed back to the precinct. The ride back was silent, each of them lost in their thoughts, the enormity of their findings sinking in.

Back at the precinct, they spread out the documents on the large conference table. Garcia joined them, his eyes widening as he took in the sheer volume of evidence.

"This is incredible," Garcia said, shaking his head. "We've got everything we need here. Names, dates, transactions... it's all laid out."

Sarah nodded, her eyes scanning the documents. "We need to start cross-referencing this with what we already have. Every piece of information needs to be verified and connected."

Ethan pointed to a series of emails. "Look at this. Direct communication between Lawson and several high-ranking officials. This is the smoking gun."

Garcia began sorting through the documents, his fingers moving quickly. "I'll get the tech team on these computers. We need to extract every bit of data we can."

As the hours passed, the team worked tirelessly, piecing together the intricate web of corruption and crime that The Broker had woven. Sarah and Ethan barely paused to rest, driven by the urgency of their mission.

Sarah looked up from her notes, her eyes meeting Ethan's. "We're getting close. But we need to be careful. The Broker will know we're closing in, and he'll do anything to protect himself."

Ethan nodded, his expression determined. "We need to move fast. The longer we wait, the more time he has to cover his tracks."

Garcia looked up from his work, a glint of excitement in his eyes. "We've got a hit. One of the emails mentions a meeting tomorrow night. It's vague, but it's our best lead."

Sarah's heart raced. "Where?"

"A warehouse near the docks," Garcia replied. "It's listed under a shell company we've linked to The Broker."

Ethan stood up, his jaw set. "We need to set up surveillance. If The Broker is going to be there, we can't afford to miss this opportunity."

Sarah nodded, feeling a surge of adrenaline. "Let's get a team together. We're not letting him slip through our fingers."

As they prepared for the operation, the atmosphere in the precinct was electric with anticipation. They were on the brink of the biggest breakthrough in the case, and no one wanted to let it slip away.

Sarah and Ethan gathered their gear, ready to face whatever the night might bring. The pursuit of justice was far from over, but they were closer than ever to bringing The Broker to justice. Each step brought them nearer to the endgame, and they were determined to see it through.

The team assembled in the briefing room, a map of the warehouse district spread out on the table. Sarah and Ethan stood at the front, outlining the plan. The air was thick with anticipation and determination; they were on the verge of capturing The Broker.

Sarah pointed to the map. "We have intel that The Broker will be meeting at this warehouse tonight. We'll set up surveillance here and here," she indicated two strategic points on the map. "We need to cover all exits and be ready to move in at a moment's notice."

Ethan added, "We're dealing with a dangerous individual who will do anything to escape. Use caution and stay sharp. Any questions?"

Officer Jenkins raised his hand. "What's our protocol if he's armed?"

Ethan's expression hardened. "If he's armed and poses a threat, you're authorized to use lethal force. But our primary objective is to take him alive. We need him to dismantle the rest of the operation."

Garcia, sitting at the back, nodded. "We've got backup units on standby, and the coast guard is ready to intercept if he tries to escape by water."

Sarah glanced around the room, meeting the eyes of each officer. "This is our chance to bring down The Broker and his entire network. Let's make sure we do it right."

As they geared up and headed out, the tension was palpable. The drive to the warehouse was silent, each officer mentally preparing for the task ahead. They arrived and quickly took their positions, the area around the warehouse shrouded in darkness.

Sarah and Ethan settled into their surveillance spot, their eyes trained on the warehouse. The minutes ticked by with agonizing slowness, the silence broken only by the occasional crackle of the radio.

Finally, a black SUV pulled up to the warehouse, and several men emerged. Ethan's heart raced. "That's him," he whispered, his eyes narrowing as he focused on the tall figure in the center.

Sarah spoke into her radio. "All units, The Broker has arrived. Hold positions and wait for my signal."

Inside the warehouse, The Broker's men began unloading crates. The Broker himself stood off to the side, his posture relaxed but alert. Sarah and Ethan watched, every muscle tensed.

After what felt like an eternity, The Broker motioned for one of his men to approach. The man handed him a briefcase, and The Broker opened it, revealing stacks of cash.

Ethan's voice was low and urgent. "This is it. We need to move now."

Sarah nodded, signaling the team. "Go! Go! Go!"

The tactical units moved in, converging on the warehouse from all sides. The Broker's men reacted instantly, drawing their weapons and firing. The night erupted into chaos as gunfire echoed through the warehouse.

Ethan led the charge, his weapon trained on The Broker. "Drop your weapon!" he shouted, his voice cutting through the noise.

The Broker turned, a cold smile on his face. "You think you can stop me?"

Sarah fired a warning shot. "This is your last chance! Drop it!"

The Broker hesitated, then threw his weapon to the ground, raising his hands. "Alright, you got me."

Ethan moved forward, cuffing him swiftly. "It's over."

The Broker's men were quickly subdued, and the warehouse fell silent. Sarah felt a wave of relief and triumph wash over her. They had done it.

As The Broker was led away, Sarah and Ethan exchanged a look of determination. "We've taken down The Broker," Sarah said, her voice steady. "Now we need to make sure the rest of the network falls with him."

Back at the precinct, the atmosphere was electric with a mix of exhaustion and exhilaration. The Broker had been captured, but there was still much to do. Sarah and Ethan sat down with The Broker in the interrogation room, ready to extract every piece of information they could.

The Broker, now looking less confident and more weary, sat across from them. Sarah began, her voice firm but calm. "You're facing serious charges, but you can help yourself by cooperating. Tell us everything about your operation."

The Broker leaned back, his eyes calculating. "And what do I get in return?"

Ethan's voice was cold. "A chance to make a deal. But it depends on how much you're willing to give us."

The Broker sighed, realizing he had little choice. "Fine. I'll talk. But I want assurances."

Sarah nodded. "You'll get them. Now start talking."

For the next hour, The Broker detailed his network, providing names, locations, and operations. Each revelation was a step closer to dismantling the entire organization.

"We have safe houses in several cities," The Broker explained. "Each one is managed by a lieutenant. They handle the day-to-day operations and report back to me."

Ethan took notes, his pen moving swiftly across the paper. "And the money? How does it flow through the network?"

The Broker leaned forward. "We use legitimate businesses as fronts. The money is laundered through various accounts before it's used for bribes and payoffs."

Sarah pressed further. "Who are your main contacts in the city government?"

The Broker rattled off a list of names, each one more shocking than the last. "These people are deeply embedded. Taking them down won't be easy."

Ethan's eyes narrowed. "We'll take care of that. Just keep talking."

As The Broker continued to divulge information, Sarah felt a sense of satisfaction and resolve. They were finally getting to the heart of the operation, and nothing would stop them now.

When The Broker finished, Sarah stood up, looking him in the eye. "You did the right thing. We'll make sure you're protected."

Ethan added, "But don't think this absolves you. You're still going to pay for what you've done."

As they left the interrogation room, Sarah felt a surge of determination. They had The Broker, and now they had the information they needed to bring down the rest of his network. The battle was far from over, but the tide had turned in their favor.

Chapter 9
The Final Threads

The precinct was a hive of activity as the final preparations for the raid were underway. Sarah Thompson and Ethan Drake had spent the past weeks tirelessly working to dismantle Marco Alvarez's criminal network. The culmination of their efforts had led them to this moment—the final strike against the mastermind himself.

Sarah stood in the middle of the bustling operations room, a large map of the city pinned to the wall behind her. Red dots marked the locations of Marco's safe houses and known associates, while a large, ominous black circle highlighted their primary target—a secluded mansion on the outskirts of the city where Marco was believed to be hiding.

Ethan approached, his expression resolute. "The teams are ready, Sarah. We've got SWAT, federal agents, and our own officers in position. Everyone's just waiting for the go-ahead."

Sarah nodded, her mind racing with the details of their plan. "Good. We need to hit hard and fast. Marco's expecting us to make a move, but he won't be ready for the scale of this operation."

Chief Donovan joined them, his face a mask of determination. "We've come a long way. This is our chance to bring him down for good. Are you both ready?"

"Ready as we'll ever be," Sarah replied, her voice steady. "We've got all the intel we need. Marco's security will be tight, but we're prepared."

Donovan nodded. "Alright. Let's brief the teams one last time."

The officers and agents gathered in the briefing room, the atmosphere charged with anticipation. Sarah and Ethan took their places at the front, facing the assembled team.

"Listen up, everyone," Sarah began, her voice clear and authoritative. "We've worked tirelessly to get to this point. Marco Alvarez is our primary target. He's dangerous and unpredictable, but we have the element of surprise on our side."

Ethan stepped forward, pointing to the map. "We'll be hitting the mansion from multiple angles. SWAT will breach the main entrance while our teams secure the perimeter and cut off any escape routes. Federal agents will handle the interior, searching for Marco and any key evidence."

A young officer raised his hand. "What do we do if Marco resists?"

"Use force as necessary," Donovan answered. "But our priority is to take him alive. We need him to face justice and to provide information on any remaining associates."

Sarah scanned the room, meeting the eyes of each team member. "Stay focused and work together. We've come too far to let anything slip through the cracks. Let's bring him down."

As the briefing concluded, the officers and agents moved out with a sense of purpose. Sarah and Ethan headed to their vehicle, their minds focused on the mission ahead.

"You think Marco knows we're coming?" Ethan asked as they drove through the city streets, their destination looming closer.

"Probably," Sarah replied, her eyes fixed on the road. "But he doesn't know how prepared we are. We've covered every angle."

They arrived at the staging area near the mansion, joining the rest of the team as final checks were made. The night air was cool, filled with the hum of quiet conversations and the rustle of gear being adjusted.

Sarah took a deep breath, feeling the weight of the moment. "This is it, Ethan. Everything we've worked for comes down to this."

Ethan placed a reassuring hand on her shoulder. "We've got this, Sarah. We've been through worse. Just another day on the job, right?"

She smiled slightly, appreciating his unwavering support. "Yeah, just another day."

The command came through their earpieces. "Teams, move into position. Operation starts in five."

Sarah and Ethan led their team to the designated entry point, their movements silent and coordinated. They crouched behind a row of hedges, the mansion looming ahead like a dark fortress.

"On my mark," Sarah whispered into her radio. "Three, two, one. Go."

SWAT breached the front entrance with a thunderous crash, the sound echoing through the night. Simultaneously, Sarah, Ethan, and their team surged forward, securing the perimeter and cutting off any potential escape routes.

Inside, the federal agents moved with precision, clearing room after room as they searched for Marco. The tension was palpable, each second stretching into an eternity.

Suddenly, a voice crackled through the radio. "We've found him. Upper floor, east wing."

Sarah and Ethan exchanged a glance, their hearts pounding. "Let's move," Sarah said, leading the way into the mansion.

They navigated the opulent hallways, their footsteps muffled by the thick carpets. The sounds of the operation were distant, a backdrop to the intense focus of their mission.

As they reached the east wing, they saw Marco, surrounded by agents, his hands raised in surrender. The sight of the man who had caused so much pain and destruction, finally subdued, filled Sarah with a profound sense of accomplishment.

"It's over, Marco," she said, her voice unwavering. "You're done."

Marco's eyes were cold, but he offered no resistance. "You think this ends with me? You're more naïve than I thought."

Ethan stepped forward, cuffing Marco securely. "We'll see about that. Right now, you're coming with us."

As they escorted Marco out of the mansion, the weight of their victory settled over Sarah. They had done it. The battle was not entirely over, but they had struck a significant blow against a powerful enemy.

Back at the precinct, the atmosphere was one of relief and subdued celebration. Sarah and Ethan debriefed the team, ensuring all evidence was secured and all protocols were followed.

Donovan approached them, a rare smile on his face. "Excellent work, both of you. This is a huge win for us."

Sarah nodded, exhaustion and satisfaction mingling in her expression. "Thank you, Chief. We couldn't have done it without the team."

Ethan added, "We've got Marco, but there's still work to be done. We need to ensure his entire network is dismantled."

Donovan agreed. "And we will. But tonight, take a moment to appreciate what you've accomplished. You've made a real difference."

As the team began to disband, Sarah and Ethan shared a moment of quiet reflection. They had faced immense challenges and uncovered a web of crime far greater than they had imagined. But together, they had persevered.

"We did it, Sarah," Ethan said, his voice filled with pride.

"Yeah, we did," she replied, a sense of fulfillment settling over her. "But like you said, there's still more to do."

Ethan nodded. "And we'll do it. One step at a time."

With a renewed sense of purpose, they were ready to continue their fight for justice, knowing that their efforts had brought them one step closer to a safer, more secure Harborview.

Back at the precinct, the air was thick with anticipation and tension. Marco Alvarez, the mastermind behind a sprawling criminal empire, sat in the interrogation room, his expression a mix of defiance and resignation. Sarah Thompson and Ethan Drake stood outside, watching him through the one-way glass, preparing for what would be one of the most critical interrogations of their careers.

Sarah took a deep breath, steeling herself. "We need to break him, Ethan. He's the key to dismantling the rest of his network."

Ethan nodded, his face serious. "We've got enough evidence to put him away, but we need him to talk. We need names, locations, operations—everything."

Sarah pushed open the door to the interrogation room and stepped inside, Ethan close behind. Marco looked up, his eyes cold and calculating.

"Marco Alvarez," Sarah began, taking a seat across from him. "You're facing multiple charges: racketeering, money laundering, drug trafficking, and conspiracy to commit murder. We've got enough to ensure you never see the outside of a cell again."

Marco smirked, leaning back in his chair. "You think locking me up will stop anything? There are others ready to take my place."

Ethan leaned forward, his eyes narrowing. "Maybe. But if you cooperate, we can make things easier for you. Help us take down the rest of your network, and we'll talk about reducing some of your charges."

Marco's smirk widened. "And why would I do that? What do I gain from betraying my own people?"

Sarah's gaze was unwavering. "Your people won't hesitate to cut you loose to save themselves. We both know loyalty is fleeting in your world. Help us, and you might see some leniency."

Marco chuckled, shaking his head. "You're wasting your time. I've survived this long because I know when to keep my mouth shut."

Ethan crossed his arms, his voice cold. "You're not in control here, Marco. We've already dismantled most of your operations. It's only a matter of time before we get the rest. Make it easier on yourself."

Marco's eyes flickered with something—fear, perhaps, or realization. "You think you've won because you've caught me? This is far from over."

Sarah leaned in, her voice low and intense. "We've got the evidence, Marco. We've got your ledgers, your emails, your associates in custody. It's over. But how it ends for you is still up to you."

Marco's bravado faltered for a moment. He looked down, considering his options. "And if I cooperate, what happens to me?"

"You help us, and we can negotiate a deal," Ethan replied. "Less time in prison, better conditions. But you need to give us something solid."

Marco sighed, rubbing his temples. "Fine. I'll give you a few names. But I want guarantees."

Sarah nodded. "We'll talk to the DA. But you need to start talking. Now."

Marco looked up, his expression a mix of defeat and resolve. "Alright. There's a warehouse on the east side. It's a major distribution point for our operations. And there's a guy named Carlos Mendoza. He handles most of the financial transactions."

Ethan took notes, his pen moving quickly across the page. "Keep going. Who else is involved?"

Marco hesitated, then continued. "There's also Luis Ramirez. He oversees the drug shipments. And Sofia Morales—she's the contact for our international partners."

Sarah exchanged a glance with Ethan. This was the break they needed. "We need addresses, locations. Where can we find them?"

Marco provided the details, his voice losing some of its earlier defiance. "I want those guarantees in writing," he insisted.

"You'll get them," Sarah assured him. "But keep talking. What else do we need to know?"

As Marco divulged more information, Sarah and Ethan felt a sense of triumph. They were getting the pieces they needed to bring down the entire network. The hours ticked by, the interrogation room filled with the details of Marco's operations.

Finally, Marco slumped back in his chair, exhausted. "That's everything. Now, I want my deal."

Sarah stood, her expression resolute. "We'll take this to the DA. If your information checks out, you'll get your deal."

Ethan added, "But understand this, Marco. If you're holding anything back, if you've lied to us, the deal's off."

Marco nodded, a hint of resignation in his eyes. "I've told you everything. Just make sure you hold up your end."

As they left the room, Sarah and Ethan felt a wave of relief and determination. They had the information they needed to strike a decisive blow against Marco's network. The final countdown had begun, and they were ready to finish what they had started.

Back in the operations room, they briefed Chief Donovan on the new intel. "Marco's given us key locations and names," Sarah said. "We need to move fast and hit these targets."

Donovan nodded, his expression one of grim satisfaction. "Good work. Let's coordinate with the federal agencies and get this done. We're taking them all down."

As the team mobilized for the final raids, Sarah and Ethan knew they were on the brink of a major victory. The fight against Marco Alvarez was nearing its end, and they were ready to see it through.

The precinct was a flurry of activity as officers and agents prepared for the final coordinated raids. The tension was palpable, every team member acutely aware of the stakes. Sarah and Ethan stood at the center of the operations room, reviewing the details one last time.

Sarah addressed the assembled teams, her voice steady and authoritative. "Listen up. We've got the intel we need from Marco. We're hitting multiple locations simultaneously to dismantle the rest of his network. Our targets are a warehouse on the east side, a financial office downtown, and a drug distribution center near the docks."

Ethan stepped forward, pointing to the marked locations on the map. "SWAT will lead the assault on the warehouse. Federal agents will handle the financial office, and our units will take the docks. Stay sharp and communicate. We can't afford any mistakes."

Chief Donovan added, "We've come this far because of your dedication and hard work. Let's finish this and bring them all to justice."

The teams nodded, their faces set with determination. They moved out swiftly, the air buzzing with anticipation.

Sarah and Ethan led the convoy to the east side warehouse, their minds focused on the mission. As they approached, they saw the massive structure looming in the distance, its shadow cast ominously in the early morning light.

They parked a block away, moving into position. "Remember, we go in fast and hard," Sarah reminded her team. "We need to secure the area and apprehend everyone inside."

The SWAT team took the lead, breaching the warehouse doors with a loud crash. Inside, chaos erupted as Marco's men scrambled to defend their stronghold.

"Police! Get down!" Ethan shouted, his weapon trained on a group of armed men.

A firefight ensued, the sound of gunfire echoing through the cavernous space. Sarah and Ethan moved strategically, covering each other as they advanced.

"Clear the left side!" Sarah ordered, her voice cutting through the noise. "Secure those exits!"

The team worked with precision, methodically taking down the defenders and securing the warehouse. As the last of Marco's men were subdued, Sarah spotted a figure trying to escape through a side door.

"Ethan, over there!" she shouted, pointing to the fleeing man.

They gave chase, cornering him in a narrow alley behind the warehouse. "Stop! Harborview Police!" Ethan commanded.

The man, panting heavily, raised his hands in surrender. "Okay, okay! Don't shoot!"

Sarah cuffed him, her expression stern. "Who are you? What's your role in this operation?"

"I'm just a runner," the man stammered. "I move shipments, that's all."

"Who do you report to?" Ethan pressed, his grip firm on the man's arm.

"Raul Garcia," the runner replied. "He's the one in charge here."

Sarah exchanged a glance with Ethan. "We've got what we need. Let's get him back to the precinct for questioning."

As they secured the scene and collected evidence, Sarah's radio crackled to life with updates from the other teams. "Team Bravo, we've secured the financial office. Multiple suspects in custody."

"Team Charlie, the docks are secure. All targets apprehended."

A sense of relief washed over Sarah. They were dismantling the network piece by piece. "Good work, everyone," she said into her radio. "Regroup at the precinct."

Back at the precinct, the atmosphere was electric with the thrill of success. The teams debriefed, each reporting their findings and the evidence collected.

Chief Donovan addressed the group, pride evident in his voice. "You've all done an outstanding job. This operation was a success because of your hard work and dedication. We've dealt a significant blow to Marco Alvarez's network."

Sarah and Ethan exchanged a look of triumph. "We did it," Ethan said, his voice filled with satisfaction.

Sarah nodded, feeling a sense of accomplishment. "Yes, but there's still more to do. We need to ensure these guys stay behind bars and that the remaining pieces of the network are taken down."

As the dust settled, the precinct returned to a semblance of normalcy. Sarah and Ethan worked tirelessly to process the evidence and prepare for the upcoming trials. The adrenaline from the raids had subsided, leaving a quiet determination to see the case through to its conclusion.

One evening, as they were wrapping up their work, Sarah glanced at Ethan. "You know, we've come a long way since the beginning of this case. It's hard to believe how much we've uncovered."

Ethan smiled, leaning back in his chair. "It's been a hell of a ride. But we couldn't have done it without the team. Everyone played a crucial role."

Sarah nodded, her eyes reflecting a mix of pride and exhaustion. "True. But now we have to make sure Marco and his associates face justice. The trials are going to be tough."

Ethan's expression grew serious. "We've got the evidence. And we've got each other's backs. We'll get through it."

As they packed up for the night, Chief Donovan approached, a rare smile on his face. "I wanted to commend you both personally. Your leadership and determination were pivotal in bringing down Marco's network."

"Thank you, Chief," Sarah said. "But it was a team effort. We couldn't have done it without everyone's dedication."

Donovan nodded. "That's true. But your perseverance and ability to see the bigger picture were essential. You should both be proud of what you've accomplished."

Ethan grinned. "We are, Chief. And we're ready for whatever comes next."

As they left the precinct, the cool night air was a welcome relief from the intensity of the past weeks. Sarah looked up at the stars, feeling a sense of closure and fulfillment.

"We did good, Ethan," she said quietly. "We made a real difference."

Ethan nodded, his gaze steady. "Yeah, we did. And we'll keep making a difference, one case at a time."

With a renewed sense of purpose, they walked into the night, ready to face whatever challenges lay ahead, knowing that together, they could overcome anything.

Chapter 10
The Trial

The morning sun cast long shadows across the precinct as Sarah Thompson and Ethan Drake prepared for one of the most significant days of their careers—the trial of Marco Alvarez. Months of relentless investigation and dangerous raids had led them to this point, and they knew the stakes were higher than ever.

Sarah sat at her desk, meticulously organizing her notes and evidence files. The trial was set to begin in a few hours, and she wanted to ensure every detail was in place. Ethan entered the room, carrying two cups of coffee, his face a mask of focus.

"Thought you might need this," he said, handing her a cup.

"Thanks," Sarah replied, taking a sip. The caffeine was a welcome boost. "We've got everything we need, right?"

Ethan nodded, sitting down beside her. "Yeah, we've got it all. Witness statements, forensic evidence, financial records. We've built a solid case."

Sarah glanced at the clock. "We should head to the courthouse soon. The DA wants to go over a few last-minute details."

Ethan stood up, grabbing his files. "Let's do it. We've come too far to leave anything to chance."

They arrived at the courthouse, the grand building looming imposingly against the clear sky. Inside, the atmosphere was charged with anticipation. Reporters and spectators filled the hallways, eager to witness the trial of one of the city's most notorious criminals.

Sarah and Ethan made their way to the DA's office, where District Attorney Linda Carlisle was waiting for them. Carlisle was a seasoned prosecutor with a reputation for being tough and unyielding.

"Detectives," she greeted them, her tone brisk. "I've reviewed your case files. You've done excellent work. We're going to need both of you to testify about the investigation and the raids."

"We're ready," Sarah said confidently. "We've been over everything multiple times. We know the case inside out."

Carlisle nodded, satisfied. "Good. We need to paint a clear picture for the jury. Marco's defense team is going to come at us hard, trying to discredit the evidence. We can't give them any openings."

Ethan spoke up, his voice steady. "We'll hold our ground. Marco's crimes are well-documented. The evidence speaks for itself."

Carlisle smiled, though her eyes remained sharp. "That's the spirit. Let's head to the courtroom. It's time to get this started."

As they entered the courtroom, the buzz of conversations hushed to a murmur. Marco Alvarez sat at the defense table, flanked by his lawyers. His expression was calm, almost smug, as if he believed he could still control the outcome.

Sarah and Ethan took their seats, the weight of the moment settling over them. The judge entered, and everyone rose.

"Be seated," the judge commanded, his voice authoritative. "We are here today to begin the trial of Marco Alvarez. The charges against him include racketeering, money laundering, drug trafficking, and conspiracy to commit murder."

The DA began her opening statement, laying out the prosecution's case with precision and clarity. She detailed the extensive investigation, the evidence collected, and the testimonies they would present.

When it was the defense's turn, Marco's lead attorney, a sharp-suited man named Victor Sanchez, stood up. "Ladies and gentlemen of the jury, my client is a victim of overzealous law enforcement. The evidence against him is circumstantial at best, and we will prove his innocence."

Sarah felt a flicker of anger but remained composed. They had anticipated this tactic, and they were prepared.

As the trial proceeded, witnesses took the stand, recounting their experiences and interactions with Marco's criminal enterprise. Each testimony was a piece of the puzzle, adding depth and detail to the picture of Marco's extensive operations.

Finally, it was Sarah's turn to testify. She took the stand, swearing to tell the truth. The DA approached her with a reassuring nod.

"Detective Thompson, can you describe the initial stages of the investigation into Marco Alvarez's activities?"

Sarah took a deep breath, her voice steady and clear. "The investigation began with a series of arson attacks linked to Marco Alvarez. As we dug deeper, we uncovered a complex network involving drug trafficking, money laundering, and other illegal activities."

The DA guided her through the key points of the investigation, highlighting the crucial evidence they had gathered. Sarah detailed the raids, the arrests, and the financial records that traced back to Marco.

When it was the defense's turn to cross-examine, Sanchez approached with a predatory smile. "Detective Thompson, isn't it true that some of the evidence you collected was circumstantial?"

Sarah met his gaze, unflinching. "All evidence was corroborated by multiple sources. We have direct links between Marco Alvarez and the illegal activities detailed in the charges."

Sanchez pressed on, trying to undermine her testimony. "Isn't it possible that someone else could have orchestrated these activities, framing my client?"

Sarah's voice remained firm. "The evidence points directly to Marco Alvarez. His involvement is undeniable."

Satisfied with her answers, the defense moved on. Ethan's testimony followed, reinforcing the case with his own experiences and observations. Together, their testimonies formed a compelling narrative that was hard to refute.

As the day drew to a close, the judge adjourned the court until the following morning. Sarah and Ethan left the courthouse, the weight of their testimonies lifting slightly.

"We did well today," Ethan said, a note of optimism in his voice. "We've laid out a strong case."

Sarah nodded, though her mind remained focused. "We did. But we need to stay vigilant. The defense will keep trying to poke holes in our evidence."

Ethan placed a reassuring hand on her shoulder. "We've got this, Sarah. We're almost there."

They walked into the evening, the courthouse behind them, but the fight for justice still ahead. The trial was far from over, but with each passing day, they moved closer to securing a conviction and bringing Marco Alvarez to justice.

Beat 2: The Crucial Evidence

The following morning, the courthouse was again filled with a sense of anticipation. The prosecution had made a strong start, but today was critical. Sarah and Ethan knew that the presentation of the most damning evidence against Marco Alvarez would be crucial in securing a conviction.

As the courtroom filled, Sarah and Ethan took their seats, ready for another intense day. The judge entered, and the proceedings began. District Attorney Linda Carlisle stood, her demeanor as sharp as ever.

"Your Honor, today we will present key evidence that directly links Marco Alvarez to the crimes he is accused of," Carlisle announced. She turned towards the jury, her expression resolute. "We have obtained financial records, communication logs, and testimonies that will prove beyond a reasonable doubt that the defendant orchestrated a vast criminal enterprise."

The first witness of the day was Agent Marcus Lawson from the FBI. He took the stand, his presence commanding. Carlisle began her questioning.

"Agent Lawson, can you describe the nature of the evidence your team collected during the investigation?"

Lawson nodded. "We collected a series of financial records from shell companies linked to Marco Alvarez. These records detailed transactions that funded illegal activities, including drug trafficking and money laundering."

Carlisle handed him a document. "Please explain to the court what this document represents."

Lawson held up the document. "This is a ledger from one of the shell companies, Green Horizon Enterprises. It shows large sums of money being transferred to accounts controlled by Marco Alvarez."

The jury murmured, the weight of the evidence palpable. Carlisle continued, "Agent Lawson, were these transactions cross-referenced with other pieces of evidence?"

"Yes," Lawson confirmed. "We matched these transactions with email communications and witness testimonies. Everything points to Marco Alvarez as the orchestrator."

Next, Carlisle introduced the communication logs. "These logs were obtained from computers seized during the raids. They contain emails and messages between Marco Alvarez and his associates, discussing the details of their operations."

She handed the logs to Lawson, who began reading aloud. "Here's an example: 'Make sure the shipment arrives by Friday. Use the usual route. Marco.' This is just one of many messages that show his direct involvement."

As Lawson stepped down, Carlisle called the next witness—Luis Ramirez, one of Marco's former associates who had agreed to testify in exchange for a reduced sentence. Ramirez took the stand, looking nervous but determined.

"Luis Ramirez," Carlisle began, "can you tell the court about your role in Marco Alvarez's operations?"

Ramirez nodded, his voice trembling slightly. "I managed the drug shipments. Marco gave the orders, and I made sure everything ran smoothly."

"And did Marco Alvarez personally oversee these operations?" Carlisle asked.

"Yes," Ramirez replied. "He was involved in everything. He made all the major decisions."

Carlisle showed him another document. "Is this one of the shipment schedules you managed?"

Ramirez glanced at the document and nodded. "Yes, this is one of them. It shows the dates, quantities, and destinations for the drugs we moved."

The jury listened intently, the evidence building a clear picture of Marco's extensive control over the criminal network.

As the day progressed, the defense tried to discredit the witnesses, but the evidence was overwhelming. The testimonies, financial records, and communication logs all pointed directly to Marco Alvarez.

During a break, Sarah and Ethan stepped outside the courtroom to catch their breath. The gravity of the trial weighed heavily on them, but they were buoyed by the strength of the case they had built.

"We're doing it, Sarah," Ethan said, his eyes reflecting determination. "We're bringing him down."

Sarah nodded, feeling a mix of relief and resolve. "We just have to keep pushing. The jury needs to see the full extent of his crimes."

As they returned to the courtroom, Carlisle prepared to introduce the final piece of evidence for the day—a video recording from one of the raids. The footage showed Marco's men discussing their operations, providing a visual confirmation of everything the witnesses had described.

The courtroom fell silent as the video played. The jurors watched intently, their expressions grim as they absorbed the reality of Marco's criminal empire.

When the video ended, Carlisle addressed the jury. "You have seen the evidence and heard the testimonies. Marco Alvarez is not just a criminal; he is the mastermind behind a network that has caused untold harm. We ask that you consider the weight of this evidence and deliver a verdict of guilty."

The defense attempted to sow doubt, but the evidence was undeniable. As the day ended and the court adjourned, Sarah and Ethan felt a growing sense of confidence. They had presented a compelling case, and it was now up to the jury to decide.

Walking out of the courthouse, Ethan turned to Sarah. "We've done everything we can. Now we just have to wait."

Sarah nodded, feeling a mix of exhaustion and hope. "I know. Let's hope the jury sees the truth."

As they headed back to the precinct, they couldn't help but feel that justice was within reach. The trial had laid bare the extent of Marco Alvarez's crimes, and now, it was only a matter of time before the verdict was delivered.

The tension in the courtroom was palpable as the jury filed back into their seats. After days of grueling testimony and overwhelming evidence, the moment of truth had arrived. Sarah Thompson and Ethan Drake sat side by side, their hearts pounding with anticipation. Marco Alvarez, flanked by his defense team, maintained a stoic facade, though a flicker of uncertainty crossed his eyes.

The judge entered and took his seat, calling the court to order. "Ladies and gentlemen of the jury, have you reached a verdict?"

The jury foreman stood, holding a piece of paper. "We have, Your Honor."

The judge nodded. "Please read the verdict."

The foreman unfolded the paper, clearing his throat. "In the case of the People versus Marco Alvarez, on the charge of racketeering, we find the defendant guilty."

A collective breath was held as the foreman continued. "On the charge of money laundering, we find the defendant guilty. On the charge of drug trafficking, we find the defendant guilty. And on the charge of conspiracy to commit murder, we find the defendant guilty."

The courtroom erupted in murmurs. Sarah and Ethan exchanged a look of relief and triumph, the weight of their efforts finally yielding the result they had hoped for.

Marco's face tightened, his composed exterior cracking ever so slightly. His lead attorney, Victor Sanchez, quickly stood. "Your Honor, we request a mistrial based on procedural errors and prosecutorial misconduct."

The judge raised a hand, silencing the courtroom. "Mr. Sanchez, your request is noted, but this court finds no grounds for a mistrial. The evidence presented was compelling and irrefutable. The defendant will be remanded into custody pending sentencing."

Sanchez protested, "Your Honor, this is an outrage. My client deserves a fair—"

The judge cut him off. "Mr. Sanchez, enough. The jury has spoken. Bailiffs, take the defendant into custody."

As Marco was led away, he turned to Sarah and Ethan, his eyes burning with anger. "This isn't over. You think you've won, but you've just started a war."

Ethan met his gaze, unflinching. "We'll be ready. You're done, Marco."

The judge banged his gavel, calling for order. "Court is adjourned."

Outside the courtroom, reporters swarmed, microphones thrust forward as cameras flashed. "Detective Thompson, Officer Drake, how do you feel about the verdict?" one reporter shouted.

Sarah held up a hand, her voice calm but firm. "Justice has been served today. We're proud of the work we've done, and we're grateful to the jury for seeing the truth."

Ethan added, "This is a victory for the people of Harborview. We've taken a dangerous criminal off the streets, and we'll continue to work tirelessly to ensure the safety of our community."

The reporters pressed for more, but Sarah and Ethan pushed through the crowd, making their way to the precinct. The sense of relief was palpable, but they knew their work was far from over.

As they entered the precinct, their colleagues greeted them with applause and cheers. Chief Donovan approached, a broad smile on his face. "Outstanding work, both of you. This is a huge win for us."

Sarah nodded, the weight of the trial beginning to lift. "Thank you, Chief. It was a team effort. We couldn't have done it without everyone's support."

Ethan added, "And there's still more to do. We need to ensure Marco's associates are taken down as well."

Donovan clapped them on the back. "One step at a time. For now, enjoy this victory. You've earned it."

Later that evening, Sarah and Ethan found themselves back at their favorite bar, the familiar setting providing a comforting backdrop for reflection. They sat in a quiet corner, nursing their drinks and soaking in the reality of their hard-won victory.

Ethan broke the silence, his voice thoughtful. "You know, it's been a long road to get here. We've faced so many obstacles, but we never gave up."

Sarah nodded, a soft smile playing on her lips. "We didn't. And it's because of that perseverance that we're here now, celebrating a major win. But it's not just about taking down Marco. It's about making a difference."

Ethan raised his glass. "To making a difference. And to the team that made it possible."

They clinked glasses, the sound a quiet affirmation of their shared journey. As they sipped their drinks, the weight of the past months slowly began to lift, replaced by a sense of accomplishment and hope for the future.

Sarah looked at Ethan, her eyes reflecting the bond they had forged. "We've come a long way, Ethan. And we've made a real impact. Here's to many more victories."

Ethan smiled, his eyes warm with camaraderie. "Many more victories, partner."

As they sat together, the challenges they had faced and the victories they had won formed the foundation of a new chapter. They were ready for whatever came next, knowing they would face it together, stronger than ever.

Chapter 11
A New Dawn

The morning sun filtered through the blinds of the precinct, casting a warm glow on the bustling activity within. The atmosphere was charged with the excitement of new beginnings as the task force geared up for its first major operation. Sarah and Ethan stood at the helm, their confidence and determination palpable.

In the briefing room, the task force members gathered around the large conference table. The whiteboard was filled with maps, photos, and notes detailing the targets they would be hitting that day. Sarah stood at the front, her eyes scanning the room, taking in the eager faces of their team.

"Alright, everyone," she began, her voice steady and commanding. "Today marks the beginning of a new chapter. We've dismantled The Broker's network, but there's more work to be done. Our first target is a major hub in the drug distribution network. We need to move quickly and efficiently."

Ethan stepped forward, adding to Sarah's briefing. "We've identified three primary locations. Each one is heavily guarded, and we suspect they're using advanced security systems. Our objective is to secure the locations, apprehend the suspects, and gather as much evidence as possible."

One of the officers, Jenkins, raised his hand. "What's our protocol if we encounter resistance?"

Sarah's gaze was unwavering. "Use non-lethal force whenever possible, but your safety comes first. These are dangerous individuals, and we need to be prepared for anything."

Garcia, who was coordinating the logistics, chimed in. "We've got backup units on standby, and medical teams ready to respond. Stay sharp and stick to the plan."

As the briefing concluded, the team moved out, each member knowing their role and the importance of the mission. Sarah and Ethan led the way, their partnership a well-oiled machine honed by countless operations.

They arrived at the first location, a sprawling warehouse on the outskirts of the city. The team moved into position, surrounding the building with practiced precision. Sarah and Ethan stood by the entrance, their ears tuned to the subtle sounds inside.

Ethan whispered into his radio. "Alpha team, ready on my mark. Three... two... one... go!"

They breached the door, flooding into the warehouse with weapons drawn. Inside, chaos erupted as the suspects scrambled to defend themselves. The task force moved swiftly, subduing the suspects and securing the area.

Sarah spotted the leader of the group, a burly man with a scar across his face, attempting to escape through a back exit. She pursued him, her footsteps echoing in the cavernous space.

"Stop! Police!" she shouted, her voice cutting through the noise.

The man turned, his eyes wild with desperation. He raised a weapon, but before he could fire, Sarah tackled him to the ground, disarming him in a swift, practiced motion.

Ethan arrived moments later, securing the suspect with cuffs. "Nice work, Sarah."

She nodded, catching her breath. "Thanks. Let's make sure we get everything."

They regrouped with the team, who were already cataloging evidence and securing the warehouse. Sarah looked around, satisfaction mingling with the adrenaline of the operation.

The radio crackled to life with Garcia's voice. "Bravo team, report."

"Bravo team here," came the reply. "Second location is secure. All suspects in custody, and we've recovered a significant amount of contraband."

Ethan's eyes met Sarah's, a shared sense of accomplishment passing between them. "Two down, one to go."

They moved to the third location, a rundown apartment building in a seedy part of town. The team approached with caution, knowing this would be the most dangerous of the three targets.

Inside, they encountered fierce resistance, the suspects determined to protect their territory. The task force fought back with equal determination, their training and coordination shining through.

Sarah found herself in a standoff with one of the leaders, a wiry man with a menacing glare. "You're not getting out of here," she said, her voice firm.

The man sneered. "You think you can stop us? We're just a small part of something much bigger."

Ethan moved in from the side, his weapon trained on the man. "It's over. Drop your weapon."

The man hesitated, then threw his gun to the floor with a clatter. "Fine. But you haven't won. There are more of us."

Sarah secured the suspect, a sense of resolve hardening within her. "We'll find them. Every last one."

As they cleared the building and gathered the evidence, the weight of their task settled over them. The battle was far from over, but they had taken a crucial first step.

Back at the precinct, the atmosphere was electric with the thrill of victory and the anticipation of the work to come. Sarah and Ethan reviewed the day's successes, their minds already turning to the next operation.

Ethan looked at Sarah, his expression serious but hopeful. "We've made a good start. There's still a lot to do, but I know we can handle it."

Sarah nodded, her determination unwavering. "Together, we can take on anything. This is just the beginning."

The following day, the task force reconvened in the briefing room, the energy from their initial success still palpable. The room buzzed with quiet conversation as officers shared updates and prepared for the next phase of their operation. Sarah and Ethan stood at the front, reviewing the latest intelligence reports.

Garcia entered the room, a tablet in hand. "We've got new intel on the remaining cells. Looks like they're scrambling, trying to regroup after yesterday's raids."

Sarah nodded, her eyes scanning the information. "Good. We need to keep the pressure on. If we move quickly, we can dismantle the entire network before they have a chance to recover."

Ethan turned to the team. "Our next targets are two major hubs identified from the decrypted files. One is a shipping facility on the waterfront; the other is a high-end nightclub downtown that's a front for their money laundering operations."

Officer Jenkins raised a hand. "What's the plan for simultaneous strikes?"

Sarah tapped the map on the whiteboard. "We'll split into two teams. Alpha team, led by me, will hit the shipping facility. Bravo team, led by Ethan, will take the nightclub. We move in at the same time, 2200 hours."

Garcia added, "We've arranged for backup units and aerial surveillance. We need to be prepared for anything."

Ethan addressed the room, his voice firm. "Remember, these are dangerous individuals. Stay sharp and watch each other's backs. Any questions?"

A young officer, Davis, spoke up. "What do we do if we encounter civilians at the nightclub?"

Ethan responded, "Priority is to secure the suspects and ensure civilian safety. Use non-lethal force whenever possible."

Sarah looked around the room, meeting the eyes of each team member. "This is a coordinated effort. We can't afford any mistakes. Trust your training and your instincts. We've got this."

The room fell silent as the teams absorbed the plan. They knew the risks, but they were ready. The task force dispersed to gear up, a sense of determination settling over them.

As they prepared, Sarah pulled Ethan aside. "We need to be in constant communication. If anything goes sideways, we need to know immediately."

Ethan nodded. "Agreed. We've come this far together; we're not taking any chances now."

At the appointed hour, the teams moved out, the city lights twinkling against the darkening sky. Sarah's team arrived at the shipping facility, the sound of waves lapping against the docks providing an eerie backdrop.

She signaled for her team to take their positions. "Alpha team in position. Bravo team, status?"

Ethan's voice crackled over the radio. "Bravo team in position. On your mark."

Sarah took a deep breath, then gave the order. "Go."

Alpha team breached the entrance of the shipping facility, moving with practiced precision. Inside, they found crates stacked high and workers scurrying to hide evidence. Sarah's team fanned out, securing the area and apprehending suspects.

Sarah spotted the facility's manager, a burly man with a shaved head, attempting to flee. She pursued him, her voice echoing through the cavernous space. "Stop! Police!"

The man ignored her, ducking behind a stack of crates. Sarah closed in, ready for a confrontation. She rounded the corner, finding him frantically searching for an exit.

"End of the line," Sarah said, her weapon trained on him.

He raised his hands, defeat etched on his face. "Alright, alright. I give up."

Sarah cuffed him, radioing Ethan. "Alpha team secure. How's it looking at the nightclub?"

Ethan's voice came through, tense but controlled. "We've got a situation. Suspects are armed, and there are civilians inside. We're handling it, but we could use some backup."

Sarah's heart raced. "We're on our way. Hold tight."

She turned to her team. "Let's move. Bravo team needs our support."

They arrived at the nightclub, the scene inside chaotic. Patrons cowered under tables as gunfire echoed through the room. Sarah's team moved in, coordinating with Ethan to subdue the armed suspects and ensure the safety of the civilians.

Ethan met Sarah's eyes across the room, relief evident on his face. "Good timing."

Sarah nodded, her focus unwavering. "Let's finish this."

Together, they worked to clear the nightclub, arresting the remaining suspects and securing evidence. The operation was intense, but their training and coordination paid off. As the last suspect was led away in cuffs, the adrenaline began to ebb, replaced by a profound sense of accomplishment.

Back at the precinct, the atmosphere was charged with victory. Officers processed evidence, debriefed the teams, and shared stories of the night's events. Sarah and Ethan found a moment of quiet in the briefing room, reviewing the final reports.

Ethan leaned back, a satisfied smile on his face. "We did it. Two major hubs taken down in one night."

Sarah nodded, her expression reflecting a mix of exhaustion and triumph. "And there's more to come. We're making a real impact."

Garcia entered, his face beaming. "Great work tonight, both of you. The mayor's already been informed. He's thrilled with the results."

Sarah smiled. "We couldn't have done it without the team. Everyone played their part."

Ethan agreed. "And we'll keep pushing. There's still more to uncover, but we're on the right path."

As they wrapped up for the night, the precinct slowly quieted, the sense of a job well done settling over them. They knew the battle against organized crime was far from over, but they were making significant strides.

Walking out into the cool night air, Sarah looked at Ethan. "We've come a long way. But there's still a lot to do."

Ethan nodded, a determined glint in his eyes. "And we'll do it together. This is just the beginning."

As they parted ways, each heading home for a well-deserved rest, they felt a renewed sense of purpose. They had taken on a formidable challenge and emerged victorious. And with each new operation, they were getting closer to making their city a safer place for everyone.

The precinct was quiet, a stark contrast to the chaos of the night before. Sarah and Ethan sat in a small conference room, the early morning light filtering through the blinds. They were going over the final reports from the previous night's operations, but their minds were already on the next steps.

Garcia walked in, holding a stack of fresh intel. "Morning. Thought you'd want to see this."

Ethan looked up, curiosity in his eyes. "What've you got?"

Garcia laid the papers on the table. "More details from the nightclub raid. Seems like we stumbled onto something big. One of the suspects was carrying encrypted files on a flash drive. Amy's working on decrypting them now, but it looks like there are plans for a major shipment coming in next week."

Sarah leaned forward, her interest piqued. "Did we get any specifics?"

Garcia shook his head. "Not yet. But if this shipment is as significant as we think, it could be the break we need to dismantle the remaining cells."

Ethan nodded. "We need to stay ahead of this. As soon as Amy has those files decrypted, we move."

Just then, Amy burst into the room, a wide grin on her face. "Got it! The files are decrypted. You're not going to believe this."

Sarah and Ethan exchanged a glance before turning back to Amy. "What did you find?" Sarah asked.

Amy pulled up the files on her tablet, showing them detailed plans for the shipment. "They're moving a massive amount of drugs and weapons through the port. Scheduled for next Tuesday, midnight."

Ethan's eyes narrowed. "That's five days from now. We need to mobilize."

Sarah nodded, her mind already racing with strategies. "We'll need a full team. Coordinated strikes at the port and any known distribution points. We can't let any of it slip through."

Garcia chimed in. "I'll start making calls. We'll need backup from the feds and the coast guard."

Sarah looked at Amy. "Can you keep monitoring their communications? We need to know if they change plans."

Amy nodded. "Already on it. I'll keep you updated with any developments."

As Amy and Garcia left the room, Sarah turned to Ethan, her expression serious. "This is it, Ethan. We can't afford any mistakes."

Ethan met her gaze, his resolve unwavering. "We won't make any. We've got this."

They spent the next few hours meticulously planning the operation, coordinating with various agencies and making sure every detail was covered. The tension in the room was palpable, but there was also a sense of determination.

Garcia returned with updates. "The feds and the coast guard are on board. They're ready to move when we are."

Sarah nodded. "Good. Let's run through the plan one more time. I want everyone clear on their roles."

Ethan began outlining the operation. "We'll have teams positioned at the port and at known distribution points. As soon as the shipment arrives, we move in. We need to secure the drugs and weapons and apprehend anyone involved."

Sarah added, "We'll also have surveillance teams monitoring the area. If they try to change plans or move the shipment, we'll be ready."

Garcia looked around the room. "Any questions?"

The team shook their heads, their faces set with determination. Sarah felt a surge of pride. They were ready.

As the day turned into evening, Sarah and Ethan took a moment to breathe. They stood outside the precinct, the cool air a welcome relief.

Ethan looked at Sarah, a small smile on his face. "We've come a long way."

Sarah nodded, her eyes reflecting the same sentiment. "We have. And we're not done yet."

Ethan's smile widened. "No, we're not. But we're getting closer. One step at a time."

They stood in silence for a moment, each lost in their thoughts. The next few days would be crucial, but they were ready for the challenge.

Sarah broke the silence. "Let's get some rest. We're going to need it."

Ethan nodded. "Good idea. See you tomorrow, Sarah."

"Good night, Ethan."

As they parted ways, Sarah felt a renewed sense of determination. They were on the brink of something big, and she knew they had the strength and resolve to see it through.

The next few days were a whirlwind of preparation. The task force worked around the clock, coordinating with federal agencies and refining their strategy. The tension was palpable, but there was also a sense of anticipation and resolve.

On the night of the operation, the team gathered in the briefing room one last time. The air was thick with the weight of what they were about to undertake. Sarah and Ethan stood at the front, their faces reflecting the gravity of the moment.

Sarah began, her voice steady. "Tonight, we bring down one of the largest criminal operations this city has ever seen. We've planned meticulously, and we're ready. Trust your training, trust each other, and stay focused."

Ethan added, "We'll have teams positioned at the port and at all known distribution points. Our objective is to secure the shipment and apprehend every suspect. No one gets away."

Garcia stepped forward, a grim expression on his face. "We've got backup units and medical teams on standby. If anything goes sideways, we're prepared."

Sarah looked around the room, meeting the eyes of each team member. "This is it. Let's bring them down."

As they moved out, the tension in the air was almost tangible. The drive to the port was silent, each member of the team mentally preparing for what lay ahead.

When they arrived, the port was shrouded in darkness, the only light coming from the occasional streetlamp. The team took their positions, their breaths visible in the cool night air.

Sarah's voice came through the radio. "Alpha team in position. Bravo team, status?"

Ethan's response was immediate. "Bravo team in position. All units, hold. We move on my signal."

Minutes felt like hours as they waited, the anticipation building with each passing second. Finally, the signal came. "Go, go, go!"

The teams moved in unison, breaching the port and surrounding the shipment. Suspects scrambled, trying to flee or hide, but the task force was ready. Within minutes, they had secured the area, the drugs and weapons confiscated, and the suspects apprehended.

Ethan's voice crackled through the radio. "Alpha team secure. All suspects in custody."

Sarah responded, her voice filled with relief. "Copy that, Bravo team. Great work, everyone."

As they began processing the scene, Sarah and Ethan found a moment to talk. Ethan's face was a mix of exhaustion and triumph. "We did it, Sarah. We brought them down."

Sarah nodded, a smile spreading across her face. "We did. And we couldn't have done it without this team."

Garcia approached, his face beaming. "This is a huge win. The mayor's going to be thrilled."

Ethan laughed. "We might even get a day off after this."

Sarah shook her head, still smiling. "Maybe. But for now, let's finish up here."

As the night wore on, the team worked tirelessly, securing evidence and ensuring all suspects were processed. The sense of accomplishment was overwhelming. They had done it. They had brought down a major criminal network and made their city a safer place.

Back at the precinct, the atmosphere was one of quiet celebration. Officers shared stories of the night's events, their faces reflecting a mix of exhaustion and pride.

Sarah and Ethan stood outside the precinct, the first light of dawn beginning to break over the horizon. Ethan looked at Sarah, his expression one of deep satisfaction. "We made a real difference tonight."

Sarah nodded, her eyes reflecting the same sentiment. "We did. And there's still more to do. But for now, let's take a moment to appreciate what we've accomplished."

Ethan smiled, a sense of peace settling over him. "Agreed. We've earned it."

As they stood there, watching the sun rise, they knew that this was just the beginning. They had faced immense challenges and emerged victorious. And together, they were ready to take on whatever came next.

Chapter 12
New Beginnings

The precinct was alive with the buzz of activity as the task force processed the final pieces of the operation. The atmosphere was a mix of exhaustion and exhilaration, the team riding high on their recent success. Sarah and Ethan stood at the center of it all, coordinating the last details and ensuring everything was in order.

Garcia approached them, a wide grin on his face. "The mayor's office just called. They want to hold a press conference to announce the bust. They're giving you both a lot of credit."

Sarah smiled, a rare moment of pride showing through her usual stoicism. "That's great news, Mark. The team deserves it."

Ethan nodded. "Absolutely. Everyone put in the work. We couldn't have done it without them."

Garcia clapped Ethan on the back. "Well, you both should get ready. The press conference is in an hour. They're expecting you at City Hall."

As Garcia walked away, Ethan turned to Sarah, a playful grin on his face. "Ready to be the face of justice?"

Sarah rolled her eyes, but there was a hint of a smile on her lips. "Let's just get this over with. I'm not a fan of the spotlight."

They made their way to City Hall, the weight of their accomplishments settling in. The grand building loomed ahead, a symbol of the authority and responsibility they carried. Inside, the atmosphere was electric with anticipation. Reporters and camera crews buzzed around, setting up for the big announcement.

Mayor Davis greeted them warmly, his smile wide and genuine. "Detectives Thompson, Blake, it's an honor to have you here. What you've accomplished is nothing short of remarkable."

Sarah nodded politely. "Thank you, Mayor. We're just doing our jobs."

Ethan shook the mayor's hand. "We're happy to be here. The team deserves the recognition."

The mayor led them to the stage, where a podium had been set up. As they took their places, the room fell silent, all eyes on them.

Mayor Davis began, his voice resonant and authoritative. "Ladies and gentlemen, we are here today to recognize the incredible efforts of our police force in dismantling one of the largest criminal networks our city has ever seen. This success is due to the tireless work and dedication of the task force led by Detectives Sarah Thompson and Ethan Blake."

The room erupted in applause, the sound filling the space. Sarah felt a wave of pride and gratitude for her team.

Ethan stepped up to the podium, his voice steady and confident. "Thank you, Mayor Davis. This operation was a team effort from start to finish. We had the support of multiple agencies, and every officer involved played a crucial role. We couldn't have done it without them."

A reporter raised her hand, and the mayor nodded to her. "Detective Blake, what's next for the task force?"

Ethan glanced at Sarah before answering. "We're not done yet. There are still remnants of the network we need to track down. We'll continue working tirelessly to ensure our city remains safe."

Sarah took her turn at the podium, her voice firm and resolute. "Our job is to protect and serve. This operation was a significant victory, but it's just one part of a larger effort. We will keep fighting until every last piece of this network is dismantled."

The reporters continued to ask questions, each one highlighting different aspects of the operation and the challenges they faced. Sarah and Ethan answered them with the same calm and determination they had shown throughout the investigation.

As the press conference drew to a close, Mayor Davis thanked them once again. "Detectives, your work has made our city a safer place. We are all in your debt."

After the conference, as they made their way back to the precinct, Ethan looked at Sarah. "You did great up there."

Sarah shrugged, a small smile playing at her lips. "Just doing my job."

Ethan chuckled. "You always say that. But you know, it's more than just a job. You're making a real difference."

She looked at him, her expression softening. "So are you, Ethan. So are you."

Back at the precinct, the atmosphere was still buzzing from the announcement. Officers congratulated them as they walked through, the sense of camaraderie and shared victory palpable.

Garcia met them with a grin. "Looks like you two are celebrities now."

Ethan laughed. "Let's hope it doesn't go to our heads."

Sarah shook her head, smiling. "No chance of that."

As they settled back into their routine, the weight of their responsibilities remained, but there was also a renewed sense of purpose. They had achieved something monumental, and they were ready to face whatever came next.

Ethan leaned back in his chair, looking over at Sarah. "So, what's the next move?"

She thought for a moment, her gaze distant. "We keep pushing. There's always more to do."

He nodded, his expression serious. "Together?"

She met his eyes, her resolve unwavering. "Always."

They turned back to their work, the sense of accomplishment fueling their determination. The city was safer because of their efforts, and they were ready to continue the fight for justice. Together, they could face anything.

The precinct hummed with a quieter, more focused energy in the days following the press conference. The task force was now firmly established, their mandate clear. They had dismantled a major criminal network, but the work of rooting out the remnants and preventing new threats from emerging was ongoing.

Sarah sat at her desk, reviewing a thick stack of reports. Each document detailed the next steps in their operations, from tracking down leads on remaining associates of The Broker to coordinating with federal agencies on broader initiatives. The coffee on her desk had long gone cold, but she barely noticed, absorbed in the intricacies of their plans.

Across from her, Ethan was similarly engrossed, his fingers flying over his keyboard as he compiled data and cross-referenced information. The room was filled with the quiet sounds of diligent work—papers shuffling, keyboards clicking, the low murmur of colleagues discussing strategy.

Occasionally, Sarah would look up, catching Ethan's eye. They shared a silent understanding, a mutual respect and trust that had been forged through the trials they had faced together. Their partnership had become a cornerstone of the task force's success.

As the morning wore on, Garcia walked over, a file in hand. "Got something interesting here," he said, setting the file down on Sarah's desk.

Sarah glanced up, intrigued. "What's this?"

Garcia leaned against the desk. "One of our sources tipped us off about a potential new player trying to fill the void left by The Broker. We don't have much yet, but it's enough to start digging."

Ethan looked over, his interest piqued. "Another power grab already? That didn't take long."

Garcia nodded. "Yeah, well, crime never sleeps. This guy goes by the name 'The Phantom.' We're still gathering intel, but if he's making a move, we need to be ahead of him."

Sarah opened the file, scanning the preliminary information. "We'll need to set up surveillance, start mapping out his connections. If he's trying to take over, he's bound to slip up somewhere."

Ethan stood, his expression resolute. "Let's get the team together. We need to hit this hard and fast."

Within minutes, the task force was assembled in the briefing room, the atmosphere tense but focused. Sarah stood at the front, the file in her hand.

"We've got a new target," she began, her voice steady and clear. "The Phantom. We don't know much about him yet, but he's trying to take over where The Broker left off. Our job is to stop him before he gets a foothold."

Ethan stepped forward, adding to Sarah's briefing. "We'll be setting up surveillance at known hotspots and tracking any unusual activity. We'll also be reaching out to our contacts for more information. This is a priority operation. We need to move quickly and efficiently."

The team nodded, their expressions reflecting the gravity of the situation. They had just come off a major victory, but there was no time to rest. The city depended on them.

As the meeting broke up, Sarah and Ethan headed back to their desks to finalize their plans. The weight of their new mission settled over them, but there was no hesitation in their movements. They knew what needed to be done, and they were ready to do it.

By late afternoon, the first surveillance units were in place, and the task force was already gathering data. Sarah and Ethan monitored the feeds, analyzing patterns and identifying potential leads. The work was meticulous and demanding, but they thrived on the challenge.

In a rare moment of quiet, Ethan looked over at Sarah. "Think we'll ever get a break?"

Sarah smiled faintly, her eyes still on the screen. "Maybe one day. But for now, there's too much at stake."

He nodded, understanding. "Just making sure you're not forgetting that vacation we talked about."

She glanced at him, her smile widening. "Not a chance. We'll get there, Ethan. Just not today."

As evening approached, the task force remained vigilant, their focus unwavering. They were on the trail of a new threat, and they wouldn't rest until it was neutralized. The city needed them, and they were ready to answer the call.

The lights in the precinct burned late into the night, a testament to their dedication and resolve. Sarah and Ethan, side by side, were prepared to face whatever challenges lay ahead. Together, they were a force to be reckoned with, and nothing would stand in their way.

In the days that followed, the task force remained on high alert. The city seemed quieter, but Sarah knew it was the calm before the storm. The Phantom was out there, and every piece of intel brought them closer to unraveling his plans.

Sarah and Ethan were in the conference room, pouring over the latest reports. The walls were lined with maps and photos, each one marking a potential lead. The task force moved around them, a well-oiled machine of dedicated officers.

Garcia entered, carrying a folder. "Got something. One of our sources confirmed a meeting. The Phantom is gathering his lieutenants tonight at an old warehouse on the east side."

Ethan looked up, his eyes narrowing. "That's our chance. We need to hit them before they can solidify their plans."

Sarah nodded, her mind already racing. "We'll need to move fast. Get a team together and brief them. We go in tonight."

As the team assembled, Sarah outlined the operation. "This is our chance to take down The Phantom. We'll move in with two teams—one through the front, the other covering the back exits. Our priority is to secure the area and apprehend everyone inside."

Ethan added, "Be prepared for resistance. These guys won't go down without a fight. Stay sharp and watch each other's backs."

The team nodded, their expressions determined. They had faced down The Broker's network, and they were ready to take on this new threat.

Hours later, they arrived at the warehouse, the night air cool and still. The building loomed ahead, its dark silhouette against the city's glow. Sarah and Ethan took their positions, the team spreading out around them.

Sarah's voice was calm but firm over the radio. "All units, in position. On my mark."

The team moved in, breaching the warehouse doors. Inside, the space was dimly lit, the air thick with the scent of oil and metal. Men scrambled to draw weapons, but the task force was swift and precise.

Ethan led the charge, his voice cutting through the chaos. "Police! Get down!"

A suspect lunged at him, but Ethan sidestepped, bringing the man to the ground in a smooth, practiced motion. Sarah moved through the room, her eyes scanning for The Phantom.

She spotted him near the back, directing his men. "There!" she shouted, pointing him out to the team.

The Phantom turned, his face a mask of cold fury. He drew a gun, but Sarah was faster, firing a warning shot. "Drop it!"

He hesitated, then threw the weapon to the ground. "You think you've won? This is just the beginning."

Ethan moved in, cuffing him. "We'll see about that."

As the team secured the warehouse, Sarah felt a sense of triumph. They had taken down The Phantom before he could establish his hold. The city was safe once more, thanks to their efforts.

Back at the precinct, the mood was celebratory but subdued. There was still work to be done, but they had achieved a significant victory.

Garcia approached Sarah and Ethan, a smile on his face. "Nice work, both of you. The mayor's already heard about the bust. He's thrilled."

Sarah nodded, her exhaustion mingling with pride. "It was a team effort. We couldn't have done it without everyone's hard work."

Ethan leaned back in his chair, a satisfied grin on his face. "And now, maybe we can finally take that break."

Sarah laughed softly. "We'll see. But for now, let's focus on wrapping this up."

As the dust settled from the operation, Sarah and Ethan found themselves in the precinct's briefing room, reflecting on the night's events. The room was quiet, save for the low hum of conversation from the officers outside.

Ethan broke the silence, his voice thoughtful. "You know, I didn't think we'd catch The Phantom this quickly. It's a testament to how far we've come as a team."

Sarah nodded, a smile playing at her lips. "We've come a long way. It feels good to see our efforts paying off."

Garcia entered, holding two cups of coffee. "Thought you two could use these. Great work tonight."

Ethan accepted his cup, nodding in gratitude. "Thanks, Mark. We couldn't have done it without your intel."

Garcia smiled. "Just doing my part. Besides, it's not every day we get to take down a major player like The Phantom."

Sarah took a sip of her coffee, her mind already racing ahead. "We need to stay vigilant. There are always more threats. But tonight, we can at least enjoy this victory."

Ethan leaned back, his expression relaxed. "Speaking of enjoying things, how about that vacation? We've earned it."

Sarah laughed, the sound light and genuine. "Alright, you win. Let's plan it. Somewhere warm, with no phones."

Garcia grinned. "Sounds like a good plan. You two deserve it."

As they talked, the camaraderie and mutual respect between them were evident. They had faced immense challenges together, and their bond had only grown stronger.

Later that night, Sarah and Ethan walked out of the precinct, the cool night air a welcome contrast to the intensity of the day. They stood by their cars, the city quiet around them.

Ethan looked at Sarah, a serious expression on his face. "You know, we've been through a lot. But I wouldn't want to do this with anyone else."

Sarah smiled, her eyes reflecting the same sentiment. "Neither would I. We make a good team, Ethan."

He nodded, a hint of a smile on his lips. "Yeah, we do. And whatever comes next, I know we can handle it."

They stood in silence for a moment, the weight of their accomplishments settling over them. The future was uncertain, but they were ready to face it together.

Sarah broke the silence, her voice soft. "So, vacation?"

Ethan laughed. "Yes, vacation. Let's make it happen."

As they parted ways, a sense of peace and anticipation filled the air. They had achieved something remarkable, and they were ready for whatever came next. Together, they were unstoppable.

The city lights twinkled around them as they drove home, a reminder of the place they had sworn to protect. They had made a difference, and they would continue to do so, one step at a time.

For now, they could rest, knowing they had done their part to make the city a safer place. And with the promise of a well-deserved break on the horizon, they faced the future with renewed strength and determination.

Chapter 13
Reflections

The morning sun cast a golden hue over the city, but the atmosphere inside the precinct was anything but serene. Detective Sarah Thompson sat at her desk, the events of the past weeks weighing heavily on her. The Architect's network was crumbling, but the fight was far from over. The final phase of their plan still loomed large, threatening to plunge the city into chaos.

Ethan Drake walked in, his expression grim but determined. He dropped a file on Sarah's desk. "We've got a lead. Interrogation of The Architect's operatives revealed a name—Jessica Kane. She's been coordinating the logistics for their operations."

Sarah looked up, her eyes narrowing. "Jessica Kane. Any idea where we can find her?"

Ethan nodded. "She's been sighted at an old warehouse on the east side. Looks like she's making a last-ditch effort to regroup."

Sarah stood, her resolve hardening. "Then we need to move fast. Get the team ready. We're going to bring her in."

As they prepared to head out, Garcia approached, a worried look on his face. "We've got another problem. There's chatter about a potential cyber attack on the city's emergency response systems. If they pull that off, we're looking at widespread panic and delayed responses to critical incidents."

Sarah's jaw tightened. "We can't let that happen. We need to split up. Ethan, you and I will go after Jessica Kane. Garcia, coordinate with cybercrimes and secure those systems. We need to cover all our bases."

Garcia nodded. "Understood. I'll keep you updated."

The drive to the warehouse was tense, the silence between Sarah and Ethan filled with unspoken thoughts. As they arrived, they saw the dilapidated building looming ahead, its broken windows and rusted exterior a stark reminder of the danger within.

Ethan parked the car, his eyes scanning the area. "Looks quiet. Too quiet."

Sarah nodded, her hand resting on her weapon. "Stay sharp. We don't know what we're walking into."

They approached the entrance, moving cautiously. Sarah signaled for Ethan to cover her as she pushed the door open. Inside, the warehouse was dimly lit, filled with crates and old machinery. The air was thick with dust, and the only sound was their footsteps echoing off the walls.

Sarah whispered into her radio, "Team Alpha, in position. Moving in."

Ethan followed closely, his eyes darting around the room. "Do you hear that?" he whispered.

Sarah listened, catching the faint sound of typing. "Someone's here. Let's move."

They advanced quietly, following the sound to a small office at the back of the warehouse. Peering inside, they saw a woman hunched over a laptop, her fingers flying over the keys. Sarah recognized her from the photos—Jessica Kane.

Sarah motioned for Ethan to take the lead. "Jessica Kane. Step away from the computer and put your hands where we can see them."

Jessica's head snapped up, her eyes wide with surprise. She hesitated for a moment, then slowly raised her hands. "You're too late," she said, a defiant edge to her voice. "The plan is already in motion."

Ethan moved forward, securing her hands behind her back. "We'll see about that. What are you working on?"

Jessica smirked. "Wouldn't you like to know?"

Sarah stepped closer, her voice cold. "We're not here to play games. Tell us how to stop the attack on the emergency response systems."

Jessica's smirk faltered slightly. "You think you can stop this? The Architect's plan is bigger than you can imagine."

Ethan tightened his grip. "Start talking, or you'll regret it."

Jessica glanced at the laptop, then back at Sarah. "There's a command center hidden in the industrial district. That's where they're launching the cyber attack from. But good luck finding it. It's well hidden."

Sarah nodded to Ethan. "Get her out of here. We need to get to that command center."

As they escorted Jessica out of the warehouse, Sarah's phone buzzed. It was Garcia. "Sarah, we've detected unusual activity in the industrial district. Looks like they're preparing for the cyber attack."

Sarah's heart raced. "We're on our way. Hold them off as long as you can."

They hurried back to the car, the urgency of the situation driving them forward. As they sped through the city streets, Sarah couldn't shake the feeling that they were running out of time.

Ethan glanced at her, his expression determined. "We'll find it, Sarah. We have to."

Sarah nodded, her resolve unwavering. "We will. And we'll stop them, no matter what it takes."

As they approached the industrial district, the tension in the car was palpable. The stakes had never been higher, and the clock was ticking down. But Sarah knew they had the skills and the determination to see this through. Together, they would uncover the command center, stop the cyber attack, and bring an end to The Architect's reign of terror.

The industrial district loomed ahead, a maze of factories and warehouses, each one a potential hiding place for the command center orchestrating the cyber attack. Sarah and Ethan drove through the narrow streets, their eyes scanning for any sign of unusual activity.

Ethan's voice broke the tense silence. "We need a starting point. If Jessica was telling the truth, the command center should be well hidden."

Sarah nodded, her mind racing. "We're looking for something out of place. Extra security, unusual power usage, anything that stands out."

Garcia's voice crackled over the radio. "I've got a lead for you. We've detected a spike in power consumption at a warehouse on Mill Street. It's off the grid, but the readings are off the charts."

Sarah's eyes narrowed. "That's our spot. We're heading there now."

They arrived at the warehouse, its exterior nondescript and unremarkable. But Sarah could feel the tension in the air. She signaled for Ethan to cover her as they approached the entrance.

Ethan whispered, "We go in fast and hard. No chances."

Sarah nodded. "On three. One, two, three."

They burst through the door, weapons drawn. Inside, the warehouse was a stark contrast to its exterior. Computers and servers lined the walls, cables snaking across the floor. In the center, a group of men and women worked furiously at their stations, their eyes widening in shock as Sarah and Ethan entered.

"Freeze! Hands up!" Sarah commanded, her voice echoing through the room.

The operatives hesitated, then began to raise their hands. But one of them, a tall man with a scar across his cheek, made a sudden move towards a control panel.

Ethan fired a warning shot. "Don't even think about it."

The man froze, his eyes glaring with defiance. "You're too late. The attack is already underway."

Sarah moved forward, her weapon trained on the man. "Shut it down. Now."

He sneered. "I'd rather die."

Ethan stepped closer, his voice cold. "That can be arranged."

The man's resolve faltered, his eyes flicking towards the screens. "Alright, alright. I'll do it."

As he moved to shut down the systems, Sarah kept her weapon trained on him, her heart pounding. "What's your name?"

"Andrew," he muttered, his hands moving over the keyboard.

Sarah watched as the screens flickered, the progress of the cyber attack slowing. "Andrew, you're going to tell us everything. Who's behind this? Where's The Architect?"

Andrew glanced at her, fear and defiance warring in his eyes. "The Architect? He's already gone. He left as soon as the attack started."

Ethan frowned. "Where did he go?"

Andrew hesitated, then sighed. "There's a safe house in the hills, just outside the city. That's where he'll be."

Sarah nodded. "Ethan, get the location from him. We need to move."

As Ethan secured the information, Sarah's phone buzzed. It was Garcia. "Sarah, we're seeing a significant drop in the attack. Whatever you're doing, it's working."

Sarah allowed herself a brief moment of relief. "We've got them shutting it down. But The Architect has fled to a safe house in the hills. We're heading there next."

Garcia's voice was firm. "Be careful. He's bound to have it heavily fortified."

Sarah ended the call and turned to Ethan. "Let's go. We need to end this."

The drive to the hills was a blur of urgency and tension. The safe house, nestled among the trees, was a stark contrast to the chaos of the city. They parked a distance away, moving in on foot to avoid detection.

Ethan surveyed the area through binoculars. "Looks quiet. Too quiet."

Sarah nodded. "He'll be expecting us. We need to be smart about this."

They moved through the forest, the underbrush crunching under their boots. As they approached the safe house, Sarah signaled for Ethan to take the rear entrance while she moved towards the front.

Sarah whispered into her radio, "On my mark. Three, two, one—move."

They breached the entrances simultaneously, sweeping through the rooms. The safe house was luxurious, a stark contrast to the grimy warehouses and factories they'd encountered before. But it was eerily empty.

Ethan's voice came through the radio. "Clear on this side. No sign of him."

Sarah frowned, moving through the lavish living room. "Keep searching. He's here somewhere."

As she entered a study, she noticed a series of monitors on the wall, each one showing different parts of the city. And there, in the center, was a live feed of the warehouse they'd just left. The Architect had been watching them.

Suddenly, a voice crackled through the speakers. "Impressive, Detective Thompson. But you're too late."

Sarah's heart pounded. "Show yourself!"

The Architect's voice was calm, almost amused. "I'm afraid I can't do that. But you've been a worthy adversary. Until next time."

The screens went dark, and Sarah felt a surge of frustration. They were so close, yet The Architect had slipped through their fingers once again.

Ethan joined her in the study, his expression grim. "He's gone, isn't he?"

Sarah nodded, her jaw clenched. "Yes. But we've weakened his network. We'll find him."

As they left the safe house, Sarah felt a mix of determination and exhaustion. The Architect was still out there, but they were getting closer. Every step brought them nearer to the final confrontation, and she was ready for it.

They drove back to the city in silence, the weight of their mission pressing down on them. Sarah knew the fight wasn't over, but with each victory, they were gaining ground. And when the time came, they would be ready to bring The Architect to justice, no matter the cost.

The precinct was a storm of motion and noise as Sarah and Ethan returned from the safe house. The air was thick with a mix of urgency and frustration. Despite shutting down the cyber attack and weakening The Architect's network, the mastermind had slipped through their fingers once again. But Sarah's determination burned brighter than ever.

Garcia met them at the entrance, his expression serious. "We've got a situation. The Architect just released a statement online, threatening another attack. He's targeting the city's main transportation hub."

Sarah's eyes narrowed. "He's trying to spread us thin. We need to regroup and hit him where it hurts."

Ethan nodded. "We need a plan. Let's get everyone into the briefing room."

The team gathered quickly, the room buzzing with anticipation. Sarah took her place at the front, her gaze steady and commanding. "Listen up. The Architect is targeting the transportation hub. If he succeeds, the entire city will be paralyzed. We can't let that happen."

Ethan stepped forward, pointing to a map of the city. "We need to secure all major entry and exit points. We'll set up checkpoints and coordinate with local law enforcement. This will be our highest priority."

Jamie, the young officer, raised her hand. "Do we have any intel on his exact plan? How he's going to strike?"

Garcia shook his head. "Not yet. But we're monitoring all communications. Any sign of unusual activity, we'll be on it."

Sarah's mind raced. "We need to anticipate his moves. Think like him. He's methodical, always one step ahead. But we have an advantage— he's under pressure now. He's making mistakes."

Ethan added, "We also need to consider the possibility of decoys. He's used them before to throw us off."

Garcia's phone buzzed. He glanced at it, then looked up, his expression grim. "We've got a lead. An informant just tipped us off about a suspicious delivery to the hub. Large crates, no paperwork. Could be explosives."

Sarah's eyes sharpened. "Alright. Ethan, you and I will head to the hub. Garcia, coordinate with the bomb squad and get units in place. Jamie, keep monitoring communications and report any new intel."

As they drove to the transportation hub, the tension was palpable. Sarah glanced at Ethan, her jaw set. "We're close, Ethan. I can feel it. He's getting desperate."

Ethan nodded, his eyes on the road. "Desperate means dangerous. We need to be ready for anything."

They arrived at the hub, a sprawling complex of terminals and warehouses. The place was bustling with activity, commuters and workers unaware of the looming threat. Sarah and Ethan moved quickly, coordinating with the officers already on site.

Sarah addressed the team, her voice firm. "We need to find those crates and secure them. Move in pairs, stay in contact, and be thorough."

Ethan added, "If you see anything suspicious, don't engage. Call it in and wait for backup."

The search began, officers fanning out through the complex. Sarah and Ethan moved through the main terminal, eyes scanning for any sign of the crates.

Just then, Jamie's voice crackled over the radio. "Detective Thompson, we've got eyes on the crates. They're in warehouse 14. Bomb squad is en route."

Sarah's heart pounded. "Copy that. We're on our way."

They sprinted to the warehouse, finding it heavily guarded by security. Sarah flashed her badge. "Police! We need access now!"

The guards stepped aside, and they rushed in, finding the crates near the back. The bomb squad was already at work, carefully inspecting the contents.

The squad leader looked up, his expression tense. "We've got explosives, alright. High-grade stuff. This could have leveled the entire hub."

Ethan's voice was calm but urgent. "Can you disarm them?"

The leader nodded. "We're on it. Just need some time."

Sarah's radio buzzed again, Jamie's voice urgent. "Detective, we've intercepted a message. The Architect knows we're here. He's sending reinforcements to stop us."

Sarah's eyes narrowed. "We need to secure this area. No one gets through."

Ethan turned to the officers. "Set up a perimeter. We hold this position until the bomb squad is done."

Minutes felt like hours as they waited, the tension thick in the air. The sound of approaching vehicles signaled the arrival of The Architect's reinforcements. Sarah and Ethan took positions, ready for the confrontation.

The first wave came quickly, armed men spilling out of black SUVs. Gunfire erupted, echoing through the warehouse. Sarah and Ethan returned fire, holding their ground.

Sarah shouted over the noise, "We can't let them get to the crates!"

Ethan fired, taking down an approaching attacker. "We've got this, Sarah. Just hold on!"

The firefight intensified, but Sarah's team held firm. The bomb squad continued their work, defusing the explosives with steady hands. Finally, the squad leader called out, "We're clear! Bombs disarmed!"

Relief washed over Sarah. "Good job! Now let's finish this."

They pushed back the remaining attackers, securing the area. As the last of The Architect's men were taken into custody, Sarah felt a surge of triumph. They had stopped the immediate threat, but the fight was far from over.

Ethan approached, his face streaked with dirt and sweat. "We did it. But we need to find The Architect. He won't stop until he's caught."

Sarah nodded, her resolve unwavering. "We will. We're closing in. He's running out of places to hide."

Back at the precinct, the atmosphere was one of cautious optimism. They had won a significant battle, but the war was still raging. Sarah and her team regrouped, reviewing the latest intel and planning their next move.

Garcia approached, a new sense of urgency in his eyes. "We've decrypted another message. It's coordinates to a location outside the city. It could be where The Architect is hiding."

Sarah's eyes met Ethan's, a steely determination in them. "Then that's where we're going. This ends now."

As they prepared to head out, Sarah felt a mix of exhaustion and resolve. They were on the brink of bringing The Architect to justice, and she was ready to see it through to the end. Together, they would stop him, no matter the cost. The final confrontation was near, and they would face it head-on, united in their pursuit of justice.

The atmosphere in the precinct was electric with tension and anticipation. Sarah Thompson stood at the center of the operations room, her team gathered around her. The decrypted coordinates from The Architect's latest message were displayed on the screen—a remote location outside the city, hidden deep in the forest. It was time to end this.

Ethan Drake was beside her, his face set with determination. "This is it, Sarah. We've tracked him to his last hideout. We need to be prepared for anything."

Sarah nodded, her gaze sweeping over her team. "We've come a long way. The Architect has thrown everything at us, but we've pushed back every time. This is our chance to bring him to justice. Stay sharp and stay safe."

Garcia stepped forward, his expression serious. "We've coordinated with the local authorities. They'll provide backup, but we'll be the first in. The element of surprise is crucial."

Sarah's voice was steady. "Alright, let's move out. We're taking two teams. Bravo team will cover the perimeter and ensure no one escapes. Alpha team, you're with me. We're going in."

The drive to the forested hideout was tense, each member of the team mentally preparing for the confrontation ahead. The sun was setting, casting long shadows over the road. Sarah's mind raced with the possibilities of what they might encounter.

Ethan broke the silence. "Sarah, whatever happens in there, we've got your back."

Sarah glanced at him, a small smile playing on her lips. "I know, Ethan. Let's finish this."

They arrived at the edge of the forest, the coordinates leading them to an old, abandoned cabin. The place was eerily quiet, the only sound the rustling of leaves in the wind. Sarah signaled for Bravo team to take their positions, surrounding the area.

Sarah's voice was barely a whisper. "On my mark. Three, two, one—move."

Alpha team advanced towards the cabin, their movements silent and coordinated. Sarah and Ethan led the way, their weapons drawn. They breached the door, entering swiftly and efficiently.

Inside, the cabin was dark and cluttered, the faint glow of computer screens illuminating the room. Sarah's eyes scanned the space, searching for any sign of The Architect.

A voice echoed from the shadows, smooth and calm. "Detective Thompson. I've been expecting you."

Sarah's heart pounded as she turned towards the source of the voice. There, standing in the doorway of an adjacent room, was The Architect, his eyes gleaming with a cold, calculated intelligence.

Sarah stepped forward, her weapon trained on him. "It's over, Architect. You're surrounded. Surrender now."

The Architect smiled, a chilling sight. "Surrounded? Perhaps. But not defeated. You've been a worthy opponent, Sarah. But this game is far from over."

Ethan moved to flank him, his voice firm. "Hands where we can see them. Now."

The Architect raised his hands slowly, his smile never fading. "You think you've won, but you haven't. My network is vast. Even if you take me down, others will rise."

Sarah's eyes narrowed. "We'll deal with them. Right now, you're coming with us."

As they moved to cuff him, The Architect suddenly reached for something in his pocket. Ethan reacted instantly, tackling him to the ground. A small device clattered across the floor, a flashing red light indicating it was some kind of detonator.

Sarah picked up the device, her voice shaking slightly. "What is this? What did you plan?"

The Architect laughed, a harsh, mirthless sound. "Insurance. If I go down, I take you all with me."

Garcia's voice crackled over the radio. "Sarah, we've detected explosives rigged throughout the cabin. You need to get out of there, now!"

Sarah's heart raced. "Everyone out! Now!"

They dragged The Architect out of the cabin, sprinting towards the safety of the trees. Just as they reached the edge of the clearing, a massive explosion rocked the ground, the cabin engulfed in flames.

Sarah and her team hit the ground, shielding themselves from the blast. When the dust settled, she looked up, her heart still pounding. The cabin was a smoldering ruin, but they were alive.

Ethan pulled The Architect to his feet, his grip ironclad. "Your plan failed. You're done."

The Architect's smile had finally faded, replaced by a look of cold fury. "You may have won this battle, but the war is far from over."

Sarah stood, her resolve stronger than ever. "We'll see about that. Take him away."

As The Architect was led to a waiting vehicle, Sarah turned to her team. "Good work, everyone. We've taken a major step today, but we can't let our guard down. There's still work to be done."

Garcia approached, a look of relief on his face. "We did it, Sarah. We stopped him."

Sarah nodded, her gaze fixed on the horizon. "Yes, but we need to dismantle his entire network. We can't let any remnants regroup."

Ethan placed a hand on her shoulder, his voice soft. "We will. Together."

As they made their way back to the precinct, Sarah felt a sense of accomplishment mingled with the weight of the ongoing battle. The Architect was in custody, but the fight for the city's safety continued. She knew that with her team by her side, they were ready for whatever challenges lay ahead.

Chapter 14
Resolute Steps

The precinct had returned to its usual rhythm, but the sense of accomplishment lingered. The task force's recent successes had brought a new level of confidence to the team. Sarah and Ethan were at their desks, reviewing the latest reports and planning their next steps.

Garcia approached, carrying a steaming cup of coffee. "Morning, you two. Looks like we've got a quiet day ahead."

Sarah glanced up, a hint of a smile on her lips. "Let's hope it stays that way. We could use a breather."

Ethan nodded in agreement. "Agreed. But knowing our luck, something's bound to come up."

Garcia chuckled, handing the cup to Sarah. "Well, enjoy it while you can. Oh, and I've got some updates on the remaining leads from The Phantom's network."

Sarah took the coffee, nodding her thanks. "Let's hear it."

Garcia pulled out a file and began reading. "We've identified a few low-level associates still at large. They're small-time players, but we should wrap them up to ensure they don't regroup."

Ethan leaned back in his chair, considering the information. "Shouldn't be too difficult. We can send a couple of teams to pick them up."

Sarah agreed. "Let's get it done. We need to close this chapter completely."

As they continued to discuss the details, a call came in over the radio. "All units, we have a report of suspicious activity near the docks. Possible drug deal in progress."

Ethan's eyes met Sarah's. "There goes our quiet day."

Sarah stood, determination in her eyes. "Let's move. Garcia, coordinate with backup units. We'll handle this."

The drive to the docks was tense, the familiar anticipation of an imminent operation settling over them. As they approached, they could see a group of men gathered near a shipping container, their movements furtive.

Ethan surveyed the scene, his jaw set. "Looks like we've got a few dealers and their buyers. We need to move in fast before they scatter."

Sarah nodded, her voice steady. "We'll split up. I'll take the left flank, you cover the right. Garcia, have the backup units ready to block any exits."

The team moved into position, the adrenaline sharpening their focus. Sarah gave the signal, and they converged on the suspects, weapons drawn.

"Police! Hands in the air!" Ethan shouted, his voice echoing off the metal containers.

The suspects froze, their eyes wide with fear. One of them made a move to run, but Sarah was faster, intercepting him and bringing him to the ground.

"Don't even think about it," she warned, cuffing him swiftly.

Ethan and the rest of the team secured the remaining suspects, the entire operation over in minutes. As they began processing the scene, Sarah and Ethan exchanged a look of satisfaction.

"Nice work," Sarah said, a smile tugging at her lips.

Ethan nodded, his expression relieved. "Looks like we can handle anything, even on a 'quiet' day."

Back at the precinct, the atmosphere was a mix of routine and residual adrenaline. Sarah and Ethan reviewed the information gathered from the docks, piecing together the connections to their ongoing investigations.

Garcia approached with a new lead. "I've been digging through the evidence we collected. Found something interesting—an address linked to a known associate of The Phantom. It might be worth checking out."

Sarah took the file, scanning the details. "This could be the last piece we need to shut down his entire network."

Ethan leaned over, looking at the address. "Let's not waste any time. We'll head there now. Garcia, coordinate with the team and have backup ready."

As they geared up and headed out, the sense of purpose was clear. They were determined to see this through to the end. The address led them to an old warehouse on the outskirts of the city, its rundown exterior belying the significance it held.

Sarah and Ethan approached cautiously, their senses heightened. They could hear faint voices from inside, and the flicker of shadows confirmed that the place was occupied.

Ethan signaled to the team, his voice low. "We go in quietly. We need to catch them off guard."

They moved in, the creak of the warehouse door barely audible. Inside, they found a small group of men huddled around a table, deep in conversation.

Sarah stepped forward, her weapon at the ready. "Police! Don't move!"

The men looked up in shock, but they were too slow. The team moved in, securing them with practiced efficiency. As they searched the warehouse, they found more documents and electronic devices, the final threads of The Phantom's network.

Ethan glanced at Sarah, his expression one of determination and relief. "This is it. We've got everything we need."

Sarah nodded, a sense of accomplishment settling over her. "We did it. Let's get this back to the precinct and wrap it up."

Back at the precinct, the team worked late into the night, processing the evidence and finalizing their reports. The sense of closure was palpable, the knowledge that they had dismantled a major criminal network bringing a sense of peace.

Sarah and Ethan stood by the windows, looking out at the city they had worked so hard to protect. The lights of the precinct cast a warm glow, a beacon of safety in the night.

Ethan broke the silence, his voice thoughtful. "We've done a lot of good, Sarah. The city's safer because of us."

Sarah nodded, her expression softening. "Yeah, it is. And we'll keep it that way."

He turned to her, a smile on his face. "Together?"

She smiled back, the bond between them stronger than ever. "Always."

As they stood there, side by side, they knew that their work was far from over. But they were ready for whatever came next, their resolve unshakeable. Together, they would continue to fight for justice, no matter the challenges ahead.

The precinct was buzzing with activity as the team processed the latest round of evidence. Sarah and Ethan were in the conference room, reviewing the documents and digital files they had seized. The atmosphere was one of focused intensity, the team driven by the recent breakthroughs.

Garcia entered the room, holding a printout. "We've got something. One of the emails we decrypted points to a meeting between The Phantom's remaining lieutenants. It's happening tomorrow night at a downtown hotel."

Sarah looked up, her eyes narrowing in determination. "We need to act on this. If we can get them all in one place, we can take down the rest of the network."

Ethan nodded, already formulating a plan. "We'll need to move carefully. These guys are dangerous, and they'll be on high alert after our recent operations."

Garcia added, "I've already started coordinating with the hotel management. They're willing to help, but we need to keep this low-key to avoid tipping off the suspects."

Sarah stood, her resolve clear. "Let's gather the team and go over the plan. We can't afford any mistakes."

The team assembled in the briefing room, the air thick with anticipation. Sarah outlined the details, her voice steady and commanding. "We'll set up surveillance around the hotel. Our goal is to apprehend the suspects without causing a scene. We'll have plainclothes officers inside, and the rest of the team will be ready to move in at a moment's notice."

Ethan added, "We'll use the hotel's security cameras to monitor their movements. Once we have confirmation of their presence, we'll move in. Be prepared for resistance. These guys won't go down without a fight."

The team nodded, their expressions serious. They knew the stakes and were ready to act. As they dispersed to prepare for the operation, Sarah and Ethan shared a look of determination.

"We've got this," Ethan said, his voice confident.

Sarah nodded, her resolve unwavering. "Yes, we do."

The next evening, they arrived at the hotel, the team taking their positions. The lobby was bustling with activity, but the task force moved with practiced precision, blending into the background. Sarah and Ethan monitored the surveillance feeds, watching for any sign of the suspects.

Garcia's voice came over the radio. "We've got eyes on the targets. They just entered the lobby."

Sarah's heart pounded with anticipation. "All units, be ready. Wait for my signal."

The suspects made their way to a private conference room, their demeanor tense and guarded. Sarah waited until they were all inside before giving the order. "Go now. Move in."

The team converged on the conference room, the suspects caught off guard by the sudden intrusion. "Police! Hands in the air!" Ethan shouted, his weapon trained on the nearest man.

The suspects hesitated, then complied, realizing they were surrounded. The team moved in, securing them with practiced efficiency. As they began to search the room, Sarah felt a surge of triumph. They had done it.

Back at the precinct, the mood was one of celebration. The remaining pieces of The Phantom's network had been dismantled, and the city was safer for it. Sarah and Ethan stood by the windows, looking out at the city they had sworn to protect.

Ethan's voice broke the silence. "We did it, Sarah. We took them down."

Sarah nodded, a smile tugging at her lips. "Yeah, we did. And we'll keep doing it, no matter what."

Later that night, the team gathered at a local bar to unwind and celebrate their success. The atmosphere was relaxed, the tension of the past weeks finally easing. Sarah and Ethan sat at a table with Garcia, enjoying the rare moment of downtime.

Garcia raised his glass, a grin on his face. "To the best damn team in the city. We did good, guys."

Everyone raised their glasses, the mood light and celebratory. Ethan leaned back in his chair, a contented smile on his face. "Feels good to take a break, doesn't it?"

Sarah laughed softly. "It does. But I have a feeling it won't last long."

Garcia nodded. "Probably not. But we'll enjoy it while we can."

As the evening wore on, the conversation turned to lighter topics, the team bonding over shared stories and experiences. Sarah found herself relaxing, the weight of her responsibilities lifting, if only for a moment.

Ethan looked at her, his expression thoughtful. "You know, Sarah, I've been thinking. We've been through a lot together. I can't imagine doing this job without you."

Sarah met his gaze, her eyes reflecting the same sentiment. "I feel the same way, Ethan. We make a good team."

He smiled, raising his glass again. "To us, and to many more victories."

They clinked glasses, the bond between them stronger than ever. As they continued to talk and laugh, the camaraderie and mutual respect they shared were evident.

The night wore on, and the bar slowly emptied. Sarah and Ethan stepped outside, the cool night air a welcome contrast to the warmth of the bar. They walked in comfortable silence, the city lights casting a soft glow around them.

Ethan broke the silence, his voice quiet. "Do you ever think about the future, Sarah? What's next for us?"

Sarah considered his question, her expression thoughtful. "I think about it sometimes. But for now, I'm focused on the present. There's still so much work to do."

He nodded, a small smile on his lips. "Yeah, there is. But whatever happens, I'm glad we're in this together."

She smiled back, the connection between them clear. "Me too, Ethan. Me too."

As they walked back to their cars, the sense of partnership and shared purpose was stronger than ever. They had faced immense challenges and emerged victorious, their bond unshakeable.

Sarah stopped by her car, turning to Ethan. "Get some rest. We've got a lot to do tomorrow."

He nodded, his smile widening. "You too, Sarah. See you in the morning."

As she drove home, Sarah felt a sense of peace and determination. They had accomplished so much, and there was still more to do. But she knew that with Ethan by her side, they could handle anything.

The city lights twinkled around her, a reminder of the place she had sworn to protect. She was ready for whatever came next, confident in her team and their ability to face any challenge. Together, they were unstoppable.

Chapter 15
New Challenges

The precinct was a hive of activity as usual, but there was a noticeable energy in the air. Sarah and Ethan had just wrapped up their morning briefing with the task force when Garcia approached them, a concerned look on his face.

"Sarah, Ethan, can I talk to you for a minute?" Garcia said, glancing around to make sure they were out of earshot of the rest of the team.

"Sure, what's up?" Ethan asked, folding his arms across his chest.

Garcia lowered his voice. "I just got word from our informant. There's a new player in town. Goes by the name 'Viper.' Apparently, he's been making some serious moves in the underworld. Word is, he's even more dangerous than The Phantom."

Sarah's eyes narrowed. "Viper? What do we know about him?"

"Not much," Garcia admitted. "But what we do know is that he's ruthless. He's been consolidating power fast, taking over territories left vacant by our recent busts."

Ethan let out a low whistle. "Sounds like we've got our work cut out for us."

Sarah nodded, her mind already racing with strategies. "We need to gather intel, find out who his associates are, and what his next move might be. We can't let him establish a foothold."

Garcia looked around the bustling precinct. "I've already got some of our best people on it. But we need to be careful. This guy is smart. He's managed to stay under the radar so far."

Ethan sighed. "Great. Just when we thought we could catch our breath."

Sarah placed a hand on his shoulder. "We'll handle it, Ethan. We always do."

Garcia nodded in agreement. "I've got faith in you two. If anyone can take down Viper, it's you."

Sarah glanced at Ethan. "Let's start by reviewing everything we have on him. We'll need to work quickly and quietly."

They moved to their desks, pulling up files and cross-referencing information. The minutes ticked by in a blur of activity, the weight of their new challenge pressing down on them.

Ethan looked up from his screen. "You think Viper could be linked to any of The Phantom's old contacts?"

Sarah considered this. "It's possible. We should cross-reference known associates and see if any names pop up."

Garcia returned with more files. "Here's everything we've got so far. It's not much, but it's a start."

Sarah took the files, flipping through them. "Thanks, Mark. We'll dig into these and see what we can find."

Ethan leaned back in his chair, rubbing his temples. "I hate feeling like we're always playing catch-up."

Sarah nodded in agreement. "I know. But we've been through worse. We'll get ahead of this."

Garcia gave them a reassuring smile. "I'll keep you posted with any new developments. We're in this together."

As Garcia walked away, Ethan turned to Sarah. "So, where do we start?"

Sarah glanced at the files. "Let's start with known associates and recent activities. We need to find a pattern, something that links him to the recent surge in crime."

Ethan nodded. "And maybe we can find someone who's willing to talk. There's always someone who knows more than they let on."

Sarah agreed. "Exactly. Let's hit the streets, talk to our informants. Someone out there has to know something."

They spent the next few hours in the field, meeting with contacts and gathering information. The name Viper came up repeatedly, each mention more concerning than the last. It was clear that they were dealing with a significant new threat.

Back at the precinct, they regrouped with Garcia to review their findings. Ethan summarized their intel. "Viper's smart, calculated. He's been systematically taking over territories, and he's got a loyal following."

Garcia frowned. "We need to find a way to disrupt his operations. Hit him where it hurts."

Sarah agreed. "We'll need to set up surveillance, monitor his known locations, and see if we can identify his key players."

Ethan nodded. "And we'll need to be ready to move fast. Once we find an opening, we have to act."

Garcia placed a hand on Sarah's shoulder. "You've got this. We're behind you all the way."

Sarah felt a surge of determination. "We'll bring him down. No matter what it takes."

Beat 2

The task force worked tirelessly through the night, analyzing data, cross-referencing information, and setting up surveillance on known locations linked to Viper. The precinct was a flurry of activity, each member focused and driven by the new threat.

Sarah and Ethan were in the conference room, a large map of the city spread out before them. Pins and notes marked key locations and potential hotspots.

Ethan pointed to a cluster of pins. "These areas have seen the most activity. If Viper is planning something big, it's likely to be here."

Sarah nodded, tracing a line with her finger. "We'll need to increase our patrols and keep an eye on these spots. Any movement, we need to know about it immediately."

Garcia entered, holding a fresh batch of reports. "Our surveillance teams are in place. We should start getting intel soon."

Sarah took the reports, flipping through them quickly. "Good. We need to stay ahead of this. The sooner we have actionable intel, the better."

Ethan leaned back, his expression serious. "I just hope we're not too late. This guy is dangerous. We need to be ready for anything."

Sarah met his gaze, her resolve unwavering. "We will be. We've faced worse and come out on top. We'll do it again."

As the night wore on, the task force remained vigilant, their eyes on the screens and ears to the ground. They were ready for whatever came next, their focus and determination unshakeable.

In the early hours of the morning, a call came in. "We've got movement at one of the surveillance sites. Looks like a meeting."

Sarah and Ethan sprang into action, rallying the team. "Let's move. This could be our chance."

They arrived at the location, a rundown warehouse on the outskirts of the city. The team moved into position, their training and experience guiding their every step.

Sarah's voice was calm but firm over the radio. "Everyone in position. On my signal."

The tension was palpable as they waited, each second stretching into eternity. Finally, Sarah gave the order. "Go now!"

The team moved in, breaching the warehouse doors and flooding the space. Inside, they found a group of men huddled around a table, their surprise quickly turning to resistance.

Ethan's voice cut through the chaos. "Police! Get down!"

The suspects hesitated, then scattered, but the task force was ready. They moved with precision, securing the suspects and the warehouse. As they searched the premises, they found documents and electronic devices that could provide crucial intel on Viper's operations.

Sarah looked around the warehouse, her heart pounding with adrenaline and triumph. They had made a significant move against Viper, but she knew this was just the beginning.

Back at the precinct, the team reviewed the evidence they had gathered. Ethan summarized their findings. "We've got names, locations, plans. This is a goldmine."

Garcia nodded, his expression serious. "We need to act on this quickly. Viper won't sit idle once he knows we're on to him."

Sarah agreed. "We'll hit them fast and hard. We need to keep the pressure on and not give them a chance to regroup."

As they prepared for the next phase of their operation, Sarah felt a surge of determination. They had a long road ahead, but with their combined strength and resolve, they would face whatever challenges came their way. Together, they would bring Viper down and ensure the safety of their city.

The following days were a whirlwind of activity as the task force dug deeper into Viper's operations. The evidence gathered from the warehouse was proving invaluable, revealing connections and plans that brought them closer to dismantling his network.

Sarah and Ethan were in the war room, poring over a large map marked with new intel. Red pins indicated known locations, blue pins potential targets, and yellow pins were leads yet to be verified.

Garcia entered with a fresh batch of files. "We've got more intel from our informants. Looks like Viper is planning a major shipment next week. This could be our chance to take him down."

Ethan looked up from the map, his eyes narrowing. "Where's the shipment coming in?"

Garcia handed over a file. "The docks. Same place we intercepted The Phantom's last operation."

Sarah took the file, scanning the details. "We'll need to set up surveillance and be ready to move in quickly. This could be the break we've been waiting for."

Ethan nodded, already planning the operation in his head. "We'll need all hands on deck for this. Let's brief the team."

As the task force gathered in the briefing room, the air was thick with anticipation. Sarah stood at the front, the map behind her.

"We've got a solid lead on Viper's next move," she began, her voice steady and authoritative. "He's planning a major shipment at the docks next week. Our objective is to intercept the shipment and apprehend everyone involved."

Ethan stepped forward, adding to Sarah's briefing. "We'll set up surveillance around the area and coordinate with the coast guard to ensure we cover all possible escape routes. This is a high-risk operation, so we need to be prepared for anything."

Garcia chimed in, "We've also got backup units on standby. They'll be ready to assist as soon as we move in."

Sarah looked around the room, meeting the eyes of each team member. "This is our chance to take down Viper and his network once and for all. Stay focused, stay sharp, and watch each other's backs."

The team nodded, their resolve clear. They knew the stakes and were ready to act. As they dispersed to prepare for the operation, Sarah and Ethan exchanged a look of determination.

"We've got this," Ethan said, his voice confident.

Sarah nodded, her resolve unwavering. "Yes, we do."

The night of the operation arrived, and the task force moved into position around the docks. The air was cool and heavy with the promise of rain, adding to the tension that hung over the team.

Sarah and Ethan were stationed in a surveillance van, monitoring the feeds from the cameras they had set up around the area. The screens showed the docks from multiple angles, each one a potential point of entry for Viper's shipment.

Ethan pointed to one of the screens. "There, a truck just pulled in. That's our target."

Sarah nodded, her heart racing with anticipation. "All units, stand by. Wait for my signal."

The truck stopped near a large warehouse, and several men began unloading crates. Sarah watched intently, looking for any sign of Viper himself. The minutes ticked by, each one stretching into eternity.

"Wait," Ethan said, his voice low. "There he is."

Sarah's eyes locked onto the figure stepping out of a black SUV. Viper. He was tall, with a commanding presence that matched the descriptions they had gathered. This was their chance.

"Move in now," Sarah ordered, her voice calm but urgent.

The task force moved with precision, converging on the warehouse from all sides. Shouts of "Police!" filled the air as the suspects scrambled to flee, but the team was ready. Within moments, the area was secured, and the suspects were in custody.

Ethan and Sarah approached Viper, who was being held by two officers. His expression was one of cold fury, but there was a hint of resignation in his eyes.

"Viper," Sarah said, her voice steady. "It's over. You're under arrest."

He glared at her but said nothing, knowing there was no escape. As the officers led him away, Sarah felt a wave of relief and triumph. They had done it.

Back at the precinct, the atmosphere was one of celebration and reflection. The task force had successfully taken down one of the city's most dangerous criminals, and the sense of accomplishment was palpable.

Garcia approached Sarah and Ethan, a wide grin on his face. "Great work, you two. We did it."

Ethan nodded, a satisfied smile on his face. "Yeah, we did. And the city's a lot safer because of it."

Sarah looked around at her team, feeling a deep sense of pride. "This was a team effort. We couldn't have done it without everyone's hard work and dedication."

As the night wore on, the team continued to celebrate their success, sharing stories and enjoying the moment. Sarah and Ethan found a quiet corner, reflecting on what they had achieved.

Ethan raised his glass. "To many more victories."

Sarah clinked her glass against his, a smile on her lips. "To us."

They stood there, side by side, ready to face whatever challenges lay ahead. Together, they were unstoppable.

Chapter 16
New Horizons

The precinct was quieter than usual, the buzz of recent victories settling into a calm sense of accomplishment. Sarah and Ethan were at their desks, catching up on the backlog of paperwork that had accumulated during the intense weeks of operations. The morning sunlight streamed through the windows, casting a warm glow over the room.

Garcia approached, a spring in his step. "Morning, you two. How's it going?"

Ethan looked up, a smirk on his face. "Morning, Mark. Just trying to dig ourselves out of this mountain of paperwork."

Sarah glanced over, a hint of amusement in her eyes. "Feels like we haven't had a breather in weeks. But I'd rather have paperwork than more crises."

Garcia chuckled. "Amen to that. By the way, I heard some interesting news from the brass. They're considering expanding the task force, maybe even turning it into a permanent unit."

Ethan raised an eyebrow. "Permanent, huh? Guess we did a good job."

Sarah nodded, her mind already racing with possibilities. "It makes sense. There's always going to be another threat. Having a dedicated unit could make a big difference."

Garcia smiled. "Exactly. And with you two at the helm, it's bound to be a success."

Ethan leaned back, considering the idea. "Well, I'm up for the challenge if you are, Sarah."

She met his gaze, her determination clear. "Absolutely. We've proven we can handle anything. Let's keep making a difference."

As they discussed the future of the task force, a familiar voice called out from across the room. "Detectives Thompson and Blake, a moment of your time?"

It was Captain Reynolds, the head of their precinct. He approached with a serious expression, but there was a glint of pride in his eyes.

"Captain," Sarah greeted him. "What can we do for you?"

Reynolds nodded at them. "I wanted to personally commend you both for your outstanding work. Taking down The Phantom and Viper in such a short time is no small feat. The city owes you a debt of gratitude."

Ethan smiled, his tone humble. "Thank you, Captain. We couldn't have done it without the team."

Reynolds continued, "That's why I'm recommending both of you for commendations. And I'll be pushing for the task force to become a permanent unit. We need leaders like you two to keep our streets safe."

Sarah felt a surge of pride. "We appreciate that, Captain. We're ready to continue the fight."

Reynolds nodded, his expression serious. "Good. Because there's always more work to be done. But for now, take a moment to enjoy your success. You've earned it."

As Reynolds walked away, Garcia leaned in, a grin on his face. "Looks like you two are moving up in the world."

Ethan chuckled. "Feels good to be recognized. But he's right, there's always more work to do."

Sarah smiled, feeling a rare moment of contentment. "And we're ready for it. Bring it on."

Later that day, as they wrapped up their paperwork, Ethan looked over at Sarah. "So, about that vacation we keep talking about…"

Sarah laughed softly. "Yeah, I think we've earned it. Any ideas?"

Ethan leaned forward, a playful glint in his eye. "How about somewhere with a beach, good food, and no cell service?"

Sarah nodded, her eyes lighting up at the thought. "Sounds perfect. Let's make it happen."

Just then, Garcia approached again, his expression more serious. "Sorry to interrupt your plans, but we've got a situation. Just got a call about a possible hostage situation at a downtown bank."

Sarah and Ethan exchanged a look, their vacation plans put on hold once again. "Let's go," Sarah said, her tone all business.

They grabbed their gear and headed out, the familiar rush of adrenaline kicking in. The drive to the bank was tense, the gravity of the situation settling over them.

As they arrived, the scene was chaotic. Police cars surrounded the building, and a crowd had gathered, watching anxiously. The SWAT team was on standby, waiting for instructions.

Sarah and Ethan approached the incident commander, a stern-faced officer named Lieutenant Davis. "What's the situation?" Sarah asked.

Davis pointed to the building. "We've got a group of armed men inside. They're holding several hostages. Demanding money and a getaway vehicle."

Ethan nodded. "Do we have eyes inside?"

Davis shook his head. "Not yet. We're trying to establish communication."

Sarah turned to Ethan. "We need to get in there and assess the situation. Can you work on getting a negotiator on the line?"

Ethan nodded. "I'm on it."

As he walked away to coordinate the negotiations, Sarah focused on the task at hand. "Alright, let's get a layout of the building and figure out our entry points. We need to be ready to move in if things go south."

The team quickly gathered information and prepared for the next steps. The tension was palpable, but they were ready. This was what they trained for.

Sarah's radio crackled to life. "Negotiator's on the line. We're trying to establish contact."

She nodded, her mind racing with strategies. "Good. Keep me updated. We need to end this peacefully if possible."

As they waited for the situation to unfold, Sarah and Ethan stood side by side, their resolve unshakeable. They had faced down countless challenges before, and they were ready to do it again.

Ethan glanced at Sarah, a determined look in his eyes. "We've got this."

Sarah nodded, her expression mirroring his. "Yes, we do. Together."

As the situation at the bank continued to develop, they knew that their teamwork and determination would see them through. They were ready for whatever came next, their bond stronger than ever.

The tension around the downtown bank was thick as Sarah and Ethan coordinated with the SWAT team and the negotiator. Every second counted, and the stakes were as high as they could be.

Ethan's voice cut through the tension as he briefed the team. "Alright, we've got a layout of the building. Entry points here, here, and here," he said, pointing to the map spread out on the hood of a police car. "We'll have SWAT ready to breach if negotiations fail."

Sarah nodded, turning to the negotiator, a calm and collected woman named Lisa. "What's the latest?"

Lisa adjusted her headset. "We've established contact with the leader. He's demanding a getaway vehicle and safe passage. Claims they'll start hurting hostages if we don't comply."

Ethan's jaw tightened. "What's our assessment? Are they bluffing?"

Lisa shook her head. "Hard to tell. He's calm, but that could mean he's serious. We need to buy time, keep them talking."

Sarah looked at Ethan. "We need to be ready to move in if things go south. Can you coordinate with SWAT?"

Ethan nodded. "On it."

As Ethan walked away to speak with the SWAT commander, Sarah turned back to Lisa. "Let's keep him engaged. What's his name?"

Lisa glanced at her notes. "He's going by 'Reed.' No other details yet."

Sarah took a deep breath. "Alright, let's do this."

Lisa spoke into her headset. "Reed, this is Lisa. We're working on getting what you asked for, but we need more time. Can you tell me how the hostages are doing?"

There was a tense pause before Reed's voice crackled through the radio. "They're fine, for now. But you're running out of time."

Lisa kept her tone even. "I understand. We just want everyone to get out of this safely. Can you tell me why you're doing this, Reed? Maybe there's another way we can help."

Reed's voice was colder now. "No more talking. Get me that vehicle, or people get hurt."

Lisa looked at Sarah, who nodded. "Keep him talking, Lisa. We need more time."

Meanwhile, Ethan was coordinating with the SWAT team. "We're going to need to breach quickly if this goes sideways. Entry points are secure. Make sure we have eyes on all exits."

The SWAT commander, a grizzled veteran named Sergeant Brooks, nodded. "We're ready, Detective. Just give the word."

Ethan's radio buzzed. "Ethan, it's Sarah. We need a distraction. Something to buy us more time."

Ethan thought for a moment. "We could stage a fake vehicle handover. Make it look like we're complying."

Sarah's voice came through, decisive. "Do it. But make sure it's convincing."

Ethan turned to Brooks. "We're staging a fake vehicle handover. Can you have a team ready to move in under the cover of the distraction?"

Brooks nodded. "Consider it done."

Back at the negotiation point, Lisa was keeping Reed engaged. "Reed, we've got your vehicle. It's on the way. But we need to ensure the hostages' safety first. Can you release one as a sign of good faith?"

Reed's voice was terse. "One hostage, when I see the vehicle."

Sarah's eyes met Lisa's. "We need to move fast."

Outside, a police car, rigged to look like a getaway vehicle, pulled up slowly. SWAT teams moved into position, ready to breach at a moment's notice.

Lisa spoke into her headset. "Reed, the vehicle is here. Can you see it?"

There was a pause. "Yeah, I see it. Sending out a hostage."

The bank doors opened, and a terrified woman stumbled out, her hands bound. Sarah moved quickly to get her to safety. "You're okay now. We've got you."

Lisa's voice remained calm. "Thank you, Reed. Now let's talk about the rest of the hostages."

But Reed wasn't buying it. "No more talking. We're coming out. If I see anything I don't like, it's over."

Ethan's voice came over the radio. "We're ready, Sarah. Just give the word."

Sarah took a deep breath. "Wait until they're fully outside. We need to minimize the risk to the hostages."

The doors opened again, and Reed and his men started to emerge, shielding themselves with hostages. The tension was unbearable, every second stretched thin.

Ethan's voice was low and urgent. "Now, Sarah. We need to move now."

Sarah nodded to Brooks. "Go, go, go!"

SWAT teams surged forward, their movements swift and precise. Shots rang out, shouts filled the air, and within moments, the scene was chaos. Sarah and Ethan moved with practiced precision, securing hostages and subduing suspects.

Reed made a break for it, dragging a hostage with him. Sarah followed, her voice steady. "Reed, let her go. It's over."

Reed's eyes were wild. "Stay back! I'll do it!"

Sarah's tone was calm but firm. "No, you won't. It's over, Reed. Let her go."

Ethan moved behind Reed, his weapon trained. "Listen to her. Let the hostage go."

Reed hesitated, then released the hostage and dropped his weapon. "Alright, alright. You win."

SWAT moved in, securing Reed. Sarah and Ethan breathed a sigh of relief as the hostages were led to safety.

Ethan looked at Sarah, his face serious. "We did it."

Sarah nodded, exhaustion and relief washing over her. "Yeah, we did. Good work, Ethan."

They stood together, watching as the scene was secured, knowing they had faced another challenge and come out victorious. Their bond, their partnership, was stronger than ever. And they were ready for whatever came next.

Back at the precinct, the adrenaline of the bank hostage situation had faded, leaving a satisfying calm in its wake. Sarah and Ethan sat in the break room, cups of coffee in hand, the tension from the day's events finally starting to dissipate.

Ethan leaned back, his eyes closed for a moment. "I swear, Sarah, I don't think I've ever felt that kind of tension before."

Sarah nodded, her expression thoughtful. "It was intense, but we handled it. Just like we always do."

Garcia walked in, a grin on his face. "I heard about the takedown. You two are becoming legends around here."

Ethan chuckled. "Legends? I think we're just doing our jobs."

Sarah smiled. "But it's nice to know our work is appreciated. Thanks, Mark."

Garcia grabbed a cup of coffee, joining them at the table. "So, what's next? Do you guys ever take a break?"

Ethan laughed. "We've been talking about a vacation for what feels like forever. Maybe now we can actually take one."

Sarah nodded. "We definitely need it. Somewhere far away from here, with no stress and no emergencies."

Garcia raised his cup. "Here's to hoping you get that break. You both deserve it."

Just then, Captain Reynolds entered the room, a serious look on his face. "Thompson, Blake, a word?"

Sarah and Ethan exchanged glances before following the captain to his office. Once inside, Reynolds shut the door behind them.

"We've got a situation," Reynolds began, his tone grave. "Intel just came in about a potential terrorist threat. It's credible and imminent."

Sarah's heart sank. "What do we know?"

Reynolds handed them a file. "A group calling themselves 'The Dawn' is planning an attack. We don't have all the details yet, but it's big. We need to move fast."

Ethan skimmed the file, his expression darkening. "This is serious. How soon do we need to act?"

"Immediately," Reynolds replied. "We're coordinating with federal agencies, but you two will lead the task force on the ground. We need to prevent this."

Sarah nodded, her mind racing with possibilities. "We'll need all available resources. Surveillance, intel gathering, everything."

Reynolds nodded. "You've got it. I trust you both to handle this. Keep me updated."

As they left the office, Ethan turned to Sarah. "Looks like our vacation will have to wait."

Sarah sighed. "Yeah, but we'll get through this. We always do."

They spent the next few hours in the war room, coordinating with federal agents and setting up surveillance on known associates of The Dawn. The weight of the new threat hung over them, but their determination was unwavering.

Ethan reviewed the latest intel reports. "We've got eyes on a few key players. We should start with these locations."

Sarah agreed. "Let's brief the team. We need to move quickly and efficiently."

The task force gathered in the briefing room, the atmosphere tense but focused. Sarah addressed the team, her voice steady. "We have a credible threat from a group called The Dawn. Our objective is to gather intel, disrupt their plans, and apprehend key members. This is a high-stakes operation. Be prepared for anything."

Ethan added, "We'll be working closely with federal agencies. Our first targets are these locations. We need to move fast and stay coordinated."

Garcia chimed in, "We've got backup units on standby and surveillance teams in place. Let's make this count."

As the team moved out, the gravity of their mission settled in. They had faced numerous challenges before, but this felt different—more urgent, more dangerous.

At the first location, a rundown warehouse, the team moved in silently. Inside, they found evidence of explosives and detailed plans for the attack. Sarah's heart raced as she realized the scale of what they were up against.

Ethan examined the plans. "They're targeting multiple locations across the city. This is huge."

Sarah nodded. "We need to notify all units and coordinate a city-wide response. We can't let this happen."

Back at the precinct, the task force worked through the night, piecing together the puzzle and coordinating with other agencies. The clock was ticking, but they were relentless in their efforts.

Ethan's voice broke the silence in the war room. "We've identified their leader. He's been spotted at a safe house on the east side."

Sarah's eyes narrowed. "Let's move. This could be our chance to stop them."

The team converged on the safe house, moving with precision. Inside, they found the leader, a man named Kane, and several of his associates. A fierce gunfight ensued, but the task force was well-prepared. They secured the suspects and gathered crucial intel that confirmed the scale of the planned attack.

Ethan looked at Sarah, his face etched with determination. "We did it. We stopped them."

Sarah nodded, relief washing over her. "Yeah, we did. Great work, everyone."

As they returned to the precinct, the mood was one of exhausted triumph. They had averted a disaster and saved countless lives. Sarah and Ethan sat together in the break room, the weight of the day's events finally lifting.

Ethan raised his coffee cup. "To us, and to never giving up."

Sarah smiled, clinking her cup against his. "To us."

They sat in comfortable silence, knowing that no matter what challenges lay ahead, they would face them together. Their bond was stronger than ever, and they were ready for whatever came next.

The dawn light filtered through the precinct windows, casting long shadows across the room. The task force had worked through the night, coordinating with federal agencies and securing the city against the threat posed by The Dawn. The sense of urgency had given way to a calm, focused determination.

Sarah and Ethan sat in the briefing room, surrounded by maps and files. Their exhaustion was palpable, but so was their resolve. They knew they had averted a major disaster, but there was still work to be done.

Garcia walked in, holding a fresh pot of coffee. "You two look like you could use this."

Ethan chuckled, accepting a cup. "You have no idea, Mark. Thanks."

Sarah took a cup as well, nodding her gratitude. "Any updates?"

Garcia nodded, setting the pot down. "We've got most of The Dawn's key players in custody. Their leader, Kane, is being interrogated right now. We're still piecing together the full extent of their plans, but it looks like we managed to stop them just in time."

Ethan leaned back in his chair, a look of relief crossing his face. "Good. The last thing we need is more surprises."

Sarah glanced at the files spread out before them. "We need to make sure we didn't miss anything. Let's review the intel one more time."

As they went through the documents, piecing together the final details, Captain Reynolds entered the room. "I wanted to personally thank you both for your outstanding work. You've saved countless lives."

Ethan looked up, a hint of a smile on his lips. "Just doing our job, Captain."

Reynolds nodded, his expression serious. "I know, but you went above and beyond. The city owes you a debt of gratitude. And on a personal note, I'm recommending you both for the highest commendations."

Sarah felt a surge of pride. "Thank you, Captain. We appreciate it."

Reynolds continued, "We'll have a debriefing later today with all the agencies involved. But for now, get some rest. You've earned it."

As Reynolds left, Garcia grinned at them. "You two are unstoppable."

Ethan laughed softly. "Feels like it sometimes. But we couldn't have done it without the team."

Sarah nodded in agreement. "Absolutely. Everyone played their part."

Just then, a call came through on the radio. "Detectives Thompson and Blake, we need you in interrogation. Kane's ready to talk."

Sarah and Ethan exchanged a look, then stood up. "Let's see what he has to say," Sarah said.

In the interrogation room, Kane sat at the table, his hands cuffed in front of him. His eyes were cold, but there was a hint of resignation in his demeanor. Sarah and Ethan took their seats across from him, the tension in the room palpable.

Ethan started, his tone calm but firm. "Kane, you're looking at serious charges. Terrorism, conspiracy, attempted murder. The best thing you can do right now is cooperate."

Kane's lips curled into a sneer. "You think you've won? There are others out there. You can't stop all of us."

Sarah leaned forward, her gaze steady. "We've stopped you, and we'll stop anyone else who tries to follow in your footsteps. But right now, you have a chance to help yourself. Tell us everything you know about The Dawn's operations."

Kane's eyes flickered with a mix of defiance and fear. "Why should I? You'll lock me up either way."

Ethan's voice was steady. "Because cooperation could mean the difference between life in prison and a chance at parole someday. It's your choice."

There was a long silence as Kane considered his options. Finally, he sighed, the fight draining out of him. "Alright. I'll talk."

Over the next hour, Kane provided detailed information about The Dawn's operations, their plans, and their associates. Sarah and Ethan listened intently, asking questions and taking notes. By the end of the session, they had a comprehensive picture of the threat they had averted and the steps needed to ensure the city's safety.

As they left the interrogation room, Ethan looked at Sarah, his expression one of cautious optimism. "I think we got everything we need."

Sarah nodded, a sense of closure settling over her. "Yeah. Let's brief the team and make sure we follow up on every lead."

Back in the briefing room, they shared the new intel with the task force. The mood was one of determination and relief. They had faced a formidable challenge and come out on top, but they knew the work wasn't over.

Garcia summarized the next steps. "We'll coordinate with federal agencies to track down the remaining associates and secure all known locations. We can't leave any loose ends."

Ethan added, "And we'll need to review our security measures to prevent any future threats. We've learned a lot from this."

Sarah looked around at the team, her expression one of pride and gratitude. "You all did an amazing job. We faced a serious threat, and we handled it together. Let's keep that momentum going."

As the team dispersed to carry out their tasks, Sarah and Ethan stood by the window, looking out at the city they had sworn to protect. The sun was rising, casting a warm glow over the skyline.

Ethan broke the silence, his voice thoughtful. "You know, Sarah, we've been through a lot together. But I feel like this is just the beginning."

Sarah smiled, her eyes reflecting the same sentiment. "I feel the same way. And whatever comes next, we'll face it together."

They stood there for a moment, side by side, knowing that no matter what challenges lay ahead, they were ready. Their bond was stronger than ever, and their resolve unshakeable. Together, they would continue to fight for justice, protecting the city they loved.

Chapter 17
A New Threat

The precinct was buzzing with a rare sense of calm after the chaos of the past few weeks. Sarah and Ethan were at their desks, catching up on routine paperwork and discussing the latest developments. The morning sunlight streamed through the windows, casting a warm glow over the bustling room.

Garcia approached with a smile. "You two finally get a chance to breathe?"

Ethan leaned back in his chair, stretching. "Feels like it. Nice to have a few quiet days for a change."

Sarah nodded. "Definitely. Gives us a chance to catch up on everything that's piled up."

Garcia chuckled. "Well, enjoy it while it lasts. You know it never stays quiet for long around here."

As if on cue, Captain Reynolds walked in, a serious look on his face. "Thompson, Blake, I need you in my office."

Sarah and Ethan exchanged glances, then followed Reynolds to his office. Once inside, Reynolds closed the door behind them.

Reynolds got straight to the point. "We've got a new situation. There's been a series of high-profile burglaries across the city. The MO suggests it's the work of a professional crew. They're hitting jewelry stores, art galleries, and high-end homes."

Ethan frowned. "Do we have any leads?"

Reynolds nodded, handing them a file. "We've got some surveillance footage and witness statements, but nothing concrete yet. I want you two to take the lead on this. We can't let this crew continue their spree."

Sarah flipped through the file, her mind already racing with possibilities. "We'll start by reviewing the footage and talking to the witnesses. If this is a professional crew, they're bound to slip up eventually."

Reynolds nodded. "Agreed. I trust you two to handle this. Keep me updated."

As they left Reynolds' office, Ethan glanced at Sarah. "Looks like our quiet days are over."

Sarah smiled, a determined glint in her eye. "Wouldn't have it any other way. Let's get to work."

They headed to the surveillance room, where Garcia was already queuing up the footage. "Got the tapes ready for you. It's not much, but it's a start."

Ethan leaned over the monitor. "Let's see what we've got."

The footage showed a group of masked individuals breaking into a high-end jewelry store. Their movements were swift and coordinated, clearly the work of professionals.

Sarah studied the screen. "Look at how they move. This isn't their first job."

Garcia nodded. "They're good. But everyone makes mistakes. We just need to find theirs."

Ethan pointed to one of the figures. "Pause it there. Look at that tattoo on his wrist. Can you zoom in?"

Garcia adjusted the controls, zooming in on the image. "Got it. Looks like a distinctive mark. We can run it through our database, see if we get any hits."

Sarah nodded. "Good. Let's also look at the witness statements. Maybe someone saw something they didn't realize was important."

They spent the next few hours reviewing the footage and cross-referencing the information with their database. The tattoo led to a known associate of a local crime syndicate, giving them their first solid lead.

Garcia handed them the printout. "Here's everything we have on him. Goes by the name 'Razor.' Small-time crook, but connected to some bigger players."

Ethan looked over the file. "Looks like Razor just moved up our list of priorities. Let's pay him a visit."

As they prepared to head out, Sarah turned to Garcia. "Keep digging into the footage and witness statements. There's more to this crew, and we need to find out who's behind it."

Garcia nodded. "Will do. Be careful out there."

Ethan and Sarah headed to their car, the sense of calm from earlier replaced by the familiar rush of a new case. As they drove to Razor's last known location, Ethan glanced at Sarah. "So, what's our approach?"

Sarah thought for a moment. "Let's start by talking to him. If he's part of this crew, he might slip up and give us something. If not, we'll go from there."

Ethan nodded. "Sounds like a plan. Let's see what Razor has to say."

They arrived at a run-down apartment building, the kind of place that had seen better days. The hallways were dimly lit, and the air smelled of stale cigarettes. They found Razor's apartment on the third floor and knocked on the door.

A few moments later, the door opened a crack, and a wary eye peered out. "What do you want?"

Sarah flashed her badge. "Detectives Thompson and Blake. We'd like to ask you a few questions."

The door opened wider, revealing a wiry man with a tattoo on his wrist. "What's this about?"

Ethan's tone was calm but firm. "We're investigating a series of burglaries. We have reason to believe you might have some information."

Razor's eyes darted around nervously. "I don't know anything about that."

Sarah stepped closer. "Mind if we come in and talk?"

Razor hesitated, then stepped aside. "Fine. But I don't know how I can help."

As they entered the apartment, Sarah and Ethan exchanged a look. They were getting closer, and they wouldn't stop until they had the answers they needed.

Sarah and Ethan entered Razor's apartment, the air thick with the scent of stale smoke and something less identifiable but equally unpleasant. The small living room was cluttered with mismatched furniture and piles of old newspapers. Razor, the wiry man with the tattoo, hovered nervously by the doorway.

Sarah took a seat on a battered armchair, gesturing for Razor to sit across from her. "Let's make this quick, Razor. We're investigating a series of high-profile burglaries. Your name came up. We need to know what you know."

Razor shifted uneasily, glancing at Ethan, who was standing by the door. "I don't know anything about that."

Ethan crossed his arms, his tone firm. "You're connected to a crime syndicate that's been very active lately. We're not here to play games, Razor. Cooperate, and this might go easier for you."

Razor licked his lips, clearly weighing his options. "Look, I don't know about any burglaries. I've been keeping my head down, trying to stay out of trouble."

Sarah leaned forward, her voice calm but insistent. "We're not buying it. We have footage of you and your crew hitting a jewelry store. You're already in deep. Help us out, and maybe we can help you."

Razor's eyes darted around the room, looking for an escape. "Okay, okay. Maybe I know something. But it's not what you think. I'm not the one in charge."

Ethan raised an eyebrow. "Then who is?"

Razor hesitated, then sighed. "There's this guy. Calls himself 'Specter.' He's the brains behind the operations. We just follow orders."

Sarah exchanged a glance with Ethan. "Specter? What else can you tell us about him?"

Razor shrugged. "Not much. He's careful, always keeps his distance. We get our instructions through intermediaries, never face-to-face."

Ethan pressed on. "Where can we find these intermediaries?"

Razor hesitated again, then gave in. "There's a bar downtown, the Silver Spur. That's where they hang out. You might find someone there who can lead you to Specter."

Sarah stood up, her expression resolute. "Thanks for the information, Razor. We'll check it out. And remember, we'll be keeping an eye on you."

As they left the apartment, Ethan turned to Sarah. "Specter, huh? Sounds like we're dealing with someone who knows how to stay hidden."

Sarah nodded. "But everyone makes mistakes eventually. Let's head to the Silver Spur and see what we can find."

The drive to the bar was filled with a tense silence, both of them lost in thought. The Silver Spur was a dive bar in a rundown part of town, the kind of place where secrets were traded over cheap drinks.

They entered the bar, the dim lighting and thick haze of smoke creating an almost oppressive atmosphere. Ethan scanned the room, his eyes landing on a group of men in a corner booth.

"That looks like our best bet," he murmured to Sarah.

Sarah nodded. "Let's split up. I'll talk to the bartender, see if he knows anything. You keep an eye on those guys."

Ethan agreed, moving to a table where he could observe the booth without being noticed. Sarah approached the bar, catching the bartender's attention.

"What'll it be?" the bartender asked, wiping a glass with a dirty rag.

"Information," Sarah replied, flashing her badge discreetly. "We're looking for someone who goes by the name Specter. Heard of him?"

The bartender's eyes flickered with recognition, but he quickly masked it. "Can't say I have. We don't get many ghosts around here."

Sarah smiled slightly. "Funny. But I think you know more than you're letting on. Help us out, and we might be able to return the favor."

The bartender sighed, leaning in closer. "Alright, but you didn't hear it from me. Specter's a ghost, alright. Runs everything from the shadows. You want to find him, you'll need to talk to his right-hand man. Name's Marcus. He's one of the guys in that booth over there."

Sarah nodded her thanks, slipping a bill across the bar. She returned to Ethan's table, relaying the information.

"Marcus is our guy," she said quietly. "We need to get him talking."

Ethan nodded. "Let's go introduce ourselves."

They approached the booth, Ethan taking the lead. "Evening, gentlemen. Mind if we join you?"

The men looked up, their expressions wary. Marcus, a burly man with a scar running down his cheek, sized them up. "Who the hell are you?"

Sarah flashed her badge. "Detectives Thompson and Blake. We have a few questions."

Marcus sneered. "We're not in the mood for questions."

Ethan leaned in, his voice low and menacing. "You'll want to make an exception. We're investigating a series of burglaries, and your name came up. Talk to us now, or we can continue this conversation downtown."

Marcus glared at them, but after a moment, he relented. "Fine. What do you want to know?"

Sarah took a seat, her eyes locked on Marcus. "Tell us about Specter. Where can we find him?"

Marcus's eyes flickered with fear. "You don't find Specter. He finds you. And if he thinks you're a threat, you're as good as dead."

Ethan's voice was cold. "That's not good enough. We need something concrete."

Marcus hesitated, then sighed. "Alright. Specter has a safe house on the west side. An old warehouse. That's the best I can give you."

Sarah stood, her expression resolute. "Thanks for the tip. We'll be in touch."

As they left the bar, Ethan turned to Sarah. "Think he's telling the truth?"

Sarah nodded. "He's scared. That means we're getting close. Let's check out that warehouse."

The night was dark as they drove across the city, the streets empty and silent. They were closing in on Specter, and they knew they had to be ready for anything. The warehouse loomed ahead, its dark silhouette a reminder of the danger that lay ahead.

As they approached, Sarah and Ethan shared a look of determination. They were ready for whatever came next. Together, they would bring Specter to justice and end his reign of terror.

The warehouse loomed large and foreboding as Sarah and Ethan parked a few blocks away, careful not to draw any attention. The building was old, its brick walls covered in graffiti and the windows either boarded up or shattered. It was the perfect hideout for someone who preferred to stay in the shadows.

Sarah adjusted her earpiece, checking in with Garcia, who was monitoring from the precinct. "We're in position. Any movement on the surveillance feeds?"

Garcia's voice crackled through the earpiece. "Negative. The place looks quiet, but be careful. This guy is good at staying hidden."

Ethan glanced at Sarah, his expression serious. "Ready?"

Sarah nodded. "Let's do this."

They approached the warehouse cautiously, their footsteps silent on the cracked pavement. Sarah motioned for Ethan to take the rear entrance while she moved to the front. They would converge inside, minimizing the risk of being ambushed.

Ethan's voice came through the earpiece. "In position. Ready when you are."

Sarah took a deep breath, then pushed open the front door, the rusted hinges creaking loudly in the silence. Inside, the warehouse was dark and musty, the air thick with dust. She moved quietly, her flashlight cutting through the gloom.

Ethan joined her a moment later, his own flashlight casting long shadows on the walls. "This place is a maze," he muttered.

Sarah nodded, her eyes scanning the area. "Stay sharp. He could be anywhere."

They moved deeper into the warehouse, the sound of their footsteps echoing in the vast, empty space. Suddenly, a noise to their left made them both freeze.

Ethan whispered, "Did you hear that?"

Sarah nodded, motioning for him to follow. They crept towards the sound, their senses heightened. As they rounded a corner, they saw a figure darting away.

"Stop! Police!" Ethan shouted, breaking into a run.

Sarah followed, her heart pounding as they chased the figure through the maze of crates and debris. The suspect was fast, but Ethan was faster. He tackled the figure to the ground, pinning him down.

"Don't move!" Ethan barked, cuffing the suspect.

Sarah approached, her flashlight revealing the man's face. It wasn't Specter, but he looked terrified.

"Who are you?" Sarah demanded. "What are you doing here?"

The man stammered, "I-I'm just a lookout. Please, don't hurt me."

Ethan tightened his grip. "Where's Specter?"

The man's eyes darted around, panic setting in. "I don't know! He doesn't tell us where he is. We just follow orders."

Sarah exchanged a look with Ethan. "He's lying. We need to find Specter, and fast."

Ethan hauled the man to his feet. "You're coming with us. Maybe a night in a cell will jog your memory."

As they led the suspect outside, Garcia's voice came through the earpiece. "Any luck?"

Sarah shook her head, even though Garcia couldn't see her. "We got a lookout, but no sign of Specter. We're bringing him in for questioning."

Back at the precinct, they sat the lookout in an interrogation room, his hands still cuffed. Sarah and Ethan stood on the other side of the glass, watching him.

Ethan sighed. "He's scared, but he knows something."

Sarah nodded. "Let's go find out what."

They entered the interrogation room, the atmosphere tense. Sarah sat across from the lookout, her gaze steady. "We need information, and we need it now. Where's Specter?"

The man's eyes were wide with fear. "I told you, I don't know! He's paranoid. Never stays in one place for long."

Ethan leaned in, his voice low and threatening. "Listen, you're in deep trouble. But you can help yourself by helping us. Give us something to go on."

The man hesitated, then nodded slowly. "Alright, alright. There's a safe house. On the west side. That's where he coordinates everything. But he won't be there long."

Sarah stood, her expression determined. "Thank you. We'll check it out."

As they left the room, Ethan turned to Sarah. "Think he's telling the truth?"

Sarah nodded. "He's too scared to lie. Let's gear up and head to the safe house. This might be our best chance to catch Specter."

They moved quickly, briefing the team and coordinating with Garcia. The safe house was their next target, and they had to act fast.

The drive to the west side was tense, the streets dark and deserted. They arrived at the safe house, a nondescript building that looked abandoned. Sarah and Ethan approached cautiously, their weapons drawn.

Garcia's voice came through the earpiece. "We've got backup units on standby. Be careful."

Sarah and Ethan nodded, then moved in. The door was unlocked, swinging open with a creak. Inside, the house was dark, but they could hear movement.

Ethan whispered, "He's here. Let's go."

They moved silently through the house, their flashlights cutting through the darkness. As they reached the back room, they saw a figure hunched over a table, packing up documents and equipment.

"Freeze! Police!" Sarah shouted.

The figure spun around, a gun in hand. It was Specter. He fired a shot, but Sarah and Ethan were quicker. They returned fire, hitting him in the shoulder. Specter dropped the gun, clutching his wound.

Ethan moved in, cuffing him. "It's over, Specter."

Specter glared at them, but there was a hint of resignation in his eyes. "You got me. But there are others. You'll never stop us all."

Sarah stood over him, her voice cold. "We'll see about that. For now, you're going to prison."

As they led Specter out of the safe house, Sarah felt a sense of relief. They had stopped a major threat, but she knew the fight wasn't over. There would always be new challenges, new threats to face. But she and Ethan were ready for whatever came next.

They returned to the precinct, the weight of their success settling in. They had brought down Specter and his crew, but there was still work to be done. As they sat together, reflecting on the day's events, Sarah felt a deep sense of pride and determination. They were making a difference, one case at a time. And they would continue to do so, no matter what.

`Back at the precinct, the weight of the recent events still hung heavily in the air. Sarah and Ethan were in the interrogation room, facing Specter across the metal table. His shoulder was bandaged, and despite the pain, his eyes were sharp and defiant.

Sarah leaned forward, her gaze unwavering. "Specter, we need to know everything. Your operation, your associates, and any other plans you have in motion."

Specter smirked, wincing slightly. "You think you've won? I'm just one piece of a much larger puzzle. You can't stop what's coming."

Ethan's expression hardened. "We've already stopped you. And we will stop anyone else who tries to pick up where you left off. Now, tell us what we need to know."

Specter leaned back, his smirk fading. "You're wasting your time. I'm not saying a word."

Sarah exchanged a look with Ethan, then turned back to Specter. "We'll see about that. We have plenty of time."

Just then, Garcia entered the room with a file in hand. "We've got something. Thought you'd want to see this."

Sarah took the file, flipping it open. Her eyes widened slightly before she composed herself. "It seems your organization isn't as secretive as you thought. We have a list of your associates and their locations."

Specter's eyes flickered with surprise before he masked it. "You're bluffing."

Ethan leaned in, his voice low and intense. "Do we look like we're bluffing? We've already started rounding them up. It's only a matter of time before your whole network is dismantled."

Sarah placed the file on the table, opening it to reveal photos and names. "Look familiar? This is just the beginning. Help us now, and maybe we can make things easier for you."

Specter stared at the photos, his facade of confidence cracking. "You think you're so smart. But you're missing the bigger picture. There are others out there, more dangerous than me."

Ethan's eyes narrowed. "Then tell us who they are. Help us stop them."

Specter hesitated, the conflict evident in his eyes. "Fine. I'll tell you what I know. But it won't be easy to bring them down. They're deeply embedded, and they won't go quietly."

Sarah nodded, her voice steady. "We're prepared for that. Start talking."

Over the next hour, Specter detailed his operation, providing names, locations, and insights into the inner workings of his network. Sarah and Ethan listened intently, asking questions and taking notes. The information he provided was invaluable, and it gave them a clearer picture of the threat they were facing.

When Specter finished, he looked at them with a mixture of defeat and defiance. "There. You have your information. Now what?"

Sarah stood, gathering the notes. "Now, we follow up on every lead. And you go to prison, where you'll stay for a very long time."

Ethan added, "Your cooperation might help reduce your sentence, but make no mistake, you're still going away."

Specter nodded slowly. "I figured as much. Just know that this isn't over. Not by a long shot."

Sarah and Ethan left the interrogation room, the weight of the new information pressing on them. They headed to the briefing room, where Garcia was waiting with the rest of the team.

Sarah addressed the team, her voice firm. "We've got new intel from Specter. Names, locations, and plans. We need to move quickly to take down the rest of this network."

Ethan added, "This is our chance to dismantle a major criminal organization. We need all hands on deck. Let's coordinate with federal agencies and get this done."

Garcia nodded, already making calls. "I'll start setting up the operations. We'll need backup and surveillance on all these locations."

As the team mobilized, Sarah and Ethan reviewed the notes, planning their next moves. The sense of urgency was palpable, but so was their determination. They had come this far, and they wouldn't stop until the job was finished.

Later that evening, as they prepared to head out for the first operation, Ethan turned to Sarah. "You ready for this?"

Sarah nodded, her resolve unwavering. "Always. Let's bring them down."

The first target was a high-end condo in the heart of the city. They arrived quietly, their team moving into position around the building. Sarah and Ethan led the entry team, their weapons drawn and senses heightened.

Ethan whispered, "On three. One, two, three."

They breached the door, moving swiftly through the condo. Inside, they found several associates of Specter, caught off guard by the sudden intrusion. The team secured the suspects and began searching the premises for evidence.

Sarah's radio crackled to life. "Clear on the second floor. We've got them."

Ethan nodded, securing the last suspect. "Good. Let's get them out of here and onto the next location."

As they moved to the next target, the sense of accomplishment was mixed with the awareness that there was still much to do. They were making progress, but the fight was far from over.

Back at the precinct, the team debriefed and prepared for the next wave of operations. Sarah and Ethan worked late into the night, coordinating with other agencies and ensuring that every detail was covered.

Ethan looked over at Sarah, a tired but satisfied smile on his face. "We're getting there. One step at a time."

Sarah nodded, her own smile mirroring his. "We are. And we'll keep going until we've taken them all down."

As the night wore on, the precinct buzzed with activity, the sense of purpose driving them forward. Sarah and Ethan knew that the road ahead would be challenging, but they were ready. They had faced down countless threats before, and they would continue to do so, together.

They stood side by side, their partnership stronger than ever, ready to face whatever came next.

Chapter 18
Unraveling the Conspiracy

The precinct was quieter than usual, an uneasy calm hanging in the air. Sarah and Ethan sat in Sarah's office, reviewing the evidence they had discovered. It was damning—phone records, financial transactions, and encrypted messages that all pointed to one person: Captain Mark Anderson.

Ethan broke the silence. "We have to confront him, Sarah. There's no way around it."

Sarah nodded, her expression grim. "I know. I just... I can't believe he'd do this. We've worked with him for years."

"Trust me, I'm having a hard time with it too," Ethan said. "But the evidence is clear. We have to get to the bottom of this."

Sarah took a deep breath and stood up. "Let's do it. We need answers."

They walked down the hall to Anderson's office, each step heavy with the weight of their discovery. Sarah knocked on the door, and they entered without waiting for a response. Anderson looked up from his desk, surprised to see them.

"Sarah, Ethan, what's going on?" Anderson asked, sensing the tension.

Sarah closed the door behind them. "Mark, we need to talk. It's important."

Anderson frowned, leaning back in his chair. "Alright. What's this about?"

Ethan placed a folder on Anderson's desk, opening it to reveal the incriminating evidence. "We found these during our investigation. Phone records, financial transactions, encrypted messages. They all trace back to you."

Anderson's eyes widened as he looked at the documents. "What are you implying?"

Sarah's voice was steady but filled with a sense of betrayal. "Mark, this evidence suggests you've been leaking information to Marco's associates. We need to know why."

Anderson's face flushed with anger. "That's ridiculous! I would never betray this team. You know me better than that."

"Do we?" Ethan countered. "Because right now, the evidence says otherwise. If you have an explanation, we're listening."

Anderson stood up, pacing behind his desk. "This is a setup. Someone's trying to frame me. You have to believe me."

Sarah's eyes softened slightly, torn between her loyalty to a longtime colleague and the overwhelming evidence. "Mark, if you're innocent, help us prove it. But we need to know the truth."

Anderson stopped pacing, his shoulders slumping. "Alright. I'll tell you everything. But you have to understand, I was trying to protect my family."

"Go on," Ethan urged, his tone cautious.

Anderson sighed, sitting back down. "About a year ago, Marco's men approached me. They had dirt on me, things from my past that could ruin my career and my life. They threatened to expose me unless I cooperated."

"And you agreed?" Sarah asked, her voice tinged with disbelief.

"I didn't see another way," Anderson admitted. "They forced me to feed them information, small things at first, but it escalated. They always made it clear—if I didn't comply, they'd go after my family."

Ethan's expression hardened. "Why didn't you come to us? We could have helped you."

"I was ashamed," Anderson said quietly. "And scared. I thought I could manage it, keep them at bay, but it just kept getting worse."

Sarah leaned forward, her tone urgent. "Mark, we need everything you know. Every detail. It's the only way we can stop them and protect your family."

Anderson nodded, a look of resignation on his face. "I'll tell you everything. Marco's network is extensive. They have people in various departments, not just ours. I've been feeding them updates on your investigation, trying to stay one step ahead of you."

Ethan shook his head. "Unbelievable. Who else is involved?"

"There are others, but I don't know all their names," Anderson confessed. "I can give you the ones I do know. They're mostly in low-level positions, but they've been crucial in keeping Marco informed."

Sarah made notes as Anderson spoke, the scope of the conspiracy becoming clearer. "This is bigger than we thought," she said. "We'll need to bring this to Donovan and expand our investigation."

Anderson looked at them, desperation in his eyes. "Please, protect my family. They had nothing to do with this."

"We will," Sarah assured him. "But you need to stay here and cooperate fully. We'll handle the rest."

As they left Anderson's office, the weight of the situation settled over them. "What do we do now?" Ethan asked.

Sarah's expression was resolute. "We bring this to Donovan, and we take down Marco's entire network. No more half-measures."

Ethan nodded. "Agreed. Let's finish this."

With a renewed sense of purpose, they headed to Captain Donovan's office, ready to expose the full extent of the conspiracy and bring justice to those who had been betrayed. The battle was far from over, but they were ready to face whatever came next, together.

The precinct's interrogation room was dimly lit, creating an atmosphere of tension and unease. Sarah and Ethan sat across from Mark Anderson, who looked visibly worn out. The revelations from their initial confrontation had shaken him, but he had agreed to cooperate fully. Sarah started the recorder and leaned forward, her eyes locked on Anderson.

"Mark, we need you to tell us everything," Sarah said, her tone firm but gentle. "We need the full picture."

Anderson took a deep breath, nodding slowly. "Alright. It all started about a year ago. Marco's men approached me with information about some mistakes I made early in my career. They had proof that could destroy my life. They gave me a choice: cooperate or be ruined."

Ethan interjected, "So you started feeding them information?"

"Yes," Anderson admitted. "At first, it was minor things, nothing that would jeopardize ongoing investigations. But as time went on, their demands grew. They wanted details about your progress on their case, your strategies, everything."

Sarah exchanged a glance with Ethan. "How did they communicate with you?"

"Burner phones," Anderson explained. "They'd drop them off at different locations, and I'd pick them up. After each call, I'd destroy the phone. They were meticulous about covering their tracks."

Ethan leaned forward, his gaze intense. "You mentioned others being involved. Who are they?"

"There are a few low-level informants in various departments," Anderson said. "But it goes higher than that. Marco has connections in the city council, the mayor's office, even some local businesses. They're all in on it, profiting from his operations."

Sarah felt a chill run down her spine. "You're saying this corruption reaches the highest levels of our city's government?"

Anderson nodded, his expression grim. "Yes. Marco has built an extensive network. He uses threats, bribes, and blackmail to keep people in line. It's how he's managed to stay ahead of you for so long."

Ethan frowned, processing the information. "Who specifically in the city council and the mayor's office? We need names."

"I don't know all their names," Anderson replied. "But I do know that Councilman Richard Hayes is one of them. He's been a key player, facilitating deals and making sure Marco's operations run smoothly."

Sarah's mind raced. "And the mayor's office?"

"There's a deputy mayor, James Carroll," Anderson said. "He's been taking bribes to look the other way. Marco's influence is widespread. He's got his hands in everything."

Ethan stood up, pacing the room. "This changes everything. We're not just dealing with a criminal network; we're dealing with systemic corruption."

Sarah nodded, her expression determined. "We need to act fast. We need to gather concrete evidence against these officials and dismantle Marco's entire network."

Anderson looked at them, his eyes filled with remorse. "I'm sorry for what I've done. I thought I could manage it, but it spiraled out of control. I just wanted to protect my family."

"We understand, Mark," Sarah said softly. "But now you have to help us bring them all down. Every detail you provide is crucial."

"I will," Anderson vowed. "Whatever it takes."

As they left the interrogation room, Sarah and Ethan walked towards Captain Donovan's office, the gravity of the situation weighing heavily on their shoulders.

"Donovan needs to know about this immediately," Ethan said, his voice tense.

"Agreed," Sarah replied. "We're going to need more resources and more allies. This isn't just about taking down Marco anymore. It's about cleaning up our entire city."

They entered Donovan's office, and Sarah quickly briefed him on Anderson's revelations. Donovan's expression grew more serious with each passing second.

"This is bigger than I thought," Donovan said, rubbing his temples. "We're going to need to coordinate with the FBI and possibly even federal prosecutors. This level of corruption requires a comprehensive strategy."

Sarah nodded. "We need to act swiftly but carefully. If we tip our hand too soon, Marco and his associates will go underground, and we might never catch them."

"Start preparing your case files," Donovan ordered. "I'll make the necessary calls. We're going to need airtight evidence to bring down officials at this level."

Ethan looked at Sarah, determination in his eyes. "We've come this far. We can't let them slip away now."

"We won't," Sarah replied firmly. "This ends here."

As they left Donovan's office to begin their preparations, the scale of their task loomed large. But with every step, they knew they were getting closer to unraveling the entire conspiracy and restoring justice to their city. The fight was far from over, but they were ready for the challenge ahead.

The conference room at the precinct was bustling with activity as Sarah, Ethan, and Captain Donovan gathered their team. The information from Mark Anderson had revealed the full extent of Marco's network, and now they had to plan their next move carefully. The stakes were higher than ever, and they couldn't afford any mistakes.

Sarah stood at the front of the room, a large map of the city spread out before her. Red pins marked key locations linked to Marco's operations and his corrupt allies within the city government.

"Alright, everyone, listen up," Sarah began, her voice clear and authoritative. "We've identified several critical targets based on Mark's intel. These include properties owned by Phoenix Holdings, Councilman Richard Hayes' office, Deputy Mayor James Carroll's residence, and a few key businesses linked to Marco's laundering operations."

Ethan pointed to the map. "Our primary objective is to execute simultaneous raids on these locations. We need to catch them off guard and secure as much evidence as possible. Coordination and timing are crucial."

Captain Donovan nodded, addressing the team. "We'll be working closely with the FBI and federal prosecutors on this. They'll provide additional manpower and support. Remember, this isn't just about bringing down Marco; it's about dismantling a network of corruption that's infected our city."

Detective Lisa Chen raised her hand. "What's the plan for communication during the raids? We need to ensure that all teams are synchronized."

Sarah pointed to the communication equipment on the table. "We'll be using encrypted radios to maintain secure communication. Each team will have a designated leader who will coordinate with the command center here at the precinct."

Ethan added, "We'll also have surveillance units in place to monitor the targets before we move in. Any signs of unusual activity will be reported immediately."

Officer Jake Martinez spoke up next. "What's the contingency plan if things go sideways? We're dealing with dangerous people who might be willing to fight back."

Donovan replied, "We'll have tactical units on standby, ready to respond to any resistance. Safety is our top priority. If any team encounters heavy resistance, they're to fall back and call for backup."

Sarah nodded in agreement. "We also need to ensure the safety of any civilians in the vicinity. Each team will have officers assigned to evacuate and secure the area if necessary."

Ethan glanced at his notes, then looked around the room. "Let's go over the assignments. Team Alpha will handle the raid on Phoenix Holdings. Team Bravo will target Councilman Hayes' office. Team Charlie will secure Deputy Mayor Carroll's residence. Team Delta will hit the businesses linked to the laundering operations."

Sarah continued, "Each team leader, make sure your members are fully briefed and equipped. We move at 0500 hours tomorrow. This gives us enough time to finalize our preparations and ensure everyone is ready."

Captain Donovan stepped forward, his expression serious. "This is a critical operation. We're not just taking down a criminal; we're restoring integrity to our city. Stay focused, stay safe, and let's bring these people to justice."

As the team dispersed to make their final preparations, Sarah and Ethan stayed behind, reviewing the plan once more. "We've covered all the bases," Ethan said, his tone confident. "Now we just need to execute."

Sarah nodded, her eyes reflecting a mix of determination and resolve. "We've come this far. We can't let anything slip through the cracks. This is our chance to make a real difference."

Ethan placed a reassuring hand on her shoulder. "We've got this, Sarah. Together, we'll see it through."

That night, the precinct was a hive of activity as the teams prepared for the operation. Equipment was checked and rechecked, briefings were held, and final instructions were given. Sarah and Ethan moved through the bustling rooms, offering words of encouragement and ensuring every detail was covered.

As dawn approached, the teams assembled, ready to move out. The air was thick with anticipation and a sense of purpose. Sarah stood before them, her voice steady and strong. "Remember, we're doing this to protect our city and bring justice to those who have been wronged. Stay sharp, stay together, and let's bring them down."

With a final nod, the teams deployed, each heading to their designated targets. The coordinated strike was about to begin, and the fate of the city hung in the balance. Sarah and Ethan watched as the convoy of vehicles disappeared into the early morning light, their hearts filled with determination. The battle was far from over, but they were ready to face whatever came next, knowing that their meticulous planning and unwavering resolve would see them through.

The city was cloaked in the gray light of early dawn as the convoy of police vehicles moved silently through the streets. Each team, fully briefed and prepared, approached their targets with precision and caution. The tension was palpable, but there was a sense of resolve and determination among the officers. This was their moment to strike a decisive blow against Marco's network.

Sarah and Ethan led Team Alpha towards the headquarters of Phoenix Holdings. The building loomed ahead, dark and silent, its glass facade reflecting the dim morning light. Sarah gave the signal, and the team moved in swiftly, breaching the entrance and spreading out to secure the area.

"Remember, we need to find Andrews and any critical evidence," Sarah whispered into her radio. "Move quickly and carefully."

The team advanced through the building, clearing each room with practiced efficiency. As they reached the main office, they found Paul Andrews hunched over a desk, frantically typing on a laptop.

"Freeze! Harborview Police!" Ethan shouted, his weapon trained on Andrews.

Andrews looked up, his face contorted with surprise and anger. He raised his hands slowly, stepping away from the desk. "You've got nothing on me," he spat.

"We'll see about that," Sarah replied, cuffing him. "Secure the evidence," she ordered her team. "Take everything."

As they gathered documents and electronic devices, Ethan's radio crackled to life. "Team Bravo to Command. Councilman Hayes is in custody. We've found several incriminating files."

"Copy that, Bravo," Ethan responded. "Good work. Continue securing the location."

Meanwhile, Team Charlie was breaching the residence of Deputy Mayor James Carroll. The heavily guarded mansion posed a challenge, but the team moved with precision, overcoming the security and apprehending Carroll, who protested loudly as he was led away in handcuffs.

"You can't do this! I'm the deputy mayor!" Carroll shouted.

"You're under arrest for corruption and conspiracy," the team leader replied. "Anything you say can and will be used against you in a court of law."

Back at Phoenix Holdings, Sarah and Ethan reviewed the evidence they had collected. It was a treasure trove of information—transaction records, communication logs, and detailed plans that outlined the extent of Marco's network and its operations.

"This is it," Sarah said, her eyes scanning the documents. "This is what we need to bring down the entire operation."

Ethan nodded, but his expression was serious. "We've captured key players, but there are still loose ends. Marco's network is extensive, and we need to address every threat."

Sarah agreed. "We need to follow up on every lead, ensure that every piece of the puzzle is in place. This is just the beginning."

Their radios buzzed with updates from the other teams. "Team Delta here. We've secured the businesses linked to the laundering operations. Multiple suspects in custody, and we've found extensive financial records."

"Copy, Delta," Sarah replied. "Bring everything back to the precinct. We'll need a full debrief and analysis."

As the teams regrouped at the precinct, the mood was one of cautious optimism. They had struck a significant blow against Marco's network, but the work was far from over. The evidence they had gathered would be crucial in dismantling the entire operation and ensuring that those involved were brought to justice.

Captain Donovan addressed the assembled teams, his voice filled with pride and determination. "Excellent work today, everyone. We've taken down key figures in this conspiracy, but we need to stay vigilant. We'll continue to analyze the evidence and pursue every lead. This is a victory, but our fight isn't over yet."

Sarah and Ethan exchanged a glance, their resolve unwavering. They had come a long way, and there was still much to do. But with each step, they were closer to unraveling the conspiracy and restoring integrity to their city.

"Let's get to work," Sarah said, her voice steady. "We've got a lot to go through."

As the team settled in to analyze the evidence and plan their next moves, the sense of purpose and determination was palpable. They had faced immense challenges and overcome significant obstacles, but they were ready for whatever lay ahead. The raid had been a success, but the mission to bring down Marco's network and restore justice was ongoing, and they were prepared to see it through to the end.

Chapter 19
Uncharted Paths

The morning sun filtered through the windows of the precinct, casting long shadows across the conference room table. It had been a long night following the successful raids, and the precinct was finally starting to quiet down as the adrenaline from the operation began to wane. Sarah and Ethan sat amidst a sea of documents and evidence bags, their exhaustion evident but their spirits high.

Sarah sifted through the piles of papers, a slight smile playing on her lips. "We did it, Ethan. We really did it."

Ethan nodded, leaning back in his chair. "Yeah, we did. It's been a hell of a ride, hasn't it?"

Sarah glanced around the room, the enormity of their accomplishments settling in. "I still can't believe how far we've come. From those initial arson cases to uncovering this massive conspiracy. It feels surreal."

Ethan's expression grew serious. "You know, when we started this, I never imagined it would lead to exposing corruption at the highest levels. It's incredible, but it's also a bit overwhelming."

Sarah sighed, leaning forward to rest her chin on her hand. "I know what you mean. The personal toll this case has taken... it's been hard. The long hours, the constant danger. It's affected all of us."

Ethan reached out, placing a reassuring hand on Sarah's shoulder. "But we've also made a real difference, Sarah. We've taken dangerous people off the streets and exposed the rot within our city's leadership. That's something to be proud of."

Sarah nodded, her eyes reflecting a mix of pride and fatigue. "You're right. It's just... sometimes I wonder if it's worth it. The sacrifices we make, the relationships that suffer."

Ethan's gaze softened. "It is worth it. Every bit of it. We've seen the impact firsthand. And as for the sacrifices, well, we knew what we were signing up for. It's part of the job."

Sarah smiled faintly. "I guess I needed to hear that. Thanks, Ethan."

Ethan returned her smile. "Anytime, partner."

They lapsed into a comfortable silence, each lost in their thoughts as they continued to review the evidence. The room was filled with the soft rustle of papers and the distant hum of activity from the rest of the precinct.

After a while, Sarah broke the silence. "So, what's next? We've got a lot of evidence to process, and we still need to follow up on the remaining leads. Marco's network might be crippled, but it's not completely dismantled yet."

Ethan nodded, his expression thoughtful. "Agreed. We need to ensure that everyone involved is brought to justice. And we also have to start thinking about rebuilding trust within the community and the department. This corruption scandal has shaken a lot of people's faith in the system."

Sarah leaned back, considering Ethan's words. "You're right. It's not just about taking down the bad guys. We need to work on healing the city and restoring integrity. That's going to be a long process, but we're up for it."

Ethan smiled. "We always are. One step at a time, right?"

"Right," Sarah replied, feeling a renewed sense of purpose.

Captain Donovan entered the room, interrupting their conversation. "How are you two holding up?"

Sarah straightened in her chair. "We're good, Captain. Just reviewing the evidence and planning our next steps."

Donovan nodded, his gaze shifting between them. "You've both done exceptional work. I wanted to personally thank you for your dedication and perseverance. This case has been a turning point for all of us."

Ethan smiled. "Thank you, Captain. We couldn't have done it without the support of the entire team."

Sarah added, "And we're not done yet. There's still a lot of work to do."

Donovan's expression grew serious. "I know. But I have no doubt that you two will see it through. Take some time to rest and recharge. We'll need you at your best for what's coming next."

Sarah and Ethan nodded, appreciating the sentiment. As Donovan left the room, they shared a look of mutual determination.

"We've come this far," Sarah said softly. "We can handle whatever comes next."

Ethan nodded, his eyes reflecting the same resolve. "Together."

As they returned to their work, the weight of the past months' efforts seemed to lighten. They had faced immense challenges and overcome significant obstacles, but they were ready for whatever lay ahead. The battle to restore justice and integrity was far from over, but Sarah and Ethan were more committed than ever to seeing it through.

The precinct was buzzing with activity as the news of their recent success spread. However, the sense of accomplishment was soon tempered by the arrival of new intelligence. Sarah and Ethan were summoned to a meeting with Captain Donovan and representatives from the District Attorney's office.

In the conference room, Assistant District Attorney Lisa Harper was waiting for them. She was a sharp, no-nonsense prosecutor with a reputation for taking on tough cases. Beside her was a young man with a laptop, who was introduced as Special Agent Kyle Reynolds from the Cybercrimes Division.

"Detectives Thompson and Drake," Harper began, her tone brisk. "Congratulations on your recent success. Your work has been exemplary. However, we have a new situation that requires your expertise."

Ethan exchanged a glance with Sarah. "What's going on, ADA Harper?"

Harper gestured to Reynolds. "Agent Reynolds, if you would."

Reynolds nodded, his fingers flying across the keyboard. "We've been tracking a series of cyberattacks targeting city infrastructure, financial institutions, and government databases. The scale and sophistication of these attacks suggest a well-funded and highly skilled group. We believe they're linked to an organized crime syndicate looking to expand their operations into cybercrimes."

Sarah leaned forward, her interest piqued. "Do we have any leads on who's behind this?"

Reynolds pulled up a map on the screen, marked with various points of interest. "Our intel suggests that these attacks are orchestrated by a group known as 'The Black Web.' They're notorious for their cybercriminal activities, including data breaches, ransomware attacks, and financial fraud."

Ethan frowned, studying the map. "How does this connect to our previous case with Marco's network?"

Harper interjected, "We've found evidence that some of Marco's associates have ties to The Black Web. It appears they're diversifying their criminal activities, and cybercrime is their new frontier. Given your success in dismantling Marco's network, we believe you're the best team to tackle this new threat."

Sarah nodded slowly. "Alright, what's our next step?"

"We're forming a special task force to address this threat," Harper explained. "You two will lead the investigative team, working closely with Agent Reynolds and other experts in cybercrime. Your objective is to identify the key players, disrupt their operations, and bring them to justice."

Ethan glanced at Sarah, then back at Harper. "We're in. What resources do we have at our disposal?"

Reynolds smiled, tapping his laptop. "You'll have access to the latest cyber forensics tools, surveillance technology, and a team of specialists in cybersecurity. We'll provide continuous intel updates and support throughout the operation."

Sarah felt a surge of determination. "When do we start?"

"Immediately," Harper replied. "The cyberattacks are escalating, and we can't afford any delays. We'll set up a command center here at the precinct, and Agent Reynolds will coordinate with his team from there."

Captain Donovan, who had been listening quietly, finally spoke up. "This is a new kind of challenge, but I have full confidence in your abilities. You've proven time and again that you can handle whatever comes your way. Just know that the entire precinct is behind you."

Sarah and Ethan stood, ready to take on the new mission. "Thank you, Captain," Sarah said. "We won't let you down."

Ethan added, "We'll need a briefing with the specialists and access to any existing data on The Black Web's activities."

Reynolds nodded. "I'll arrange it. Let's get to work."

As they left the conference room, Sarah turned to Ethan, her mind already racing with the possibilities and challenges ahead. "This is going to be different from anything we've faced before."

Ethan nodded, a determined look in his eyes. "Yeah, but we'll adapt. We always do."

Back in their office, they started organizing their approach. Sarah began by reviewing the intel provided by Reynolds, while Ethan coordinated with the cyber forensics team.

"We need to understand their methods and patterns," Sarah said, scanning through a series of reports. "If we can predict their next move, we can set a trap."

Ethan nodded, pulling up additional data on his computer. "We should also look into any known associates or front companies. These groups often use legitimate businesses as a cover for their activities."

Just then, Agent Reynolds entered their office with a stack of files. "Here's everything we have on The Black Web so far. It's not much, but it's a start."

Sarah took the files, her determination growing. "Thanks, Kyle. We'll go through this and start piecing together their network."

As they delved into the new case, the weight of the challenge ahead became clear. This wasn't just about catching criminals—it was about protecting their city from a new and evolving threat. But Sarah and Ethan were ready. They had faced insurmountable odds before and emerged victorious. This time would be no different.

"We've got this," Ethan said, his voice steady. "One step at a time."

Sarah nodded, feeling the same resolve. "Let's get to work."

Together, they began the meticulous process of unraveling the complex web of cybercrime, determined to bring justice to those who threatened their city. The path ahead was uncharted, but they were ready to navigate it with the same tenacity and skill that had brought them this far.

The task force assembled in the main briefing room, a mix of seasoned detectives, cybersecurity experts, and federal agents. The atmosphere was tense but focused, as everyone understood the gravity of the mission ahead. Sarah and Ethan stood at the front, ready to lead the briefing.

Sarah began, addressing the room. "Thank you all for being here. As you know, we're dealing with a highly sophisticated group of cybercriminals known as The Black Web. They've been behind a series of escalating cyberattacks targeting our city's infrastructure, financial institutions, and government databases."

Agent Kyle Reynolds stepped forward, his laptop connected to the projector. "Our intelligence suggests that The Black Web is not only well-funded but also highly skilled. They employ cutting-edge technology and have a decentralized structure, making them difficult to track and even harder to dismantle."

A hand shot up from the back of the room. It was Detective Lisa Chen. "Do we know who's leading this group?"

Reynolds nodded. "We believe the leader goes by the alias 'Cypher.' He's a ghost in the cyber world, with no known physical identity. Our goal is to unmask him and bring down the entire network."

Ethan took over, pointing to a series of slides. "We've identified several key targets linked to The Black Web's operations. These include data centers, safe houses, and financial fronts. Each of these locations could hold crucial information about their activities and personnel."

Special Agent Maria Torres, a cyber forensics expert, spoke up. "We'll need to secure and analyze all digital evidence from these sites. It's crucial that we move quickly to prevent them from wiping their data."

Sarah nodded. "That's why we'll be executing simultaneous raids, similar to our previous operation. Coordination and timing are everything. We need to hit them hard and fast, leaving no room for them to escape or destroy evidence."

Reynolds pulled up a detailed map of the city, highlighting the targets. "Teams will be divided as follows: Team Alpha will handle the main data center in the downtown area. Team Bravo will target the financial front in Midtown. Team Charlie will raid the suspected safe house in the industrial district."

Ethan added, "Each team will have a mix of field agents and cyber experts. This ensures we can secure physical locations while also capturing and analyzing digital data on-site."

Sarah glanced around the room, ensuring everyone was following. "We'll be using encrypted communications to coordinate during the raids. Each team leader will report directly to the command center here at the precinct, where we'll be monitoring everything in real-time."

Detective Jake Martinez raised a concern. "What about contingencies? These guys are smart and might have countermeasures in place."

Reynolds replied, "We've planned for that. Each team will have a secondary objective to secure potential escape routes and alternative data storage locations. We're also coordinating with utility companies to prevent any intentional blackouts or disruptions."

Sarah continued, "We need to be prepared for anything. These criminals are resourceful and won't go down without a fight. Safety is paramount—if you encounter heavy resistance, fall back and call for backup."

Ethan looked at the assembled team, his voice firm. "This is a new kind of battle for many of us, but we're ready. We've proven we can adapt and overcome. Let's use every tool at our disposal to bring these criminals to justice."

Agent Torres added, "We'll also be conducting post-raid analysis to track any digital footprints they might leave behind. This will help us understand their network better and prevent future attacks."

Sarah wrapped up the briefing, her tone resolute. "We've faced immense challenges before and come out on top. This time will be no different. We're up against a formidable enemy, but together, we can and will take them down."

As the team dispersed to make final preparations, Sarah and Ethan stayed behind to review the last-minute details with Reynolds and Torres.

"Are we ready for this?" Ethan asked, his voice a mix of determination and concern.

"We have to be," Sarah replied. "We've done everything we can to prepare. Now it's time to execute."

Reynolds nodded. "We've got the best people on this. Let's show The Black Web what happens when they mess with our city."

Torres added, "And remember, every piece of data we secure brings us one step closer to Cypher. Stay sharp and focused."

With a final nod, the leaders joined their teams, the weight of the mission heavy but the resolve to succeed even stronger. The fight against cybercrime was on, and they were ready to lead the charge.

The night was dark and filled with tension as the task force prepared for their first major operation. The command center buzzed with quiet urgency, each team member focused on their tasks. Sarah, Ethan, and Agent Reynolds stood by the large screen displaying the real-time feed from their surveillance units.

Sarah took a deep breath and addressed the assembled teams. "Alright, everyone, this is it. Our first major operation against The Black Web. Team Alpha will hit the data center, Team Bravo targets the financial front, and Team Charlie handles the safe house. Stay sharp, stay safe, and let's bring these criminals down."

Ethan added, "Remember, our primary goal is to secure digital evidence and apprehend key members. Be prepared for anything."

Agent Reynolds nodded. "We're going in hot. Let's move out."

The teams dispersed, each unit heading to their respective targets. Sarah and Ethan joined Team Alpha, riding in the lead vehicle towards the data center. The streets were eerily quiet, the tension palpable.

As they approached the data center, Ethan glanced at Sarah. "You ready for this?"

Sarah nodded, her eyes steely with determination. "Always. Let's do this."

The convoy came to a halt, and the team quickly exited their vehicles, taking up positions around the building. Ethan signaled to move in, and the team breached the entrance, spreading out to secure the area.

Inside, the data center was a maze of servers and cables, the hum of machinery filling the air. Sarah led the way, her weapon drawn, as they moved deeper into the facility.

"Clear," called out an officer as they swept through each room, ensuring there were no hidden threats.

Reynolds and his cyber team set up their equipment, quickly accessing the servers. "We're in," Reynolds reported. "Downloading data now. This will take a few minutes."

Ethan nodded. "Keep us updated. We need to move fast."

Meanwhile, Team Bravo had reached the financial front in Midtown. Detective Lisa Chen led the team, her eyes scanning the area for any signs of resistance. They breached the building, encountering a few guards who were quickly subdued.

"Secure the area and start collecting evidence," Lisa ordered. "We need to find any financial records linking back to The Black Web."

Back at the data center, the tension mounted as the download continued. "We're almost there," Reynolds said, his eyes fixed on the screen. "Just a little longer."

Suddenly, the lights flickered, and an alarm blared. "We've been detected," Sarah said, her voice steady. "Everyone, stay alert."

The team tensed, ready for any threat. Moments later, the power stabilized, and the download completed. "Got it!" Reynolds exclaimed, pulling out the storage device. "We have everything we need."

Ethan signaled to move out. "Let's go, people. Time to exfil."

As they made their way back to the vehicles, Sarah's radio crackled to life. "Team Bravo to Command. We've secured significant financial records and apprehended several suspects. No casualties."

"Good work, Bravo," Sarah replied. "Regroup at the rendezvous point."

Team Charlie reported in next. "Safe house is secure. We've found additional evidence and detained three suspects. All clear."

Sarah felt a surge of relief. "Copy that, Charlie. Excellent work. Regroup at the rendezvous point."

The teams reconvened at the designated location, their vehicles forming a secure perimeter. Sarah and Ethan debriefed the teams, reviewing the evidence collected and ensuring all suspects were secured.

Reynolds approached them, his expression a mix of triumph and concern. "We've got a lot of data to sift through, but it's a start. This will give us a better understanding of their network."

Sarah nodded. "Great job, everyone. This was a significant first step. But remember, this is just the beginning. We've exposed a small part of their operation, but there's much more to uncover."

Ethan added, "Stay vigilant. We've hit them hard tonight, but they'll regroup and retaliate. We need to be ready for anything."

As the task force dispersed, returning to the precinct with their prisoners and evidence, Sarah and Ethan stood together, reflecting on the night's success.

"We set the tone tonight," Sarah said, a note of satisfaction in her voice. "We showed them we're not afraid to take the fight to them."

Ethan nodded, his expression resolute. "But we also saw how complex and dangerous they are. We need to stay one step ahead, always."

"We will," Sarah replied. "We have a strong team and the determination to see this through. Let's get back and start analyzing the data. The more we know, the better prepared we'll be for the next operation."

As they drove back to the precinct, the first light of dawn breaking over the horizon, Sarah felt a renewed sense of purpose. They had faced a new and formidable enemy and emerged victorious. But the battle was far from over. With each operation, they would dismantle The Black Web's network piece by piece, bringing justice to those who had been wronged and restoring safety to their city.

Chapter 20
Shifting Shadows

The precinct was a whirlwind of activity as the team prepared for what they hoped would be the final operation against The Architect's network. Sarah Thompson stood in the operations room, her eyes scanning the flurry of reports and intel that filled the screens around her. The Architect had been in custody for a week, but his network was proving resilient, with operatives still active and threats still looming.

Ethan Drake entered, carrying a fresh stack of files. "We've got new intel from one of the captured operatives. They've confirmed the location of the central command for the remaining cells. It's an abandoned military bunker outside the city."

Sarah's eyes lit with determination. "This is it, Ethan. We take out that command center, and we dismantle what's left of his network."

Garcia approached, looking grim. "We've intercepted communications suggesting they're planning one last major attack. They're desperate, and that makes them dangerous."

Sarah nodded, her mind racing. "We can't give them that chance. Gather the team. We need to move fast."

The team assembled in the briefing room, the air thick with anticipation. Sarah stood at the front, her gaze steady. "Listen up. We've identified the command center for the remaining cells. It's in an abandoned military bunker here." She pointed to the location on the map. "This is our chance to end this. We go in, secure the site, and take down anyone who resists."

Ethan stepped forward, pointing to the schematic of the bunker. "The bunker is heavily fortified. We'll need to breach multiple levels. Alpha team will enter through the main entrance, while Bravo team will secure the rear. Once inside, we need to move quickly and efficiently."

Jamie, the young officer, raised her hand. "What kind of resistance are we expecting?"

Garcia answered, "Expect heavy resistance. These are their most loyal operatives. They know this is their last stand."

Sarah's voice was firm. "We've faced worse. Stick to the plan, watch each other's backs, and we'll get through this. Let's move out."

The drive to the bunker was tense, each member of the team focused on the mission ahead. The sun was setting, casting a crimson glow over the landscape. As they approached the bunker, the imposing structure loomed ahead, a stark reminder of the challenge they faced.

Sarah and Ethan led Alpha team to the main entrance, while Garcia took Bravo team to the rear. Sarah's voice was calm but commanding as she addressed her team. "On my mark, we breach. Remember, we're dealing with highly trained operatives. Stay focused."

Ethan added, "Keep your formation tight. We clear each room before moving on."

Sarah took a deep breath. "Three, two, one—breach!"

The doors were blown open, and the team moved in swiftly. The interior of the bunker was dark and labyrinthine, filled with narrow corridors and heavy steel doors. They advanced cautiously, weapons at the ready.

A sudden burst of gunfire erupted from ahead. "Contact!" Sarah shouted, ducking behind a crate. "Return fire!"

The team responded with precision, their training evident as they pushed forward. Ethan flanked the attackers, taking down two operatives with swift, well-placed shots. "Area clear," he called out.

They moved deeper into the bunker, encountering pockets of resistance at every turn. The operatives were well-armed and determined, but Sarah's team was relentless. They cleared each room methodically, the tension thickening with each step.

Garcia's voice crackled over the radio. "Bravo team has secured the rear entrance. We're moving to rendezvous with you."

Sarah acknowledged. "Copy that. We're approaching the central command room."

They reached a heavy steel door, the final barrier to the command center. Sarah signaled for the breaching charge. "This is it. Be ready for anything."

The door exploded inward, and the team stormed the room. Inside, they found a group of operatives huddled around a large table, covered in maps and equipment. The leader, a tall man with cold, calculating eyes, turned to face them.

Sarah stepped forward, her weapon trained on the leader. "It's over. Surrender now."

The leader sneered. "You think you've won? You have no idea what's coming."

Ethan's voice was cold. "We've heard that before. Hands where we can see them."

The operatives hesitated, then slowly raised their hands. Sarah felt a surge of relief, but she kept her focus. "Secure them. And check the room for any hidden surprises."

As the team moved to secure the operatives and sweep the room, Sarah approached the table, scanning the maps and documents. She felt a chill as she realized the scale of the plans laid out before her.

"Ethan," she called, her voice tense. "These plans… they're bigger than we thought. They've been coordinating attacks in multiple cities. This isn't just about us. We need to alert the other agencies."

Ethan nodded, his expression serious. "We'll deal with it. Right now, let's secure this place and get these guys back to the precinct."

As they led the captured operatives out of the bunker, Sarah felt a mix of exhaustion and determination. They had struck a significant blow against The Architect's network, but the fight was far from over. With each step, they moved closer to dismantling the entire operation, ensuring that the threat was neutralized for good. The road ahead was still fraught with challenges, but Sarah knew they were ready to face whatever came next.

Back at the precinct, the tension was palpable as Sarah and her team prepared to interrogate the captured operatives. The leader, identified as Anton, sat in the dimly lit interrogation room, his hands cuffed to the metal table. His cold eyes scanned the room, betraying no fear or regret. Sarah and Ethan stood outside the observation window, discussing their strategy.

Sarah glanced at Ethan, her expression resolute. "We need to break him. He's the key to unraveling the rest of their network."

Ethan nodded. "Agreed. Let's see what he knows."

They entered the room, the door closing with a heavy thud. Sarah took a seat across from Anton, while Ethan stood by the door, his presence a silent warning.

Sarah started, her voice calm but firm. "Anton, we know you're one of The Architect's top lieutenants. Cooperate, and things might go easier for you."

Anton leaned back, a smirk playing on his lips. "You think you can intimidate me, Detective? I've faced worse than you."

Ethan stepped forward, his tone icy. "This isn't a game, Anton. You're looking at serious charges. Terrorism, conspiracy, attempted murder. Your best bet is to start talking."

Anton's smirk faded slightly, but he maintained his defiant posture. "You think capturing me changes anything? The plan is already in motion."

Sarah's eyes narrowed. "What plan? What's the next target?"

Anton remained silent, his gaze fixed on Sarah. She leaned in, her voice dropping to a steely whisper. "You're not protecting anyone by staying quiet. The Architect doesn't care about you. You're just a pawn."

Anton's eyes flickered with a hint of uncertainty. "You don't know anything. The Architect has planned for every contingency."

Ethan's patience was wearing thin. "We've already dismantled most of your network. Your cells are falling apart. It's over, Anton."

Anton's jaw tightened, a sign of his internal struggle. "You think you've won, but you haven't. The Architect always has a backup plan."

Sarah seized the moment. "Then tell us about the backup plan. Help us stop it."

Anton hesitated, his resolve cracking. "It's too late. The next phase... it's already underway. Multiple cities, simultaneous attacks. You can't stop it."

Ethan's eyes widened. "Which cities? When?"

Anton shook his head. "I don't know the details. Only The Architect knows everything."

Sarah pressed on. "We need specifics. Give us something to work with."

Anton looked down, a hint of defeat in his eyes. "There's a safe house in the city. The Architect's fallback point. You might find more information there."

Ethan moved closer, his tone urgent. "Where is it?"

Anton sighed, his shoulders slumping. "An old factory on the outskirts of town. You'll find what you're looking for there."

Sarah nodded, standing up. "Thank you, Anton. This might help you in the long run."

As they left the room, Sarah turned to Ethan. "We need to move fast. If what he says is true, we're running out of time."

Ethan nodded, already dialing Garcia. "Garcia, we've got a new lead. An old factory on the outskirts of town. We need to mobilize immediately."

Garcia's voice crackled through the phone. "Copy that. I'll get the teams ready."

Sarah and Ethan gathered the team, briefing them quickly on the new intel. "We're heading to the old factory. This could be our last chance to stop The Architect's plans."

Jamie raised her hand. "What about the simultaneous attacks? Should we alert other agencies?"

Sarah nodded. "Good point. Garcia, coordinate with federal agencies. They need to be aware of the threat."

As they geared up, Ethan glanced at Sarah. "This could be it. Are you ready?"

Sarah took a deep breath, her determination unwavering. "I've never been more ready. Let's finish this."

The drive to the factory was tense, each member of the team focused and prepared for what lay ahead. The factory loomed in the distance, its shadow stretching across the barren landscape.

They arrived and spread out, taking positions around the building. Sarah signaled for the breach, and the team moved in, their movements swift and precise.

Inside, the factory was a labyrinth of machinery and old equipment. Sarah led the way, her senses heightened. They reached a central room filled with computers and maps. It was clear this was the command center.

Ethan moved to one of the computers, quickly scanning the files. "Sarah, look at this. Detailed plans for attacks on multiple cities. We need to get this to the agencies immediately."

Sarah nodded, her eyes scanning the room. "We've got what we need. Let's secure the area and get out."

As they secured the factory, Sarah felt a sense of closure. They had struck a significant blow against The Architect's network. But as they exited the building, her phone buzzed with a message. It was from an unknown number.

The message read: "You've won this round, Detective. But the game is far from over."

Sarah's eyes narrowed. The Architect was still out there, but for now, they had the upper hand. She turned to her team, her voice steady. "Good work, everyone. Let's get this intel back and prepare for the next phase. This isn't over yet, but we're ready."

As they drove back to the precinct, Sarah felt a renewed sense of purpose. They had come a long way, and there was still more to do. But with her team by her side, she knew they were ready for whatever challenges lay ahead.

The precinct hummed with a sense of urgency as the team returned from the factory, carrying the critical intel that Anton had reluctantly provided. Sarah Thompson wasted no time in mobilizing her team to analyze the information. The Architect's plan for simultaneous attacks on multiple cities needed to be unraveled and thwarted, and time was of the essence.

Sarah stood at the center of the operations room, surrounded by monitors displaying maps, intercepted communications, and schematics of potential targets. Ethan Drake and Garcia were by her side, their faces etched with determination and focus.

Ethan scanned through the newly retrieved data. "We've identified at least six major cities targeted for these attacks. Each one has a critical infrastructure component at risk—power grids, water supplies, transportation hubs."

Sarah nodded, her mind racing. "We need to alert the federal agencies and coordinate with local law enforcement in each of these cities. Garcia, get me the contacts for the DHS and FBI. This is going to require a coordinated effort."

Garcia hurried to his station, dialing numbers and relaying information. The room buzzed with activity as officers and analysts worked tirelessly to decode the remaining files.

Sarah turned to Ethan. "We need a plan to secure our city while also assisting the others. Any insights on the most immediate threat?"

Ethan pointed to the screen showing the city's water supply system. "This seems to be their primary target here. If they contaminate the water supply, it could cause widespread panic and chaos."

Sarah agreed. "Then we need to prioritize securing the water treatment plants and distribution centers. Let's get teams out there immediately."

Ethan nodded, already reaching for his radio. "All units, prepare to mobilize to the following locations. We have a potential imminent threat."

As the teams moved into action, Sarah's phone buzzed. It was a call from Captain Reynolds. "Thompson, I've been briefed on the situation. What's our status?"

Sarah quickly filled him in. "We're coordinating with federal agencies and have units securing key locations. We're doing everything we can to prevent these attacks."

Reynolds' voice was steady. "Good work. Keep me updated on any developments. And Sarah, be careful out there."

She hung up and looked at Ethan. "We need to divide our forces strategically. You take a team to the main water treatment plant. I'll handle the distribution centers."

Ethan's expression was resolute. "Got it. We'll secure the plant and ensure nothing gets through."

They moved swiftly, each taking their teams to the designated locations. The drive to the distribution center was tense, the city's lights blurring past as Sarah navigated through the streets. She could feel the weight of the responsibility on her shoulders, knowing that the safety of thousands depended on their success.

Arriving at the first distribution center, Sarah and her team quickly set up a perimeter. She instructed her officers, "Check every vehicle, every person coming in and out. We can't afford any lapses."

An officer approached, his face serious. "Detective Thompson, we found a suspicious package near the entrance. Bomb squad is on the way."

Sarah's heart raced. "Secure the area and evacuate anyone nearby. We need to contain this immediately."

As the bomb squad worked to neutralize the threat, Sarah's radio crackled with Ethan's voice. "Sarah, we've secured the water treatment plant. No signs of tampering so far, but we're staying vigilant."

Sarah felt a brief moment of relief. "Good. Keep your eyes open for anything unusual. We can't let our guard down."

The bomb squad finally confirmed that the package was a decoy, designed to sow fear and distraction. Sarah's jaw tightened with frustration. The Architect's tactics were becoming more desperate, but they were not losing their resolve.

Returning to the operations room later that night, Sarah found the team still hard at work. Garcia approached with an update. "We've received confirmation from the other cities. They've managed to secure their critical infrastructure thanks to our intel. It looks like we've prevented a major catastrophe."

Sarah allowed herself a small sigh of relief. "Excellent work, everyone. But we need to stay on high alert. The Architect is still out there, and we can't let him slip away."

Ethan joined her, his expression both exhausted and determined. "We've dealt a serious blow to his plans, but he's not going to stop. We need to find him and end this for good."

Sarah met his gaze, her resolve unwavering. "And we will. Let's keep pushing forward. We're getting closer."

As the team continued to work through the night, Sarah felt a renewed sense of purpose. They had faced down a formidable adversary and emerged stronger. The Architect's network was crumbling, and soon, they would bring the mastermind himself to justice. The final confrontation was near, and they were ready to face it together, no matter the cost.

The operations room was abuzz with coordinated efforts as the team worked tirelessly to ensure the safety of their city and assist in securing other targeted locations. The tension was palpable, but there was a sense of determination and focus that permeated the room. Sarah Thompson stood at the helm, her eyes scanning the screens and her mind racing through every possible scenario.

Garcia approached with an urgent expression. "Sarah, we've decrypted another communication from The Architect. It looks like a final directive to his remaining operatives. He's planning to make a last stand."

Sarah's eyes narrowed. "Where?"

Garcia pointed to the map on the screen. "An abandoned industrial complex on the outskirts of the city. It's heavily fortified, but it's our best shot at capturing him."

Ethan joined them, his face set with resolve. "We've been waiting for this. It's time to end this once and for all."

Sarah nodded. "Agreed. Gather the team. We're moving out immediately. This is our chance to bring him in and dismantle his network for good."

The team assembled quickly, their expressions grim but determined. Sarah briefed them on the plan. "We'll be splitting into two teams. Alpha team will secure the perimeter and ensure no one escapes. Bravo team, led by Ethan and myself, will breach the complex and apprehend The Architect. We need to be swift and precise. Any questions?"

Jamie raised her hand. "What kind of resistance are we expecting?"

Sarah met her gaze. "Heavy. These are his most loyal operatives. They'll be prepared for us, but we're going in with the element of surprise."

As they geared up and moved out, the weight of the mission hung heavily over them. The drive to the industrial complex was tense, each officer mentally preparing for the confrontation ahead. The sun had set, casting long shadows over the landscape as they approached their destination.

Sarah and Ethan led Bravo team through the dense underbrush surrounding the complex, moving silently and efficiently. The old industrial buildings loomed ahead, their darkened windows and rusted exteriors a stark reminder of the danger within.

Sarah whispered into her radio. "Alpha team, report."

Garcia's voice crackled back. "Perimeter secure. No movement detected. Ready on your mark."

Sarah signaled to her team. "On three. One, two, three—move."

They breached the entrance, moving swiftly through the narrow corridors. The interior was a maze of machinery and storage rooms, the air thick with dust and the faint smell of rust. Sarah and Ethan led the way, their senses heightened as they navigated the labyrinthine layout.

Suddenly, a burst of gunfire erupted from a side corridor. "Contact!" Sarah shouted, diving for cover. "Return fire!"

The team responded with precision, their training evident as they pushed forward. Ethan flanked the attackers, taking down two operatives with well-placed shots. "Clear!"

They advanced deeper into the complex, encountering pockets of resistance at every turn. Sarah's heart pounded as they approached the central control room. The door was heavily reinforced, but they had come prepared.

"Ethan, get the breaching charge," Sarah ordered, her voice steady despite the adrenaline coursing through her veins.

Ethan nodded, placing the charge on the door. "Ready to breach."

Sarah took a deep breath. "On my mark. Three, two, one—breach!"

The door exploded inward, and the team stormed the room. Inside, they found The Architect, standing calmly amidst a bank of computers and monitors. His eyes were cold and calculating as he turned to face them.

"Detective Thompson," he said, his voice eerily composed. "I've been expecting you."

Sarah raised her weapon. "It's over, Architect. Surrender now."

The Architect smiled, a chilling sight. "You've been a worthy opponent, Detective. But do you really think capturing me will change anything?"

Ethan stepped forward, his tone firm. "Hands where we can see them. Now."

The Architect hesitated, then slowly raised his hands. "Very well. But know this—my network is vast. Others will rise in my place."

Sarah's eyes remained fixed on him. "We'll deal with them. Right now, you're coming with us."

As they cuffed The Architect and secured the control room, Sarah felt a mixture of relief and resolve. They had captured the mastermind, but the fight against his network was far from over. She knew they had dealt a significant blow, but vigilance was crucial to ensure the safety of their city.

Outside, Alpha team had secured the perimeter and detained the remaining operatives. Garcia approached, his expression one of satisfaction. "We did it, Sarah. We've got him."

Sarah nodded, looking around at her team. "Excellent work, everyone. This is a major victory, but we need to stay alert. There's still more to do."

Ethan placed a hand on her shoulder. "We'll be ready. Together."

As they transported The Architect back to the precinct, Sarah felt a sense of accomplishment tempered with the awareness of ongoing challenges. They had made significant progress, but the journey was not over. With her team by her side, she was confident they could face whatever came next, ensuring justice and security for their city.

Chapter 21
Reflections and Revelations

The morning sun bathed the city in a golden light, casting long shadows and highlighting the remnants of the night's rain. Sarah and Ethan stood outside the precinct, savoring the rare moment of calm. The task force had successfully dismantled the network, and the sense of triumph was still fresh in the air.

Sarah took a deep breath, feeling the crisp air fill her lungs. "It's almost surreal, isn't it? After everything, we've finally brought them down."

Ethan nodded, his eyes reflecting the same sense of accomplishment. "Yeah, but I can't shake the feeling that this is just the beginning. There's always another case, another challenge."

Sarah smiled, a hint of amusement in her eyes. "True, but let's enjoy this victory while we can. We've earned it."

Garcia approached, holding two cups of coffee. "Thought you two might need a pick-me-up. Great work last night."

"Thanks, Mark," Sarah said, accepting the coffee. "We couldn't have done it without the whole team."

Garcia grinned. "You're being modest. You two were the backbone of this operation. Everyone knows it."

Ethan took a sip of his coffee, savoring the warmth. "What's next on the agenda?"

Garcia shrugged. "Captain Reynolds wants to debrief us on the operation and discuss the next steps. But for now, enjoy your coffee. You've earned a little downtime."

As they stood there, watching the bustling activity of the precinct, Sarah couldn't help but reflect on how far they had come. The challenges they had faced, the victories they had achieved, and the bond that had grown between her and Ethan. It had been a long and arduous journey, but one that had forged them into a formidable team.

Inside the precinct, the mood was one of subdued celebration. Officers congratulated each other, and the sense of camaraderie was palpable. It was a rare and welcome respite from the usual tension and urgency of their work.

Later that morning, the task force gathered in the briefing room for the debriefing. Captain Reynolds stood at the front, his expression a mix of pride and seriousness. "First, let me congratulate all of you on a job well done. The operation was a success, and we've dealt a significant blow to organized crime in this city."

He looked around the room, his gaze settling on Sarah and Ethan. "You two were instrumental in this success. Your dedication and hard work have not gone unnoticed."

Sarah felt a surge of pride but remained focused. "Thank you, Captain. It was a team effort."

Reynolds nodded. "Indeed. Now, we need to discuss the next steps. We've dismantled this network, but there are always more threats on the horizon. We need to stay vigilant and prepared."

Ethan leaned forward. "What's our priority moving forward?"

Reynolds gestured to the map on the wall. "We've identified several smaller cells that were connected to the main network. They're scattered across the city, and our job is to track them down and dismantle them before they can regroup."

Sarah glanced at Ethan, a determined look in her eyes. "Sounds like we've got our work cut out for us."

Reynolds smiled. "I have no doubt that you'll handle it. Let's get to work."

As the meeting concluded, the team dispersed to their respective tasks. Sarah and Ethan headed back to their desks, already discussing their strategy for tackling the remaining cells.

Ethan pulled up a list of names on his computer. "We've got a lot of ground to cover. Where do you want to start?"

Sarah scanned the list, her mind racing. "Let's start with the most active cells. If we can disrupt their operations, it'll make it harder for them to regroup."

They spent the next few hours poring over the data, identifying patterns and planning their next moves. The sense of urgency had returned, but so had their resolve.

Garcia approached, holding another stack of files. "Looks like we've got a lead on one of the cells. A warehouse on the east side. It's been flagged for suspicious activity."

Sarah nodded, taking the file. "Let's check it out. If we can catch them off guard, we might get some valuable intel."

Ethan grabbed his jacket. "I'll get the team ready."

As they prepared to head out, Sarah couldn't help but feel a sense of anticipation. The thrill of the chase, the satisfaction of bringing criminals to justice—it was what drove her. And with Ethan by her side, she knew they could face whatever challenges lay ahead.

The drive to the warehouse was tense, each of them focused on the mission at hand. They arrived at the location, a dilapidated building that looked abandoned from the outside. But they knew better.

Ethan surveyed the area, his eyes sharp. "Looks quiet. Too quiet."

Sarah nodded, her hand on her weapon. "Stay alert. We don't know what we're walking into."

They approached the building cautiously, their movements silent and coordinated. As they reached the entrance, Sarah signaled for the team to spread out and cover all exits.

Inside, the warehouse was dark and musty, the air thick with dust. They moved through the shadows, their flashlights cutting through the gloom. As they reached the central area, they heard the faint sound of voices.

Ethan whispered, "Sounds like we've found our suspects."

Sarah nodded. "On my mark."

They burst into the room, weapons drawn. "Police! Hands up!"

The suspects froze, their eyes wide with shock. One of them, a burly man with a scar running down his face, reached for a weapon, but Ethan was quicker. "Don't even think about it," he growled, kicking the weapon away.

Sarah moved forward, securing the suspects. "We've got them. Let's see what they were up to."

As they examined the area, they found evidence of illegal activities, including weapons and drugs. It was clear that this cell had been preparing for something big.

Ethan looked at Sarah, a grim smile on his face. "Looks like we got them just in time."

Sarah nodded, feeling a sense of satisfaction. "Yes, but there are still more out there. Let's get these guys back to the precinct and see what we can learn from them."

As they escorted the suspects out of the warehouse, Sarah couldn't help but feel a renewed sense of purpose. The challenges were far from over, but they were ready to face them head-on. Together, they would continue to protect their city and bring justice to those who sought to disrupt its peace.

Back at the precinct, the suspects from the warehouse raid were processed and taken to holding cells. Sarah and Ethan headed to the interrogation rooms, ready to extract the information they needed to dismantle the remaining cells. The tension in the air was thick as they prepared to face their suspects.

Ethan glanced at Sarah. "Which one do you want to start with?"

Sarah thought for a moment. "Let's go with the leader. The one with the scar. He'll know the most."

They entered the interrogation room, where the burly man sat with his hands cuffed to the table. He looked up as they entered, his eyes cold and defiant.

Sarah took a seat across from him, her expression calm but determined. "We need to talk. The sooner you cooperate, the sooner this will be over."

The man sneered. "I'm not saying a word. You've got nothing on me."

Ethan leaned against the wall, his gaze steady. "We've got enough to put you away for a long time. Weapons, drugs, conspiracy. The works. But if you help us, we might be able to make things easier for you."

The man's eyes flickered with uncertainty. "What do you want to know?"

Sarah leaned forward. "We need information on the remaining cells. Who's leading them, where they're hiding, and what their plans are. Give us that, and we can talk about a deal."

The man hesitated, then sighed. "Alright. But I want protection. These guys don't mess around. If they find out I talked…"

Ethan nodded. "We'll make sure you're safe. Now start talking."

The man took a deep breath. "There are three main cells left. One's led by a guy named Hector. He's holed up in an old factory on the west side. The second is run by a woman named Carla. She's got a place near the docks. The third… well, that's the tricky one. It's led by a ghost. No one's ever seen his face, but he's the most dangerous of them all. He goes by the name Viper."

Sarah's eyes narrowed. "What can you tell us about Viper?"

The man shook his head. "Not much. He's a ghost, like I said. Keeps his operations tight. But if you want to find him, you'll need to start with Hector. He's Viper's right-hand man."

Ethan exchanged a look with Sarah. "Looks like we've got our next target."

As they left the interrogation room, Garcia met them in the hallway. "What did you get?"

Sarah handed him her notes. "Three main cells left. Hector, Carla, and Viper. We need to take them down, starting with Hector."

Garcia nodded. "I'll get the team ready. We'll hit the factory tonight."

Sarah and Ethan spent the next few hours preparing for the raid. The factory on the west side was a known hideout for criminal activities, but they had never been able to gather enough evidence for a raid—until now. The task force assembled, each member briefed on their role and the layout of the factory.

As they drove to the location, the tension in the air was palpable. The sun had set, casting the city in a blanket of darkness. The factory loomed ahead, its silhouette stark against the night sky.

Ethan parked the car, his eyes scanning the area. "Looks quiet. Too quiet."

Sarah nodded, her hand resting on her weapon. "Stay sharp. We don't know what we're walking into."

They approached the factory, their movements silent and coordinated. Sarah signaled for the team to spread out and cover all exits. They moved through the shadows, their flashlights cutting through the darkness.

As they reached the entrance, Sarah heard the faint sound of voices inside. She turned to Ethan, her voice a whisper. "They're in there. Ready?"

Ethan nodded. "On your mark."

Sarah counted down silently, then kicked the door open. "Police! Hands up!"

Chaos erupted as the suspects scrambled to flee. The task force moved in, weapons drawn, securing the area with practiced precision. Sarah and Ethan led the charge, taking down suspects and securing evidence.

In the midst of the chaos, Sarah spotted Hector, a tall man with a fierce expression. He reached for a weapon, but Sarah was quicker. "Don't move!" she shouted, training her gun on him.

Hector froze, his eyes narrowing. "You're making a big mistake, detective."

Ethan moved in, cuffing Hector's hands behind his back. "The only mistake here was yours. You're going away for a long time."

As they secured the remaining suspects, Sarah felt a sense of accomplishment. They had taken down another key player, but the battle was far from over. They still had to deal with Carla and the elusive Viper.

Back at the precinct, they processed the suspects and began sifting through the evidence. The mood was one of focused determination. They had made significant progress, but the most dangerous part of their mission still lay ahead.

Sarah and Ethan sat at their desks, reviewing the information they had gathered. "We're getting closer," Sarah said, her voice steady. "We need to hit Carla next, before she has a chance to regroup."

Ethan nodded. "Agreed. We'll move first thing in the morning."

As they prepared for the next phase of their operation, Sarah couldn't help but feel a sense of anticipation. The road ahead was fraught with danger, but she knew they were ready to face it head-on. Together, they would bring justice to those who sought to disrupt the peace of their city.

Chapter 22
The Docks of Deception

The morning sun cast a golden hue over the city as Sarah and Ethan prepared for the next phase of their operation. The precinct was buzzing with activity as the task force assembled, ready to take down Carla's cell near the docks. The tension was palpable, the stakes higher than ever.

Sarah stood in front of the assembled team, her expression resolute. "We've made significant progress, but we're not done yet. Carla is our next target. She's dangerous and resourceful, so we need to be ready for anything."

Ethan nodded in agreement. "We'll be hitting her safe house near the docks. It's a known hub for smuggling and illegal activities. We need to move quickly and efficiently."

Garcia, standing off to the side, chimed in. "We've got backup units in place, and the area is under surveillance. Let's make this count."

As they geared up and headed out, the drive to the docks was filled with a focused silence. The early morning fog clung to the water, creating an eerie atmosphere that matched the gravity of their mission. They parked a few blocks away, opting to approach on foot to maintain the element of surprise.

Ethan glanced at Sarah, his voice a low whisper. "We need to be careful. Carla's known for her traps and evasive tactics."

Sarah nodded, her eyes scanning the area. "Stay alert. We move in fast and cover all exits. No one gets away."

They moved through the shadows, their footsteps silent against the damp pavement. The docks were a maze of shipping containers and warehouses, the perfect cover for illicit activities. As they neared the safe house, they could hear the faint sounds of activity inside.

Ethan signaled for the team to spread out and take their positions. "On my mark. Three, two, one—move!"

They burst through the doors, weapons drawn. "Police! Hands up!"

Chaos erupted as the suspects scrambled to flee. Sarah and Ethan moved with practiced precision, taking down suspects and securing the area. In the midst of the chaos, Carla emerged, a tall woman with sharp features and a cold smile.

"Well, well, detectives. I was wondering when you'd show up," she said, her voice dripping with sarcasm.

Sarah kept her weapon trained on Carla. "It's over, Carla. Surrender now, and no one gets hurt."

Carla's smile widened. "You really think it's that simple? You have no idea what you're dealing with."

Ethan stepped forward, his tone firm. "We've dismantled most of your network. It's only a matter of time before we get the rest. Make it easy on yourself."

Carla laughed, a harsh sound that echoed through the warehouse. "You're too late. The real power behind this network is already moving on to the next phase. You think you've won, but you've only just begun to understand the scope of what's happening."

Sarah's eyes narrowed. "Who's behind this? Who is Viper?"

Carla's expression turned icy. "Viper is more than just a person. He's an idea, a force. And you'll never stop him."

Ethan moved in, cuffing Carla's hands behind her back. "We'll see about that."

As they secured the remaining suspects, Sarah and Ethan began searching the warehouse for evidence. They found crates filled with weapons, drugs, and documents detailing their operations. It was clear that Carla's cell had been a major hub for illegal activities.

Back at the precinct, the task force processed the evidence and began debriefing the suspects. The atmosphere was one of grim determination. They had made significant progress, but Carla's words about Viper lingered in the back of their minds.

Garcia approached Sarah and Ethan, holding a file. "We've got something. Carla's been less cooperative than we'd hoped, but we found a lead in the documents we recovered. It mentions a meeting place—a remote cabin outside the city. It could be where Viper is operating from."

Sarah took the file, her mind racing. "We need to check it out. If Viper is there, this could be our chance to take him down once and for all."

Ethan nodded. "I'll get the team ready. We can't afford to waste any time."

As they prepared for the next phase of their mission, the weight of Carla's words hung heavy in the air. The real challenge was just beginning, and they knew that Viper would be their most formidable adversary yet.

Sarah looked at Ethan, her expression resolute. "We've come this far. We'll see this through to the end."

Ethan's eyes met hers, filled with the same determination. "Together."

They stood side by side, ready to face whatever lay ahead. The path was fraught with danger, but they were united in their mission to bring justice to those who sought to disrupt the peace of their city. With each step, they moved closer to uncovering the truth and dismantling the network that had caused so much chaos.

The cabin stood isolated in the woods, a stark contrast to the bustling city they had just left. The air was cool and crisp, filled with the sounds of nature—an eerie calm before the storm. Sarah and Ethan led their team through the dense forest, each step bringing them closer to what they hoped would be the final piece of the puzzle.

Ethan paused, scanning the area with a pair of binoculars. "The cabin looks deserted, but we can't be too careful. This could be a trap."

Sarah nodded, her eyes focused on the distant structure. "We move in quietly. No sudden moves. If Viper is in there, we need to take him by surprise."

They signaled for the team to spread out and take their positions. The approach was slow and methodical, each member of the task force moving with practiced precision. As they reached the perimeter of the cabin, Sarah motioned for everyone to halt.

"We go in on three. One, two, three—move!"

They burst through the door, weapons drawn. "Police! Hands up!" Ethan shouted.

The inside of the cabin was dimly lit, filled with the smell of damp wood and something metallic. There was a moment of silence, then the sound of footsteps retreating deeper into the cabin. Sarah and Ethan moved swiftly, following the sound.

They found Viper in a back room, hunched over a table covered in documents and computer equipment. He looked up, a cold smile spreading across his face. "Detectives. I've been expecting you."

Sarah kept her weapon trained on him. "It's over, Viper. Surrender now, and no one gets hurt."

Viper's smile widened. "You really think it's that simple? You have no idea what you're dealing with."

Ethan stepped forward, his voice firm. "We've dismantled your network. Your associates are in custody. It's only a matter of time before we get you too."

Viper laughed, a chilling sound that echoed through the small room. "You may have won a few battles, but the war is far from over. You see, I'm just a small part of a much larger operation."

Sarah's eyes narrowed. "Who are you working for? Who's behind all of this?"

Viper shook his head. "You'll never understand. This isn't about money or power. It's about changing the world, disrupting the status quo. And you can't stop it."

Ethan moved in, cuffing Viper's hands behind his back. "We'll see about that. You're coming with us."

As they secured Viper and began collecting evidence from the cabin, the sense of accomplishment was tempered by the realization that this might just be the beginning. The documents and equipment suggested a network far larger and more sophisticated than they had anticipated.

Back at the precinct, the task force worked tirelessly to analyze the data they had recovered. The atmosphere was charged with a mix of urgency and determination. They had captured Viper, but now they needed to understand the full scope of his operation.

Garcia approached Sarah and Ethan, holding a stack of printouts. "We've found something. These documents detail a series of planned attacks on major infrastructure—power grids, communication networks, even financial systems. This is bigger than we thought."

Sarah took the printouts, her mind racing. "We need to coordinate with federal agencies. If these attacks go through, the consequences could be catastrophic."

Ethan nodded. "We'll need all the help we can get. This isn't just a local issue anymore."

As they coordinated with federal agents and briefed the task force, the scale of their mission became clear. They were no longer just dealing with a criminal organization; they were facing a threat to national security.

The task force assembled in the briefing room, the tension palpable. Captain Reynolds stood at the front, his expression serious. "We've made significant progress, but this is far from over. The documents recovered from the cabin indicate a series of attacks that could destabilize the entire country. We need to act fast and work together to prevent them."

Sarah stood up, addressing the team. "We've faced incredible challenges before, and we've come out on top. This is our biggest challenge yet, but I have no doubt that we can handle it. We need to stay focused, stay vigilant, and work as a team."

Ethan added, "We have the resources, we have the skills, and we have the determination. Let's use everything at our disposal to bring these people to justice and protect our city—and our country."

The team members nodded, their faces reflecting a mixture of determination and resolve. They knew the road ahead would be difficult, but they were ready to face whatever challenges came their way.

As they prepared to move out, Sarah and Ethan shared a moment of quiet reflection. They had come so far, faced so many obstacles, and grown stronger as a team. The challenges were far from over, but they were ready to face them together.

Ethan looked at Sarah, his expression resolute. "We've got this, Sarah. We'll see it through to the end."

Sarah nodded, her eyes reflecting the same determination. "Together."

They stood side by side, ready to face whatever lay ahead. The path was fraught with danger, but they were united in their mission to bring justice to those who sought to disrupt the peace of their city—and their country. With each step, they moved closer to uncovering the truth and dismantling the network that had caused so much chaos.

The precinct buzzed with urgency as the task force reviewed the data recovered from the cabin. Every screen flickered with maps, documents, and encrypted messages. The weight of their discovery pressed down on everyone, but none more so than Sarah and Ethan.

Sarah stood at the head of the briefing room, addressing the team. "The documents indicate multiple targets, all high-value infrastructure points across the city. We're looking at potential attacks on power grids, communication networks, and financial systems. This isn't just a criminal network; it's a coordinated effort to destabilize the city."

Ethan added, his voice firm, "We need to prioritize these targets and coordinate with federal agencies. Time is not on our side. Let's divide into teams and cover each potential attack point."

Garcia, standing by the door, nodded. "I've already contacted Homeland Security and the FBI. They're sending reinforcements, but we need to act now to prevent any immediate threats."

Sarah's phone buzzed with an incoming call. She glanced at the screen and saw it was from an unknown number. "Sarah Thompson," she answered.

A distorted voice replied, "Detective Thompson, I believe you have something that belongs to me. If you want to avoid a citywide catastrophe, you'll release Viper and drop this investigation."

Sarah's eyes narrowed. "Who is this?"

The voice chuckled. "Someone who can make your life very difficult. You have until midnight to comply, or you'll start seeing the consequences."

The call ended abruptly, leaving Sarah with a knot in her stomach. She turned to the team. "We've just been threatened. They want Viper released and for us to drop the investigation. We can't let that happen."

Ethan's jaw tightened. "They're getting desperate. That means we're close. We need to use this to our advantage."

Sarah nodded. "Agreed. Let's set a trap. We'll act like we're complying, but we'll have teams in place to intercept them."

The team quickly mobilized, setting up surveillance and coordinating with federal agents. The air was thick with tension as they prepared for the showdown.

As the clock ticked closer to midnight, the team was in position. Sarah and Ethan waited in an unmarked van, monitoring the situation. The streets were eerily quiet, the city holding its breath.

Sarah glanced at Ethan. "You ready for this?"

Ethan nodded. "Always. They won't know what hit them."

At precisely midnight, a black SUV pulled up to the designated meeting spot. Two men stepped out, looking around cautiously. Sarah's earpiece crackled to life with Garcia's voice. "We've got eyes on the suspects. Hold your position."

Sarah watched as one of the men pulled out a phone, likely to make the call confirming Viper's release. She took a deep breath, steadying her nerves.

"Now," she whispered into her earpiece.

The task force moved in with swift precision, surrounding the SUV and apprehending the suspects. Ethan and Sarah exited the van, approaching the scene as the men were handcuffed and searched.

One of the men sneered at Sarah. "You think this changes anything? You're too late."

Sarah stared him down. "We'll see about that. Who are you working for?"

The man's sneer widened. "You'll find out soon enough. This city is just the beginning."

Ethan stepped forward. "We can protect you if you cooperate. Tell us who's behind this."

The man laughed, a cold, hollow sound. "You can't protect anyone. They're everywhere."

As the suspects were taken away, Sarah and Ethan regrouped with the team. The night was far from over, and the sense of urgency had only increased. They had managed to intercept a threat, but the battle was clearly escalating.

Back at the precinct, they pored over the new information obtained from the suspects. The leads pointed to a larger, more intricate network than they had anticipated.

Lisa, the tech analyst, approached with a new set of decrypted files. "These documents indicate a central command center. It's heavily fortified and located in an abandoned building in the industrial district."

Sarah's eyes met Ethan's. "This could be it. The heart of their operation."

Ethan nodded. "We need to move fast. If we take out the command center, we can cripple their entire network."

They coordinated with the federal agencies, planning a joint operation to raid the command center. The tension was palpable as they geared up, each member of the task force aware of the high stakes.

As they approached the industrial district, the night was dark and filled with a sense of impending confrontation. The abandoned building loomed ahead, a silent fortress guarding the secrets within.

Sarah signaled for the team to spread out and take their positions. "Stay sharp. We don't know what we're walking into."

Ethan's voice was steady. "On my mark. Three, two, one—move!"

They breached the building, weapons drawn, ready to face whatever awaited them. The operation was a culmination of their efforts, a decisive strike against the shadowy network that had threatened their city. Each step brought them closer to the truth, and each heartbeat echoed with the promise of justice.

The task force moved with silent precision through the darkened corridors of the abandoned building. The air was thick with tension, each step echoing ominously against the concrete walls. Sarah and Ethan led the team, their senses heightened, ready for any sign of danger.

Ethan held up a hand, signaling the team to halt. He pointed to a doorway at the end of the hall, where a faint light flickered. "That's it," he whispered. "The command center."

Sarah nodded, her grip tightening on her weapon. "We go in fast and take control. Be prepared for anything."

They approached the door, their movements synchronized and silent. Ethan counted down with his fingers. Three, two, one. He kicked the door open, and they burst into the room, weapons drawn.

"Police! Hands up!" Sarah shouted.

The room was a hive of activity. Several men and women sat at computer terminals, while others stood around a large table covered in maps and documents. The sudden intrusion threw them into chaos, but they quickly scrambled to reach for weapons.

Ethan fired a warning shot into the ceiling. "I said hands up! Now!"

Reluctantly, the suspects complied, raising their hands as the task force moved in to secure them. Sarah's eyes scanned the room, taking in the sophisticated setup. This was clearly the nerve center of their operations.

One of the men, a tall figure with sharp features and a cold demeanor, glared at them. "You have no idea what you've done. This isn't over."

Sarah approached him, her eyes narrowing. "You're going to tell us everything. Who are you working for?"

The man's lips curled into a sneer. "You think you can stop us? We're just a small part of a much larger plan."

Ethan stepped forward, his voice firm. "Who's behind this? Who is Viper?"

The man laughed, a harsh, grating sound. "Viper is just a name, a symbol. You can take us down, but there will always be others to take our place."

Sarah's patience wore thin. She grabbed the man by the collar, pulling him close. "Tell us what we need to know, or this will get a lot worse for you."

The man's eyes flickered with uncertainty, but he remained defiant. "You're wasting your time."

Ethan motioned for one of the officers to take the man away. "We'll see about that. Secure the others and start going through their files. We need every piece of information we can get."

As the team began to search the room, Sarah and Ethan moved to the large table, examining the maps and documents spread out before them. It was clear that this was the epicenter of their operations, with detailed plans for attacks and a network of connections that spanned far beyond the city.

Sarah pointed to a map marked with several red dots. "These are their targets. Power grids, communication hubs, financial institutions. If they had succeeded, the impact would have been catastrophic."

Ethan nodded, his expression grim. "We've stopped them for now, but we need to find out how deep this goes. There could be other cells operating independently."

Garcia entered the room, carrying a laptop. "We've found something. One of the computers was still logged in. It's connected to a remote server. Lisa's working on tracing it now."

Sarah and Ethan gathered around the laptop, watching as Lisa typed furiously. "I'm in," she said, her eyes focused on the screen. "The server is encrypted, but I'm breaking through. Just a few more seconds."

The tension in the room was palpable as they waited. Finally, Lisa let out a triumphant shout. "Got it! The server is linked to multiple locations across the country. This is much bigger than we thought."

Ethan's jaw tightened. "We need to alert Homeland Security and the FBI. This isn't just a local issue anymore."

Sarah nodded, turning to the team. "Everyone, double your efforts. We need to gather all the information we can and shut this operation down completely. We can't leave any stone unturned."

As the task force worked tirelessly through the night, the scope of the operation became clear. The network was vast, with connections to other cities and even international elements. Each new piece of information painted a broader picture of the threat they were facing.

Hours later, as dawn began to break, Sarah and Ethan stood outside the building, watching the first light of day chase away the darkness. The weight of their discovery hung heavily in the air, but so did the sense of accomplishment.

Ethan broke the silence. "We did it, Sarah. We stopped them."

Sarah nodded, her eyes reflecting both relief and determination. "We did. But this is just the beginning. We've uncovered a much larger threat, and we need to be ready for whatever comes next."

Ethan's gaze met hers, filled with the same resolve. "We will be. Together."

They stood side by side, the dawn of a new day signaling both the end of one battle and the beginning of another. Their mission was far from over, but they were ready to face it, united in their pursuit of justice and the protection of their city and country.

Chapter 23
A New Dawn

The first light of dawn cast a soft glow over the precinct, signaling the end of a long and grueling night. The task force had worked tirelessly, pouring over the data recovered from the abandoned building, tracing the vast network of connections that extended far beyond their city. The enormity of their task was daunting, but the sense of purpose and determination among the team was palpable.

Sarah sat at her desk, her eyes scanning the latest reports. The information they had uncovered painted a picture of a sophisticated and far-reaching operation, one that required coordination and resources on a scale they hadn't fully grasped until now. She felt a mixture of exhaustion and resolve, knowing that their work was far from over.

Ethan approached, holding two steaming cups of coffee. "Thought you could use this," he said, setting one down in front of her.

Sarah looked up, offering a tired but grateful smile. "Thanks, Ethan. How's the team holding up?"

He took a seat across from her, his expression reflecting the same weariness. "They're tired, but focused. We've made significant progress, but there's still a lot to do. The connections we've traced so far indicate operations in multiple cities. It's bigger than we thought."

Sarah nodded, taking a sip of her coffee. The warm liquid provided a brief moment of comfort in the midst of the chaos. "We need to keep pushing. Every lead, every connection—if we miss anything, it could mean disaster."

Garcia walked over, a thick folder in hand. "Morning. I've got the latest updates. We've managed to decrypt more files from the server. It looks like they were planning simultaneous attacks across several major cities."

Sarah took the folder, her eyes narrowing as she flipped through the pages. "This is worse than we anticipated. We need to alert the federal agencies and coordinate a nationwide response."

Ethan agreed. "I'll handle the coordination with Homeland Security and the FBI. We need to move quickly and ensure every potential target is secured."

The precinct buzzed with activity as the team mobilized, each member driven by a shared sense of urgency. Phones rang incessantly, and the low hum of conversations filled the air as they communicated with agencies across the country, sharing vital information and planning their next moves.

Sarah stood at the center of the operations room, her mind racing as she issued directives and fielded questions. "We need to prioritize our resources. Focus on the highest-risk targets first. Make sure every team is fully briefed and equipped."

Ethan returned, a phone pressed to his ear. "I've got Director James from the FBI on the line. They're sending additional agents to assist us. We're also getting support from the National Guard for high-profile targets."

Sarah nodded, feeling a sense of relief. "Good. We'll need all the help we can get. Make sure our teams are in constant communication with the federal agents. We can't afford any mistakes."

As the day progressed, the task force continued to gather and analyze data, their efforts revealing more about the structure and reach of the network they were up against. Each new piece of information brought them closer to understanding the full scope of the threat, but also highlighted the challenges they still faced.

Lisa, the tech analyst, approached with a worried expression. "Sarah, we've identified another potential attack point. A major financial hub in the city. If they hit it, the economic impact would be devastating."

Sarah's eyes hardened. "We can't let that happen. Mobilize a team immediately and secure the location. We'll coordinate with the National Guard to ensure it's fully protected."

The hours slipped by in a blur of activity and urgency. The weight of responsibility pressed heavily on Sarah and Ethan as they navigated the complexities of the operation. But amidst the chaos, there was a growing sense of solidarity and resolve. They were in this together, fighting to protect their city and country from a threat unlike any they had faced before.

As evening approached, the team gathered for a brief moment of respite. The room was filled with the low murmur of conversations, the shared experience of a long and challenging day bonding them in ways words couldn't express.

Sarah looked around, feeling a deep sense of pride and gratitude for her team. "We've made incredible progress, but there's still work to be done. Stay focused, stay vigilant, and remember—we're in this together."

Ethan placed a reassuring hand on her shoulder. "We've got this, Sarah. We'll see it through."

The task force dispersed, each member returning to their posts with renewed determination. The night was far from over, but they were ready to face whatever challenges lay ahead, united in their mission to bring justice and protect the peace of their city and country.

As the sun set, casting long shadows across the precinct, Sarah and Ethan stood side by side, their resolve unwavering. They had come this far, faced countless obstacles, and grown stronger with each challenge. And as they prepared for the next phase of their mission, they knew that together, they could overcome anything.

The precinct's operations room buzzed with the frenetic energy of a team on the brink of a major breakthrough. Screens flickered with real-time data, maps, and encrypted messages. The urgency was palpable as Sarah and Ethan coordinated with federal agencies to secure the identified targets.

Sarah stood at the center of the room, issuing directives. "We need all teams on high alert. Prioritize the financial hubs and communication centers. Ensure every location has backup."

Ethan nodded, speaking into his headset. "Team Alpha, proceed to the primary financial hub. Secure the perimeter and set up surveillance. Team Bravo, you're on the communication center. Maintain a low profile but be ready to act."

Garcia approached, his expression tense. "We've got another update. There's chatter about a possible attack on a major transportation hub. This could be a coordinated effort to paralyze the city's infrastructure."

Sarah's eyes narrowed. "We can't let that happen. Dispatch Team Charlie to the transportation hub. Make sure they cover all entry and exit points."

Ethan relayed the orders, his voice steady despite the mounting pressure. "Team Charlie, your new objective is the transportation hub. Full lockdown, no one in or out without clearance."

Lisa, the tech analyst, called out from her station. "I've intercepted another encrypted message. It's mentioning a 'final phase' set to commence at midnight. They're planning something big."

Sarah's heart raced. "Can you pinpoint the origin of the message?"

Lisa's fingers flew over the keyboard. "Give me a second... Got it! It's originating from an abandoned warehouse on the outskirts of the city."

Ethan's eyes met Sarah's. "We need to hit that warehouse. If this is their command center, we can cut the head off the snake."

Sarah nodded. "Garcia, assemble a strike team. We move in fast and hard. No room for error."

Garcia spoke into his radio. "Strike team, assemble at the designated location. We're heading to the warehouse. Full tactical gear. This is it, people."

As the team geared up, Sarah and Ethan reviewed the plan. "We go in silent," Sarah said. "We don't know what we're walking into, so be prepared for anything."

Ethan checked his weapon. "Silent but ready. Let's end this."

The drive to the warehouse was filled with a tense silence. Each member of the team was lost in their thoughts, preparing for the imminent confrontation. The warehouse loomed ahead, a dark silhouette against the night sky.

Sarah signaled for the team to spread out. "Remember, we need to take control quickly and efficiently. Ethan, you take the lead."

Ethan nodded, leading the team to the entrance. "On my mark. Three, two, one—move!"

They breached the door, weapons drawn. "Police! Hands up!" Ethan shouted.

The warehouse erupted into chaos. Figures scrambled to flee, but the task force was quick and precise. Sarah moved through the shadows, her weapon trained on the fleeing suspects.

A man emerged from the darkness, a sinister smile on his face. "Welcome, detectives. You're just in time for the grand finale."

Sarah kept her weapon steady. "Who are you? What's the final phase?"

The man laughed. "You think you've won, but this is just the beginning. The final phase is already in motion. You can't stop it."

Ethan stepped forward, his voice cold. "Tell us what you're planning, or we'll find out the hard way."

The man's smile faded. "You're too late. The city will descend into chaos at midnight. All your efforts will be for nothing."

Sarah's mind raced. "What's the target?"

The man remained silent, defiant.

Ethan moved closer, his tone menacing. "We will stop you. One way or another."

The man laughed again. "Midnight. Watch the city burn."

Sarah and Ethan exchanged a look. They didn't have much time. "Secure him," Sarah ordered. "We need to find out what he's planning."

As the team apprehended the suspects, Sarah and Ethan regrouped. "We need to warn the city," Sarah said. "Activate all emergency protocols. We have less than an hour."

Ethan nodded, speaking into his headset. "All units, this is a code red. Prepare for immediate deployment to all critical infrastructure points. This is not a drill."

Garcia approached with urgency. "We've decrypted more messages. They're targeting multiple locations: power plants, water supply, and key government buildings."

Sarah's eyes widened. "We need to split our forces. Ethan, take a team to the power plant. Garcia, you cover the water supply. I'll handle the government buildings."

Ethan grabbed his gear. "Stay safe, Sarah. We'll get through this."

Sarah nodded, determination in her eyes. "We will. Let's move."

The teams dispersed, each heading to their designated locations. Sarah drove through the city, her mind focused on the task at hand. The stakes had never been higher, and failure was not an option.

As she approached the government building, she saw the faint glimmer of dawn on the horizon. The new day symbolized hope, a chance to thwart the impending disaster. She parked her car and rallied her team.

"Stay sharp," she said, scanning the surroundings. "We need to secure this area and ensure no one gets through."

Her phone buzzed with an update from Ethan. "We're in position at the power plant. No sign of trouble yet, but we're ready."

Sarah replied, "Good. Keep me posted. Garcia, status update?"

Garcia's voice came through, calm but alert. "We've secured the water supply. Extra patrols in place. All clear so far."

Sarah felt a surge of pride for her team. They were ready, united, and determined. As she prepared for the final showdown, she knew that together, they could overcome any challenge.

––––––––

Sarah stood in front of the government building, the early dawn casting long shadows across the city streets. Her team was positioned around the perimeter, their eyes scanning for any sign of trouble. The urgency of the situation weighed heavily on her mind, but she remained focused, ready to face whatever came next.

Her phone buzzed with an incoming call. "Sarah, it's Ethan. We've secured the power plant. No unusual activity so far, but we're staying alert."

"Good to hear, Ethan. Keep me updated," Sarah replied, her eyes never leaving the building in front of her.

Garcia's voice crackled over the radio. "Water supply is secure. Extra patrols are in place. All clear on our end."

Sarah nodded, feeling a slight sense of relief. "Stay vigilant, everyone. We're not out of the woods yet."

Suddenly, a figure emerged from the shadows, approaching the building. Sarah's heart raced as she recognized the man from the warehouse. "Hold your position," she whispered into her radio, watching him closely.

The man stopped at the entrance, looking around before speaking into a hidden earpiece. "We're in position. Prepare for phase one."

Sarah's mind raced. "He's communicating with someone. We need to intercept that signal."

Lisa's voice came through her earpiece. "I'm on it, Sarah. Give me a minute."

The man entered the building, and Sarah signaled for her team to move in. "We need to stop him before he can initiate whatever they're planning. Move quietly and stay low."

They approached the entrance, their movements silent and coordinated. Sarah whispered into her radio, "Team Alpha, move to the left. Team Bravo, cover the right. We'll go in through the main entrance."

As they breached the door, the man turned, surprise flickering across his face. "Detective Thompson. I should have known."

Sarah kept her weapon trained on him. "It's over. Surrender now."

The man smirked. "You're too late. The countdown has already begun."

Ethan's voice came through the earpiece. "Sarah, I've intercepted the signal. They're coordinating a series of explosions. The first one is set to go off in ten minutes."

Sarah's heart pounded. "Where's the detonator?"

The man laughed. "You'll never find it in time."

Ethan spoke again, urgency in his voice. "We're tracing the signal. It's coming from inside the building. We need to find it now."

Sarah gestured for her team to search the area. "Fan out and look for anything suspicious. We don't have much time."

As they searched the building, the tension grew. Every second felt like an eternity. Finally, one of the officers called out. "I've found something! It's a device, hidden in the basement."

Sarah and Ethan rushed to the basement, where a small device was secured to the wall. Wires snaked out from it, leading to various parts of the building. Ethan examined it closely. "It's a remote detonator. We need to disarm it carefully."

Sarah watched as Ethan worked, her heart in her throat. "Can you do it?"

Ethan nodded, his hands steady. "I need to cut the right wires in the right order. One mistake, and this whole place goes up."

The team held their breath as Ethan carefully cut each wire, the seconds ticking away. Finally, with a snip, the device powered down. Ethan let out a sigh of relief. "It's disarmed."

Sarah's earpiece crackled to life with Lisa's voice. "I've traced the signal to another location. They have a backup plan. We need to move quickly."

Sarah turned to her team. "You heard her. We need to find the secondary device and disarm it. Let's move!"

As they raced to the new location, the urgency was palpable. They reached the building, a rundown warehouse on the edge of the city. Sarah signaled for her team to surround the building. "This is it. We go in fast and take control. No mistakes."

They breached the door, weapons drawn. "Police! Hands up!" Sarah shouted.

The room was filled with computer equipment and several men working frantically. One of them reached for a weapon, but Ethan was quicker. "Don't even think about it."

Sarah approached the leader, her eyes steely. "Where's the device?"

The leader sneered. "You think you've won? There are more of us than you can count. We'll never stop."

Ethan stepped forward, his voice cold. "Where. Is. The. Device?"

The leader hesitated, then nodded toward a back room. "You're too late."

Sarah and Ethan moved quickly, finding the device hidden behind a stack of crates. Ethan examined it, his expression tense. "It's the same setup as before. We need to disarm it."

As Ethan worked, Sarah kept her weapon trained on the door, her senses heightened. Finally, Ethan cut the last wire, and the device powered down. "We did it."

Sarah's earpiece crackled with Garcia's voice. "All clear on our end. The city is safe."

Sarah let out a breath she didn't realize she'd been holding. "Good job, everyone. Let's get these guys back to the precinct."

As they escorted the suspects out of the warehouse, the first light of dawn broke through the clouds, casting a golden glow over the city. Sarah and Ethan stood side by side, watching as the city came to life.

Ethan looked at Sarah, a smile tugging at his lips. "We did it."

Sarah nodded, a sense of accomplishment washing over her. "Yes, we did. Together."

The city was safe, but they knew their work was far from over. As the sun rose, they prepared to face whatever challenges lay ahead, united in their mission to protect and serve.

Back at the precinct, the atmosphere was a mixture of relief and exhaustion. The task force had successfully thwarted the coordinated attacks, but the sense of urgency still lingered. Sarah and Ethan stood in the operations room, surrounded by their team, as they debriefed the events of the morning.

Garcia approached, a weary but satisfied expression on his face. "All suspects are in custody. Homeland Security and the FBI are coordinating with us to ensure there are no further threats."

Sarah nodded, her mind still racing with the events of the past few hours. "Good work, everyone. This was a team effort, and we couldn't have done it without each of you."

Ethan placed a reassuring hand on her shoulder. "We made a great team. But we need to stay vigilant. This network is bigger than we thought."

Lisa, the tech analyst, joined them, holding a tablet. "I've been going through the data we recovered from the warehouse. There are still a lot of unanswered questions, but we've managed to disrupt their operations significantly."

Sarah looked around at her team, a sense of pride swelling within her. "Let's take a moment to appreciate what we've accomplished. We've saved countless lives today. But our work isn't done. We need to stay on top of this and ensure we dismantle every part of their network."

Garcia nodded. "We'll keep digging. Every piece of information we uncover brings us closer to shutting them down for good."

Ethan turned to Sarah, his eyes reflecting the same determination she felt. "We've got momentum on our side. Let's use it."

Sarah agreed. "Absolutely. Let's get some rest and regroup. We'll hit the ground running tomorrow."

As the team dispersed, Sarah and Ethan headed to the break room, where they finally allowed themselves a moment of respite. The adrenaline was wearing off, leaving behind a bone-deep exhaustion.

Ethan handed Sarah a bottle of water. "You did great out there, Sarah. I couldn't have asked for a better partner."

Sarah smiled, taking the bottle. "Thanks, Ethan. We make a good team. I couldn't have done it without you."

Ethan leaned back in his chair, a thoughtful expression on his face. "You know, I've been thinking. This whole operation has shown us just how important it is to stay connected and work together. We need to keep building on that."

Sarah nodded. "Agreed. It's easy to get caught up in the daily grind and forget why we do this. But today reminded me of our purpose."

Ethan's gaze softened. "We've been through a lot together, and we've come out stronger. No matter what comes next, I know we can handle it."

Sarah felt a wave of gratitude. "Thank you, Ethan. For everything."

Their moment of reflection was interrupted by Garcia, who entered the room with a determined look. "Sorry to interrupt, but we've got new intel. Looks like there's still some activity we need to address."

Sarah and Ethan stood, ready to dive back into the fray. "What do you have, Garcia?" Sarah asked.

Garcia handed them a file. "We've identified a potential safe house where some of the remaining network members might be hiding. It's in a remote location, heavily guarded. We'll need to plan a careful approach."

Ethan glanced at Sarah. "Looks like our break is over."

Sarah took the file, her eyes scanning the details. "Let's get the team together. We need to move quickly and decisively."

Within minutes, the task force was reassembled, and Sarah outlined the plan. "We'll approach the safe house from multiple angles. Our goal is to capture the suspects and gather any remaining intel. This could be our chance to finally dismantle the rest of the network."

Ethan added, "Stay alert and communicate. We don't know what we're walking into, so be prepared for anything."

As they geared up and prepared to head out, the sense of determination was palpable. The team moved with a renewed sense of purpose, each member driven by the shared goal of protecting their city and bringing the criminals to justice.

The drive to the safe house was filled with a tense silence. Sarah and Ethan led the convoy, their minds focused on the mission ahead. The safe house came into view, a secluded building surrounded by dense forest.

Ethan signaled for the team to stop. "We'll go in on foot from here. Remember, stealth is key."

They moved through the trees, their movements silent and coordinated. As they approached the safe house, Sarah signaled for the team to take their positions. "On my mark," she whispered.

They breached the door, weapons drawn. "Police! Hands up!" Sarah shouted.

The suspects inside scrambled to react, but the task force was too quick. Within moments, the room was secured, and the suspects were in custody. Sarah and Ethan began searching the premises for any remaining evidence.

Ethan opened a hidden compartment in the floor, revealing a stash of documents and electronic devices. "Looks like we hit the jackpot."

Sarah nodded, feeling a sense of triumph. "Let's get this back to the precinct. We've got a lot of work ahead of us."

As they escorted the suspects out and secured the evidence, the weight of their mission settled over them once more. They had made significant progress, but the fight was far from over.

Back at the precinct, the team began analyzing the new data, their efforts focused and relentless. Sarah and Ethan stood side by side, ready to face whatever challenges lay ahead.

Ethan looked at Sarah, a determined glint in his eyes. "We're getting closer. We won't stop until this network is completely dismantled."

Sarah nodded, feeling a renewed sense of purpose. "Together, we'll see it through to the end."

As they dove back into the investigation, the city outside began to stir, the first light of dawn breaking through the clouds. The new day brought with it a sense of hope and determination, a reminder of why they fought so hard to protect their city.

And as Sarah and Ethan continued their work, they knew that whatever challenges lay ahead, they would face them united, driven by their shared mission to uphold justice and safeguard the peace of their home.

Chapter 24
The Calm Before

The precinct was unusually quiet the following morning. The intense flurry of activity from the night before had given way to a calm, almost eerie silence. The dawn light filtered through the large windows, casting long shadows across the floor. Sarah sat at her desk, the soft glow of her computer screen illuminating her face as she reviewed the latest reports.

Ethan approached, carrying two cups of coffee. "Morning," he said, setting one down in front of her. "How are you holding up?"

Sarah took the cup, offering a small smile. "Better now, thanks. Just going through the data from last night. We've made some significant progress, but there's still a lot to sift through."

Ethan nodded, taking a seat beside her. "We've got a few hours before the briefing with Captain Reynolds. Anything stand out?"

Sarah leaned back, rubbing her temples. "A few things. We've identified several key figures in the network, but they're scattered. It's going to take a coordinated effort to bring them all in."

Ethan took a sip of his coffee, his brow furrowing. "I'll reach out to our contacts in Homeland Security and the FBI. We'll need their resources to track these guys down."

Sarah glanced at the clock on the wall. "Good idea. We need to stay ahead of this. The longer they're out there, the more dangerous it gets."

Just then, Garcia walked in, holding a folder. "Morning, detectives. Got the latest intel from our friends at the Bureau. Thought you might want to see this before the briefing."

Sarah took the folder, quickly scanning its contents. "Interesting. It looks like they've tracked some of the key players to a safe house in the northern part of the city. We could be looking at another raid."

Ethan nodded. "We need to be careful. If they know we're closing in, they might scatter again."

Garcia leaned against the desk. "I've already put a team on standby. Just say the word."

Sarah handed the folder back to Garcia. "Let's go over this with the Captain. We need to make sure we're all on the same page."

The three of them made their way to the briefing room, where Captain Reynolds was waiting. He looked up as they entered, a look of determination on his face. "Morning, team. What have you got for me?"

Sarah took a seat, laying out the key points. "We've tracked several high-level members of the network to a safe house in the northern part of the city. It's heavily guarded, but if we move quickly, we can take them down before they have a chance to regroup."

Reynolds nodded, his eyes narrowing. "What's the plan?"

Ethan leaned forward. "We'll need a coordinated strike. Our team will handle the entry and capture, while Homeland Security and the FBI provide support and cover any escape routes."

Garcia added, "We've got a team on standby, ready to move at a moment's notice. We'll need to act fast and hit them hard."

Reynolds considered this for a moment, then nodded. "Alright. Let's move forward with the plan. Make sure everyone is briefed and ready. We can't afford any mistakes."

As the team dispersed to prepare for the raid, Sarah felt a renewed sense of determination. They were getting closer to dismantling the network, but the stakes were higher than ever. Each step brought them closer to the endgame, and there was no room for error.

Back at her desk, Sarah reviewed the details of the operation, her mind racing with the possibilities. She knew that this raid could be a turning point in their investigation, but it also carried significant risks. They were walking into unknown territory, and anything could happen.

Ethan approached, his expression serious. "Ready for this?"

Sarah looked up, meeting his gaze. "As ready as I'll ever be. Let's do this."

They gathered the team, issuing final instructions and ensuring everyone was clear on their roles. The air was thick with anticipation as they geared up, each member of the task force focused and ready.

As they drove to the northern part of the city, the sun was just beginning to rise, casting a warm glow over the buildings. The calm of the early morning was a stark contrast to the tension inside the vehicles. Sarah and Ethan rode in silence, mentally preparing for the operation ahead.

They arrived at the location, a nondescript building that blended seamlessly with its surroundings. Sarah signaled for the team to take their positions, her heart pounding with adrenaline. This was it—the moment they had been working towards.

"On my mark," she whispered into her radio. "Three, two, one—move!"

The team moved with practiced precision, breaching the entrance and spreading out to secure the area. Shouts of "Police! Hands up!" echoed through the building as they swept through each room, clearing it of suspects.

In the back room, they found the high-level members they had been searching for. Sarah and Ethan approached cautiously, their weapons drawn. "It's over," Sarah said firmly. "Surrender now."

One of the men, a tall figure with a cold expression, smirked. "You think you've won? This is just the beginning."

Ethan stepped forward. "We'll see about that. You're coming with us."

As they secured the suspects and began searching the premises for additional evidence, Sarah felt a sense of accomplishment. They had made significant progress, but she knew there was still a long road ahead.

Back at the precinct, the team began processing the evidence and debriefing the suspects. The mood was one of cautious optimism—they had achieved a major victory, but the fight was far from over.

Sarah and Ethan stood outside the precinct, watching as the sun climbed higher into the sky. The new day symbolized a new phase in their investigation, filled with both challenges and opportunities.

Ethan looked at Sarah, a smile playing at the corners of his mouth. "We did good today."

Sarah nodded, feeling a sense of pride. "Yeah, we did. But there's still work to be done."

Ethan's eyes reflected the same determination she felt. "We'll see it through, Sarah. Together."

As they turned to head back inside, the precinct buzzed with renewed energy. The task force was ready for whatever came next, united in their mission to protect and serve.

Back at the precinct, the atmosphere was charged with a mix of anticipation and tension. The task force was fully engaged in processing the evidence and interrogating the suspects from the morning raid. Sarah and Ethan were at the center of it all, coordinating the next steps and ensuring that no detail was overlooked.

Sarah sat at her desk, her eyes scanning through a mountain of paperwork. The recent operation had been a success, but the information they had gathered pointed to even more complex and widespread activities. Her thoughts were interrupted by a knock on the door.

"Got a minute?" Ethan asked, stepping into her office.

Sarah looked up, pushing aside the files. "Sure, what's up?"

Ethan closed the door behind him, his expression serious. "I've been going through the interrogation reports. One of the suspects mentioned something about a 'final shipment' that's supposed to go down tonight. It sounds like it could be significant."

Sarah leaned forward, her interest piqued. "Did they say where?"

Ethan shook his head. "No, but they hinted that it's happening at one of the major shipping docks. If it's as important as they're making it out to be, we can't afford to miss it."

Sarah nodded, a plan already forming in her mind. "We need to act fast. Get Garcia and Lisa in here. We'll need their input on this."

Minutes later, Garcia and Lisa joined them, their faces reflecting the urgency of the situation.

"What's the latest?" Garcia asked, settling into a chair.

Ethan filled them in. "One of our suspects mentioned a major shipment going down tonight at the docks. We don't have a specific location, but we know it's happening soon."

Lisa's fingers flew over her tablet. "I can pull up the shipping manifests and cross-reference them with known aliases and company names we've been tracking. It might give us a lead."

Sarah nodded. "Do it. Garcia, I need you to coordinate with the port authorities. We'll need their cooperation to secure the area and intercept this shipment."

Garcia stood, ready to act. "Consider it done."

As Lisa worked her digital magic, Sarah and Ethan discussed their approach. "We'll need to split the team," Sarah said. "One group at the docks to intercept the shipment, and another on standby to respond to any diversions they might try to create."

Ethan agreed. "I'll lead the team at the docks. You handle the standby unit. We'll stay in constant communication."

An hour later, the task force was assembled and briefed. The tension in the room was palpable as they geared up for what could be a pivotal operation.

Ethan addressed the team. "We're dealing with dangerous individuals. Stay sharp and follow the plan. Our priority is to intercept the shipment and gather as much intel as possible. Any questions?"

A young officer raised her hand. "What if we encounter resistance?"

Sarah stepped in. "We proceed with caution. Use non-lethal force if possible, but don't hesitate to protect yourselves. We need to get this right."

With the plan set, the teams moved out. The drive to the docks was filled with a tense silence, each member of the task force mentally preparing for the operation ahead. The sun was beginning to set, casting a warm glow over the city as they approached the sprawling complex of shipping containers and cranes.

Ethan's voice crackled over the radio. "Team Alpha, take positions near the entrance. Team Bravo, you're with me. We'll sweep the area and look for any suspicious activity."

Sarah responded from the standby unit. "Copy that. We're in position and ready to move if needed."

The teams spread out, moving through the shadows with practiced precision. The docks were a labyrinth of towering containers and narrow passageways, the perfect setting for an illicit transaction.

Ethan's team moved quietly, scanning the area for signs of the shipment. They spotted a group of men near one of the larger containers, their movements furtive and hurried.

Ethan signaled for his team to approach. "This is it. Stay alert."

As they neared the group, one of the men looked up, his eyes widening in alarm. "Police! Hands up!" Ethan shouted, his weapon drawn.

The men scattered, but the task force was ready. They moved quickly, securing the area and apprehending the suspects. One of the men, a burly figure with a scar across his face, tried to resist, but Ethan was on him in an instant, bringing him to the ground.

Sarah's voice came through the radio. "We've got movement near the eastern side. Team Bravo, head over there and secure the perimeter."

Ethan nodded, signaling for part of his team to move. "Roger that. Bravo, on me."

They sprinted across the docks, arriving just in time to see a group of men loading crates into an unmarked truck. Ethan's team moved in, surrounding the suspects and cutting off any escape routes.

"Drop your weapons!" Ethan commanded. The men hesitated, then complied, realizing they were outnumbered and outgunned.

Sarah and the standby unit arrived moments later, securing the area and ensuring all suspects were apprehended. As they began to inspect the crates, they found them filled with illegal weapons and contraband, confirming their suspicions.

Ethan turned to Sarah, a look of satisfaction on his face. "We did it. This shipment was meant to fuel their operations. We've dealt them a major blow."

Sarah nodded, feeling a sense of accomplishment. "But we're not done yet. We need to interrogate these guys and find out what else they're planning."

Back at the precinct, the task force worked late into the night, processing the evidence and questioning the suspects. The atmosphere was one of determination and resolve. They had made significant progress, but the battle was far from over.

Sarah and Ethan stood in the operations room, reviewing the latest reports. "We've uncovered a lot, but there's still more to do," Sarah said, her voice steady.

Ethan nodded. "We'll get there. One step at a time."

As the first light of dawn began to break, the task force continued their work, united in their mission to bring justice and protect their city from the looming threat. The challenges were far from over, but they were ready to face them head-on, together.

The precinct hummed with the energy of a team that had tasted victory but knew the battle was far from over. Sarah and Ethan worked side by side, poring over the latest intel from the intercepted shipment. The evidence pointed to a larger conspiracy, one that required careful navigation and relentless pursuit.

Sarah looked up from the documents spread across her desk. "We need to piece together how this shipment fits into the larger network. It can't be just about the weapons. There's something bigger at play here."

Ethan nodded, his brow furrowed in concentration. "Agreed. I've been reviewing the interrogation transcripts. The suspects are tight-lipped, but a few of them mentioned a name—'The Broker.' It sounds like he's a key player."

Garcia approached, holding a tablet. "Got something interesting here. One of the suspects had a burner phone with messages from an encrypted number. Our tech team managed to decrypt some of it. They're coordinating another meeting, likely to regroup after the bust."

Sarah's eyes lit up. "Do we have a location?"

Garcia nodded. "An old warehouse on the outskirts of the city. It's remote, perfect for a clandestine meeting."

Ethan glanced at Sarah. "We need to move fast. If 'The Broker' is involved, we can't let this opportunity slip."

Sarah stood, grabbing her jacket. "Let's assemble the team. We're not letting these guys get away."

Minutes later, the task force was briefed and ready. The drive to the warehouse was tense, the sun setting behind them and casting long shadows on the road ahead. The anticipation of the impending confrontation was palpable.

Ethan broke the silence. "This could be our chance to cut off the head of the snake. 'The Broker' might be the key to unraveling the entire network."

Sarah nodded, her mind focused on the task ahead. "We need to be prepared for anything. They'll be on high alert after the bust. We go in fast and hard."

They arrived at the warehouse, a dilapidated structure surrounded by overgrown weeds and rusting metal. Sarah signaled for the team to take their positions. "Remember, stay sharp. We move on my mark."

Ethan spoke into his radio. "Team Alpha, cover the exits. Team Bravo, you're with me. We're going in through the main entrance."

The team moved silently through the shadows, their weapons at the ready. Sarah's heart pounded as they approached the door. She signaled for Ethan to proceed.

Ethan kicked the door open, his voice ringing out. "Police! Hands up!"

Chaos erupted inside the warehouse. Men scrambled to reach for weapons, but the task force was swift and precise. Ethan and his team secured the entrance while Sarah moved deeper into the building, her eyes scanning for any sign of 'The Broker.'

She found him in a back room, surrounded by a group of armed men. His face was calm, almost amused. "Detective Thompson, I presume. I've heard a lot about you."

Sarah kept her weapon trained on him. "It's over, Broker. Surrender now, and no one gets hurt."

The Broker smiled. "You think it's that simple? My operations span continents. Taking me down won't stop anything."

Ethan entered the room, flanking Sarah. "We'll see about that. You're coming with us."

The Broker's smile faded. "I wouldn't be so sure." He nodded to his men, who lunged forward, weapons drawn.

A firefight ensued, the sound of gunfire echoing through the warehouse. Sarah and Ethan moved with practiced precision, taking down the armed men with calculated efficiency. The Broker tried to flee, but Ethan was on him in an instant, tackling him to the ground.

As they secured The Broker and his remaining men, Sarah felt a rush of adrenaline. They had captured a key figure, but the operation wasn't over. They needed to extract every piece of information he had.

Back at the precinct, The Broker sat in the interrogation room, his demeanor calm despite the situation. Sarah and Ethan stood outside, watching through the one-way glass.

Ethan turned to Sarah. "He's not going to break easily. We need to approach this carefully."

Sarah nodded. "Let's start by showing him what we have. Make him realize how much trouble he's in."

They entered the room, and The Broker looked up, his expression unreadable. "Detectives. Ready to negotiate?"

Sarah sat down across from him, placing a file on the table. "We have enough evidence to put you away for a long time. But if you cooperate, things might go easier for you."

The Broker leaned back, considering her words. "And what exactly do you want from me?"

Ethan leaned forward. "Names, locations, operations. We want everything. You give us that, and we can talk about a deal."

The Broker's eyes narrowed. "You think you can dismantle my entire network with a few names and locations? You're naive."

Sarah met his gaze, unflinching. "We've already taken down your shipment. Your men are in custody. Your network is crumbling. Help us, and maybe you can salvage something from this."

There was a long pause, the tension in the room thick. Finally, The Broker sighed. "Alright. I'll talk. But this doesn't end with me. There are others out there, more powerful than you can imagine."

Ethan nodded. "We'll handle them. Start talking."

As The Broker began to divulge the details of his operations, Sarah and Ethan exchanged a glance. They had made significant progress, but this was just the beginning. The road ahead was fraught with challenges, but they were ready to face them together, determined to bring justice to those who sought to disrupt their city's peace.

The night wore on as they gathered every piece of information, each revelation bringing them closer to dismantling the network that had plagued their city. The sense of purpose and resolve among the team was stronger than ever, united in their mission to protect and serve.

The interrogation of The Broker had given the task force a wealth of new information. As dawn broke over the city, Sarah and Ethan reviewed the details, their exhaustion overshadowed by a sense of accomplishment. The precinct was abuzz with activity as the team worked tirelessly to follow up on the new leads.

Sarah sat at her desk, her fingers tapping rhythmically on the keyboard as she entered data into the system. She looked up as Ethan approached, a cup of coffee in each hand. "Thought you could use this," he said, handing her one.

"Thanks," Sarah replied, taking a grateful sip. "We've got a lot to go through. The Broker's intel is extensive."

Ethan nodded, pulling up a chair beside her. "It's almost overwhelming, but this is the break we needed. We've identified several key figures and locations. If we move quickly, we can dismantle the entire network."

Sarah clicked on a document, bringing up a list of names. "These are the top players. We need to prioritize them. Start with the ones who pose the greatest threat."

Ethan leaned over, studying the list. "Agreed. We should also coordinate with the federal agencies. This operation is too big for us to handle alone."

Just then, Garcia walked in, a determined look on his face. "I've spoken with Homeland Security and the FBI. They're ready to assist. We've got backup units and additional resources on standby."

Sarah felt a surge of relief. "Good. We'll need all the help we can get. Let's organize the teams and start planning the raids."

Ethan stood, ready for action. "I'll brief the teams. We need to be ready to move out within the hour."

The task force assembled in the briefing room, the atmosphere charged with anticipation. Sarah and Ethan outlined the plan, detailing the key targets and the roles each team would play.

"We'll be hitting multiple locations simultaneously," Sarah explained. "Our goal is to capture the leaders and secure any evidence. Stay focused and follow the plan. We can't afford any mistakes."

Ethan added, "Remember, these people are dangerous. Use caution and watch each other's backs. We've come this far, and we're not backing down now."

The teams nodded, their expressions resolute. They dispersed to gear up and prepare for the operation, the weight of the mission heavy on their shoulders.

As Sarah and Ethan headed to the staging area, Sarah glanced at her partner. "We've faced a lot of challenges together, but this might be the biggest one yet."

Ethan met her gaze, a determined look in his eyes. "We're ready for it, Sarah. We'll see this through."

The drive to the first target was tense, the silence in the vehicle underscoring the gravity of the situation. They arrived at a luxurious mansion on the outskirts of the city, the suspected hideout of one of the key figures in the network.

Sarah signaled for the team to take their positions. "Remember, stay sharp. We don't know what we're walking into."

Ethan led the way, his weapon at the ready. They breached the front door, moving swiftly through the opulent interior. "Police! Hands up!" Ethan shouted.

The occupants scattered, but the task force was quick and efficient. Within minutes, they had secured the area and apprehended the suspect, a man with a commanding presence and a look of cold calculation.

Sarah approached him, her eyes steely. "You're under arrest. We know about your involvement in the network. It's over."

The man sneered. "You think this changes anything? There are more of us. You'll never stop the operation."

Ethan stepped forward. "We'll see about that. You're coming with us."

As they escorted the suspect to the waiting vehicle, Sarah couldn't shake the feeling that this was just the beginning. They had made significant progress, but the road ahead was still fraught with challenges.

The rest of the day was a blur of coordinated raids and strategic captures. Each successful operation brought them closer to dismantling the network, but it also revealed the vast scope of the conspiracy. The task force worked tirelessly, driven by their shared mission to bring justice and protect their city.

Back at the precinct, the team gathered for a debriefing. Captain Reynolds stood at the front, his expression reflecting a mix of pride and determination. "You've all done incredible work. We've made significant progress, but there's still more to be done. Stay vigilant and stay focused. We're not finished yet."

Sarah and Ethan exchanged a look of mutual resolve. They had come a long way, but they knew their journey was far from over. As the team dispersed to continue their work, Sarah felt a renewed sense of purpose.

She turned to Ethan. "We've faced a lot together, but I have a feeling the biggest challenges are still ahead."

Ethan nodded, a confident smile on his face. "We'll face them, just like we've faced everything else—together."

As they prepared for the next phase of their mission, the precinct buzzed with activity and determination. The task force was ready, united in their pursuit of justice and the protection of their city. The night was long, but their resolve was unwavering, and they knew that together, they could overcome any obstacle that lay ahead.

Chapter 25
The Unseen Threat

The precinct buzzed with a sense of urgency. The task force had spent days dismantling the network, capturing key figures and uncovering layers of the conspiracy that had threatened their city. Sarah and Ethan had barely slept, their determination to see this through fueling their every move.

Sarah stood at the operations center, her eyes glued to a large map dotted with pins marking the locations of recent raids. Ethan joined her, holding a stack of fresh reports. "Got the latest intel from the interrogations. We've confirmed that 'The Broker' was funneling resources to an even higher figure. Someone they only refer to as 'The Architect.'"

Sarah's eyes narrowed as she processed the information. "The Architect. Any idea who this person is?"

Ethan shook his head. "Not yet. But we know they're the mastermind behind the entire network. Everything points back to them."

Garcia approached, looking grim. "We've got another problem. Our tech team intercepted a communication that indicates 'The Architect' knows we're closing in. They're planning something big, and soon."

Sarah's heart pounded. "What's the target?"

Garcia handed her a tablet. "We don't have the specifics yet, but the message mentioned 'the heart of the city.' It could be an attack on a major landmark or infrastructure."

Ethan's jaw tightened. "We need to find out where and when. We can't let this happen."

Sarah nodded, her mind racing. "We'll need to divide our resources. Ethan, you and Garcia focus on gathering intel and pinpointing the target. I'll coordinate with Homeland Security and the FBI to increase security around key locations."

As they moved to action, the atmosphere in the precinct became even more charged. The stakes had never been higher, and every second counted.

Hours later, Sarah was on the phone with Director James from Homeland Security. "We need immediate support. Increase patrols around major landmarks and infrastructure. We have credible intel about a potential attack."

James's voice was steady but urgent. "Understood. We're mobilizing additional units now. Keep us updated on any developments."

As she hung up, Ethan approached, his face etched with concern. "We've narrowed it down. Based on the intercepted communication and recent activity, we believe the target is the central subway station. If they hit it during rush hour, the casualties would be catastrophic."

Sarah's stomach churned. "We need to evacuate the area and secure the station immediately. There's no time to lose."

Garcia joined them, already on his radio. "I'm coordinating with the transit authority and emergency services. We'll get everyone out and lock down the area."

The team mobilized with precision, their movements a well-oiled machine honed by months of intense operations. As they raced to the subway station, the city around them continued its bustling pace, unaware of the looming threat.

Upon arrival, the scene was chaotic but controlled. Officers directed commuters away from the station while SWAT teams moved in to secure the perimeter. Sarah and Ethan led their team into the station, their senses on high alert.

Ethan spoke into his radio. "All units, proceed with caution. Look for any suspicious packages or individuals. We need to neutralize this threat before it can be activated."

Sarah scanned the crowd, her eyes searching for anything out of place. The station was a labyrinth of platforms and tunnels, each one a potential hiding spot for the device they feared was hidden somewhere within.

"Over here!" One of the officers called out, pointing to an unattended bag near one of the benches. Sarah and Ethan rushed over, their hearts pounding.

Ethan carefully examined the bag, his hands steady. "It looks like a bomb. I need the bomb squad here, now."

Sarah nodded, her voice calm despite the fear gripping her. "Everyone, clear the area. Move back, now!"

As the bomb squad arrived and began their work, Sarah and Ethan coordinated the evacuation, ensuring that every person was safely out of the danger zone. The minutes stretched into an eternity as they waited for word from the bomb squad.

Finally, the bomb squad leader approached, his expression grim but determined. "We've disarmed it. The device was set to go off within the hour. You got here just in time."

Relief washed over Sarah. "Thank you. Great work, everyone. Let's make sure the area is secure and start the investigation into who planted this."

As they began to comb through the evidence, Sarah and Ethan felt the weight of their responsibility more than ever. They had averted disaster, but the threat of 'The Architect' still loomed large.

Back at the precinct, the mood was one of cautious optimism. They had saved countless lives, but the fight was far from over. Sarah gathered the team for a debriefing, her expression serious but resolute.

"We did good work today, but we can't let our guard down. 'The Architect' is still out there, and they know we're closing in. We need to stay vigilant and keep pushing forward."

Ethan added, "We're making progress, but it's going to take everything we've got to bring this to an end. Let's stay focused and support each other."

The team nodded, their determination unwavering. As they dispersed to continue their work, Sarah and Ethan stood together, ready to face whatever challenges lay ahead.

Sarah looked at Ethan, a sense of resolve in her eyes. "We'll get through this. Together."

Ethan nodded, a confident smile playing on his lips. "Absolutely. We're just getting started."

The task force was in full swing, following every lead that pointed toward "The Architect." The central subway station incident had only heightened the urgency. Sarah and Ethan were in the operations center, their eyes glued to the large screens displaying real-time data and surveillance footage.

Sarah glanced at Ethan, her face lined with determination. "We need to find The Architect before they can plan another attack. What's our next move?"

Ethan, scanning the latest intel, replied, "We've identified a few potential safe houses linked to The Architect's network. We should start with the one in the industrial district. It's the most active according to our sources."

Garcia approached, holding a tablet. "We've got additional surveillance footage from the subway station. There's a suspicious figure seen leaving just before the bomb was discovered. We're running facial recognition now."

Sarah nodded, her eyes sharp. "Good. Let's get a positive ID and see if we can link him to any of the safe houses. Every connection matters."

The facial recognition software beeped, and a match appeared on the screen. Ethan leaned in, reading the details. "John Mendez. Known associate of several criminal organizations, but no recent activity until now. Looks like he's resurfaced."

Garcia added, "We've got a last-known address on Mendez. It's close to one of the safe houses we've been monitoring."

Sarah turned to Ethan. "Let's gear up and pay Mendez a visit. If he's involved, he might lead us straight to The Architect."

The team assembled quickly, their movements coordinated and efficient. The drive to the industrial district was tense, the air thick with anticipation. As they approached the address, Sarah and Ethan reviewed the plan.

"We'll split into two teams," Sarah instructed. "Ethan, you take the back entrance with Bravo. Garcia and I will cover the front. Move in quietly and be ready for anything."

Ethan nodded, signaling for Bravo team to follow him. "Stay alert. We don't know what we're walking into."

They moved through the shadows, reaching the building's back entrance. Ethan signaled for Bravo to take positions, then nodded to Sarah through their comms. "In position. Ready when you are."

Sarah responded, "On my mark. Three, two, one—move!"

They breached the entrances simultaneously, moving swiftly and silently through the building. The interior was a maze of abandoned machinery and dimly lit corridors. As they advanced, they heard muffled voices coming from a room at the end of the hall.

Sarah signaled for the team to halt. "We've got voices ahead. Move in carefully."

Ethan nodded, leading Bravo team down a side corridor to flank the room. They burst in, weapons drawn. "Police! Hands up!"

The occupants scrambled, but the task force was quick. Mendez, a wiry man with a scarred face, was among them. He reached for a weapon, but Ethan was faster, pinning him to the ground.

Sarah approached, her weapon trained on Mendez. "It's over, Mendez. You're under arrest."

Mendez spat on the floor, defiant. "You think this changes anything? You're just scratching the surface."

Ethan secured Mendez's hands behind his back. "You're going to tell us everything you know about The Architect."

Mendez laughed, a harsh sound. "The Architect? You'll never find them. They're always ten steps ahead."

Sarah leaned in, her voice cold. "We've already stopped one attack. We'll stop the next one too. Start talking, or things will get much worse for you."

Mendez's eyes flickered with uncertainty. "You're too late. The Architect's plan is already in motion. It's bigger than you can imagine."

Ethan tightened his grip. "Where's the next target? Tell us now."

Mendez hesitated, then smirked. "You'll find out soon enough."

As they escorted Mendez out, Sarah and Ethan exchanged a look of grim determination. They had a major player in custody, but the clock was ticking.

Back at the precinct, Mendez was placed in an interrogation room. Sarah and Ethan stood outside, reviewing the evidence they had collected. Garcia approached with new intel.

"We've decrypted more of Mendez's communications. There's mention of a high-profile meeting tonight. It's vague, but it sounds like they're planning something big."

Sarah's eyes narrowed. "Where's the meeting supposed to take place?"

Garcia showed her the decrypted message. "An old warehouse on the waterfront. It's a known spot for clandestine deals."

Ethan straightened. "We need to get down there. If The Architect is involved, this could be our chance to catch them."

Sarah nodded. "Let's move. We need to intercept this meeting and find out what they're planning."

The team quickly geared up and headed out. The drive to the waterfront was filled with a tense silence, each member of the task force preparing for what could be the most critical operation yet.

As they approached the warehouse, Sarah signaled for the team to spread out and take their positions. "Remember, we need to catch them in the act. Move in quietly and wait for my signal."

Ethan led Bravo team around to the back entrance, while Sarah and Garcia took the front. The warehouse loomed ahead, a dark silhouette against the night sky.

Inside, the sound of voices and footsteps echoed through the cavernous space. Sarah's heart pounded as she watched the figures moving in the dim light.

"We're in position," Ethan whispered through the comms. "Ready when you are."

Sarah took a deep breath. "On my mark. Three, two, one—go!"

The task force moved in, their presence a sudden shock to the occupants of the warehouse. "Police! Hands up!" Ethan shouted.

The room erupted into chaos as men scrambled to escape. Sarah's eyes locked onto a figure at the center of the group, his face partially obscured by shadows.

"The Architect," she whispered, moving forward with her weapon raised. "You're surrounded. There's no way out."

The Architect turned, his eyes cold and calculating. "Detective Thompson, I presume. You're too late. The plan is already in motion."

Sarah's grip tightened. "We'll see about that. Take him down!"

As the task force secured the remaining suspects, Sarah and Ethan closed in on The Architect. The mastermind's expression was one of icy calm, a stark contrast to the chaos around them.

Ethan cuffed The Architect, his voice steady. "You're coming with us."

The Architect smirked. "You think you've won? This is just the beginning."

As they escorted The Architect out of the warehouse, Sarah couldn't shake the feeling that their battle was far from over. They had captured a key figure, but the true scope of the threat remained hidden.

Back at the precinct, The Architect was placed in a high-security cell. Sarah and Ethan stood outside, the weight of their mission heavy on their shoulders.

"We've made progress," Ethan said quietly. "But we need to stay vigilant. The Architect's network is vast. This isn't over."

Sarah nodded, her resolve unwavering. "We'll keep fighting. We'll protect this city, no matter what it takes."

As the dawn light filtered through the precinct windows, Sarah and Ethan prepared for the next phase of their mission. The battle against The Architect was just beginning, and they were ready to face whatever came next. Together, they would uncover the truth and bring justice to those who sought to disrupt their city's peace.

The Architect sat in the interrogation room, his demeanor calm and collected despite the situation. Sarah and Ethan watched through the one-way glass, preparing for what they knew would be a challenging interrogation. They had captured the mastermind, but now they needed to extract every piece of information he had about his network and their plans.

Sarah turned to Ethan. "This guy is smart. He's not going to break easily. We need to approach this carefully."

Ethan nodded. "Agreed. Let's start with what we know and make him realize we're in control. He needs to see that cooperating is his best option."

They entered the room, and The Architect looked up, his expression unreadable. Sarah took a seat across from him, while Ethan stood nearby, his presence imposing.

Sarah began, her voice steady. "You've been orchestrating attacks across the city. We've stopped most of them, but we know there's more. You need to tell us everything you know."

The Architect leaned back in his chair, a slight smile on his lips. "You think you've stopped anything significant? What you've done is merely delay the inevitable."

Ethan stepped forward, his tone firm. "We've dismantled your network piece by piece. We've arrested your associates, intercepted your communications, and foiled your plans. You're out of options."

The Architect's smile faded slightly. "You're thorough, I'll give you that. But you underestimate the depth of my operations. I'm just a part of a larger machine."

Sarah leaned in, her eyes locked on his. "Then tell us about the machine. Who are you working with? What are their plans?"

He hesitated, his eyes flickering with indecision. "You won't get far. They're too powerful, too entrenched."

Ethan's voice was cold. "We'll see about that. You have a choice: help us stop this, or spend the rest of your life in a cell, knowing you could have made a difference."

The Architect's facade cracked just a little, revealing a hint of uncertainty. He leaned forward, lowering his voice. "There's a meeting tonight. High-level members. If you want to make an impact, that's where you need to be."

Sarah's heart raced. "Where's the meeting?"

The Architect smirked. "An old factory on the east side. But be warned, they'll be expecting trouble. It won't be easy."

Ethan and Sarah exchanged a glance, their resolve strengthening. "We'll take our chances," Ethan said. "Thank you for your cooperation."

They left the room, closing the door behind them. Garcia was waiting, his expression tense. "What did he say?"

Sarah relayed the information quickly. "There's a meeting tonight at an old factory on the east side. High-level members. We need to move fast."

Garcia nodded. "I'll get the team ready. We'll need backup from Homeland Security and the FBI for this one."

Ethan added, "And make sure we have aerial support. If they're expecting trouble, we need to be prepared for anything."

As the task force mobilized, the tension in the air was palpable. They had a chance to strike a decisive blow against the network, but the risks were higher than ever.

The drive to the factory was silent, each member of the task force lost in their thoughts, mentally preparing for the confrontation ahead. The factory loomed ahead, its dilapidated exterior hiding the danger within.

Sarah briefed the team one last time. "We go in fast and hard. Secure the perimeter first, then move inside. Remember, we're dealing with high-level operatives. They won't go down without a fight."

Ethan led the way, his weapon at the ready. They breached the entrance, moving swiftly through the darkened corridors. The factory was a maze of old machinery and narrow passageways, each turn potentially hiding a threat.

Sarah's voice came through the comms. "Team Alpha, cover the north side. Team Bravo, you're with me. Let's move."

They advanced methodically, clearing each room and securing the area. As they approached the main hall, they heard voices and saw the glow of flashlights.

Ethan signaled for the team to halt. "This is it. On my mark, we move in."

The task force burst into the hall, their presence a shock to the gathered operatives. "Police! Hands up!" Ethan shouted.

Chaos erupted as the suspects tried to flee, but the task force was ready. Sarah and Ethan moved with precision, taking down operatives and securing the area. In the midst of the chaos, Sarah spotted a familiar face—one of The Architect's top lieutenants.

Sarah cornered him, her weapon trained on him. "It's over. You're under arrest."

The lieutenant glared at her. "You think this will stop us? We're everywhere."

Ethan secured the lieutenant's hands behind his back. "We'll see about that. You're coming with us."

As the task force rounded up the remaining operatives, Sarah and Ethan began to search the premises for any additional evidence. They found documents, electronic devices, and maps detailing future operations.

Back at the precinct, the mood was one of cautious optimism. They had struck a significant blow against the network, but the fight was far from over. Sarah and Ethan reviewed the evidence, their minds already on the next steps.

Sarah looked at Ethan, a sense of determination in her eyes. "We've made progress, but we can't let up now. We need to keep pushing."

Ethan nodded. "We will. We've got momentum on our side. Let's use it."

As the task force continued their work, the dawn light filtering through the windows symbolized a new phase in their mission. They had faced incredible challenges and overcome significant obstacles, but their resolve was stronger than ever.

Together, they would continue to fight, uncovering the truth and bringing justice to those who sought to disrupt their city's peace. The battle was far from over, but they were ready for whatever lay ahead.

The interrogation room was silent except for the ticking of a clock. The Architect sat across from Sarah and Ethan, his demeanor still composed despite the situation. The weight of the recent arrests and the confiscation of key evidence was heavy in the air.

Sarah broke the silence, her voice steady but firm. "We have enough evidence to put you away for a long time. Help us stop this, and maybe you can avoid a lifetime in prison."

The Architect's eyes flickered with a hint of defiance. "You think prison scares me? I've prepared for every eventuality. My network will continue, with or without me."

Ethan leaned in, his tone cold. "We've dismantled most of your operations. Your associates are in custody. It's over."

The Architect smirked. "You're mistaken, detective. What you've done is merely slow us down. The real power lies beyond your reach."

Sarah's eyes narrowed. "Then tell us about this 'real power.' Who's behind all of this?"

The Architect chuckled softly. "Even if I told you, you wouldn't understand. The system we've built is too intricate, too far-reaching."

Ethan's patience was wearing thin. "Try us."

The Architect leaned back, considering his options. "There's a reason we've been so successful. It's not just about the individuals. It's about the ideology. We believe in disrupting the status quo, creating chaos to usher in a new order."

Sarah pressed on. "And who leads this new order? Who are you working with?"

He sighed. "There are several key figures, each with their own role. But the one you should be worried about is 'The Shadow.' They're the true mastermind, pulling the strings from the shadows."

Ethan exchanged a glance with Sarah. "Where can we find The Shadow?"

The Architect's expression turned serious. "You don't find The Shadow. They find you. But if you're determined to chase this ghost, you'll need to follow the money. Every operation, every attack is funded through a complex web of financial transactions."

Sarah nodded. "We've traced some of your funding already. Offshore accounts, shell companies. But we need specifics. Names, locations."

The Architect shrugged. "I can give you some leads. But understand this: catching The Shadow won't be easy. They're a phantom, a myth. Many believe they don't even exist."

Ethan's voice was resolute. "We'll take our chances. Start talking."

Over the next hour, The Architect detailed a series of transactions and connections, each more complex than the last. Sarah and Ethan listened intently, their minds racing with the new information.

The Architect paused, his eyes locking onto Sarah's. "Even with this information, you're still at a disadvantage. The Shadow is always one step ahead."

Sarah met his gaze, unflinching. "We'll see about that."

As they left the interrogation room, Garcia approached them, his face lined with concern. "Did you get anything useful?"

Ethan nodded. "He gave us some leads. We need to follow the money trail. It's our best shot at finding The Shadow."

Garcia sighed. "This just keeps getting deeper. I'll get the financial crimes unit on it right away."

Sarah turned to Ethan. "Let's review the intel and start cross-referencing with what we already have. If we can piece this together, we might finally get ahead of them."

Hours passed as they pored over the information, tracing the web of transactions and connections. The scale of the network was staggering, but each new piece of data brought them closer to understanding its full scope.

Ethan looked up from his computer screen. "I think I've found something. A series of large transfers linked to a private security firm. It's a shell company, but the timing matches with several of the attacks we've intercepted."

Sarah joined him, examining the data. "This could be the break we've been looking for. If we can tie this firm to The Shadow, we might have a way in."

Garcia entered the room, a sense of urgency in his voice. "I've just spoken with Homeland Security. They've identified a potential safe house linked to the security firm. It's heavily guarded, but it's our best lead."

Sarah nodded. "Let's gear up. We're going in."

The task force assembled quickly, their determination evident in their focused movements. As they drove to the location, the gravity of the mission weighed heavily on them. This could be their chance to finally catch The Shadow.

Ethan briefed the team one last time. "We're dealing with high-level operatives. Stay sharp and follow the plan. We need to secure the area and capture anyone inside."

They approached the safe house, its exterior deceptively quiet. Sarah signaled for the team to take their positions. "Remember, we need to take them by surprise. On my mark."

The task force moved in with practiced precision, breaching the entrance and sweeping through the building. Shouts of "Police! Hands up!" echoed through the halls as they secured each room.

In the basement, they found a sophisticated command center, complete with computers, surveillance equipment, and stacks of documents. At the center of it all was a figure who matched the description of The Shadow.

Sarah stepped forward, her weapon trained on the figure. "It's over. You're under arrest."

The Shadow looked up, a calm smile on their face. "You've done well to get this far, but you've only scratched the surface. The real game is just beginning."

Ethan secured The Shadow's hands behind their back. "We'll see about that. You're coming with us."

As they escorted The Shadow out, Sarah couldn't help but feel a mix of relief and apprehension. They had made a significant capture, but the true depth of the network remained unknown.

Back at the precinct, The Shadow was placed in a high-security cell. Sarah and Ethan reviewed the evidence, their minds already on the next steps.

Ethan looked at Sarah, determination in his eyes. "We've made progress, but we need to stay vigilant. The network is vast, and there's still much to uncover."

Sarah nodded. "We'll keep fighting. Together, we'll bring them to justice."

As they prepared for the next phase of their mission, the precinct buzzed with renewed energy. The battle against The Architect and The Shadow was far from over, but they were ready for whatever came next, united in their pursuit of justice and the protection of their city.

Conclusion

The bustling cityscape of Harborview gleamed under the morning sun, a city reborn through the tireless efforts of its defenders. In the precinct's conference room, Sarah Thompson and Ethan Blake stood before their assembled team, the air buzzing with a palpable sense of accomplishment and camaraderie. It had been a long, arduous journey, but one that had finally borne fruit.

Captain Donovan stepped forward, his voice filled with pride. "Ladies and gentlemen, we have achieved something extraordinary. We've dismantled Marco's criminal network and exposed corruption at the highest levels of our city. Your dedication and perseverance have not only brought justice to the victims but have also restored integrity to our community."

Sarah glanced at Ethan, a silent acknowledgment passing between them. Their partnership, forged in the crucible of danger and adversity, had become the bedrock of their success. Together, they had navigated the murky waters of deception and crime, emerging stronger and more united than ever.

The team erupted in applause, a celebration of their hard-won victory. Yet, amidst the jubilation, Sarah's thoughts turned to the future. The battle against cybercrime, spearheaded by their new task force, was just beginning. The Black Web, though weakened, still posed a significant threat.

Ethan's voice cut through her thoughts. "We did it, Sarah. But there's still work to be done."

She nodded, a determined smile playing on her lips. "Absolutely. We've come this far, and we'll keep pushing forward. The city needs us."

Agent Kyle Reynolds and Special Agent Maria Torres joined them, their faces reflecting the same resolve. "The data we recovered from the first operation has given us a blueprint of The Black Web's network," Reynolds said. "We can dismantle it piece by piece."

Torres added, "And we have the best team to do it. Your leadership and the skills of this task force are unparalleled."

As the celebration continued, Sarah and Ethan took a moment to step outside. The city, bathed in the golden light of dawn, felt different. Safer. More hopeful.

"It's amazing how much has changed," Ethan mused, leaning against the railing. "We started with a string of arson cases, and now look where we are."

Sarah laughed softly. "Yeah, who would have thought? But every step we've taken has brought us closer to this moment. Harborview is on the path to healing because we refused to give up."

Ethan turned to her, his expression serious yet filled with admiration. "And it's because of you, Sarah. Your relentless pursuit of justice, your unwavering commitment—it's been the cornerstone of our success."

She shook her head modestly. "It wasn't just me, Ethan. It was all of us. This team, this partnership—we did it together."

They stood in silence for a moment, the weight of their journey settling into a comfortable place in their hearts. The challenges they had faced had not only tested their mettle but had also forged an unbreakable bond between them.

As they rejoined the team, the sense of purpose and unity was stronger than ever. The war against crime and corruption was far from over, but they were ready for whatever lay ahead. Together, they would continue to fight for justice, for their city, and for each other.

In the end, it wasn't just about solving cases or catching criminals. It was about making a difference, about standing up for what was right, no matter the cost. And as long as they had each other, Sarah and Ethan knew they could face any challenge that came their way.

The shadows that had once loomed over Harborview were now dissipating, replaced by the light of hope and justice. And with each new day, the city grew stronger, ready to face whatever the future held.

Milton Keynes UK
Ingram Content Group UK Ltd.
UKHW010643080724
445166UK00001B/45

9 798227 573377